Doctor's Bitter Pill

By

Sharon G. Clark

Paperback ISBN: 978-1-61929-460-8
Hardback ISBN: 978-1-61929-462-2

Flashpoint Publications First Edition: July, 2024

Printed in the United States of America.

Cover design by TreeHouse Studio

www.flashpointpublications.com

Dedication

For Keira Nicole and Alexia Haylee-Jean, the best granddaughters
in the world.

To my son, Jeremy, the wonderful father who gave? sired? these
shining stars so they shine in the orbit of my life.

Chapter One

Maple Woods, Colorado
August 1909

Six miles of county road separated Elspeth Keillor and Colonel Gardiner from the mansion, and with each bit of distance, they relaxed to enjoy the beauty of the day. They were close to their regular destination, and the Colonel began to slow the buggy, bringing it to a stop under a stand of trees overlooking a vast field of green. He looped the reins in the metal ring attached to the floorboard and leaned back. "Can you imagine anything more inspiring, Elspeth?"

"No, Colonel, I cannot." Elspeth turned to stare at the man beside her quizzically. In the weeks of their shared outings, the buggy only slowed enough to turn around for the return trip; it never came to a complete stop. Colonel Reginald Muir Gardiner, still a sturdy and healthy man, even at eighty-two years of age, had only brought her into his service because of a fall he'd taken in the home. And at the insistence of family that he have round the clock nursing. Elspeth suspected the family desired someone to keep him confined to his room, and out of their way, which is one reason Elspeth suggested they take in the fresh air at least twice a week. Her concern only for his health, she'd defended. They both needed the escape, in truth. Yet, today he seemed more preoccupied than was his usual. "I'm going to miss our little outings, now you're better, sir."

The Colonel cleared his throat loudly. "The very reason I wanted to take this occasion to have a private word with you."

"Are you not well, after all?" Elspeth asked with shocked concern. "I had no idea—" She calmed herself with a deep inhale of breath. "I could propose the doctor to visit you later today."

"No, dear, I'm as well as can be expected for a man of my advanced years." When she snickered, he smiled broadly, which pulled the curls of his mustache full across his face. Quick as the smile appeared, so did it vanish into seriousness. "I don't doubt any conversation between we two is held in the strictest confidence but would ask that what I'm about to share with you go no further than here, in this spot."

"And it shall be." Worry began to fill Elspeth. "Sir, maybe you should get straight to the point. I'm getting more than a bit concerned."

"Very well, dear, however, I must know something before I can continue. Please, answer honestly and without thought of my ulterior motives as I'm about to imply something. Something construed as insulting, if not criminal, to some. I don't wish to destroy the camaraderie I feel we've obtained."

With a hesitant nod, her stomach muscles bunched in nervous anticipation, Elspeth said, "Colonel, speak your piece, and I'll worry about any injury to my feelings later."

A deep breath and he blurted, "You have tender feelings for Giselle?"

Elspeth could feel the heat of embarrassment flush her face. Her heart pounded erratically within her chest. It wasn't as if she should, or even could, confirm falling in love with the vivacious young woman. Nor could she openly acknowledge any kind of feeling other than friendship without severe repercussions to her job, her reputation, and her very person. "Um, she's a remarkable woman, Colonel, with a fascinating sense of humor." She gulped hard. She hoped to swallow the fear that her secret was visible to other people in the household. She entwined her fingers tighter on her lap. "Why do you ask?" she inquired, even as Elspeth hoped the nervous squeak in her voice wasn't too noticeable.

As he placed a warm hand over her tightly clasped ones, Elspeth could feel just how paper-thin his skin had become, aware of how certain things made his age obvious. "I'm not judging, child. I've seen too much in my life and wouldn't presume your feelings are anything more than evident in your platonic interactions." He shifted his gaze to the scenery beyond the buggy. "Your private matters are your own, Elspeth, and I've no wish to intrude there. You needn't have a fear of me or my motives. I simply hope I haven't misread you for what I'm about to impart. I've reason to suspect something horrible is about to transpire, possibly something fatal."

"What do you mean?" Elspeth didn't understand where a conversation which started so personally could lead to fatality.

He shook his head sadly. "I made the mistake of announcing my plans to Edwin, plans to bequeath a large amount of my fortune to charities for less fortunate children." Elspeth nodded solicitously. Dr. Edwin Merrick was the son-in-law to the lady of the home where she and the Colonel presently resided. She never cared for Edwin, though Elspeth noted Colonel Gardiner and Edwin Merrick shared many talks about current events and news, historical facts, and such, regularly. "I fear I may have made a colossal misjudgment of the man. Though Edwin attempted to hide anger at my news, his subsequent behavior since has me concerned."

"Do you think he'd truly bring you harm?" Elspeth asked in surprise.

"I wish I could know for certain. Most of my

misgivings on Edwin's behalf could be unjustified, more a result of my ailing body in my waning years." He shook his head. "Mayhap I am overreacting. With this statement in mind, I have done a bit of introspection and instituted a series of events on players who are unaware they are in my little game, as it were. You, my stoic Elspeth, are one such player."

Elspeth knew without a doubt the Colonel wasn't infirm though his current ramblings were quickly suggesting otherwise. "I'm afraid I'm not following."

"I know about the old estate your family left you and your half-brother. I also know you haven't the funds to maintain the property at this time, let alone build the care facility you have in mind for the property. So, I've set up an account in your name. The funds should cover every aspect of fixing, furnishing, and maintaining the facility for at least five years. Share with your brother as you see fit. When I learned who your brother was, I felt better about my decision."

Elspeth stiffened.

"Don't get your back up, young lady. It's not what you're thinking." He paused, then snorted. "Aw, hell, it is what you think. But, in my defense, it's because he can give support and aid, and no one will question him as a doctor—as a man. The financial assist should give you time to make a go of the business. You intend the home to become a care facility for the elderly, do you not?"

"How do you—"

Colonel Gardiner held up a hand. "I'm a rich man with access to much for the right price. As such, here is what I propose, my dear. Soon, I will not need your nursing services. I also have an irrational fear something untoward is about to happen, as I've said. Whether it does or does not transpire, Giselle needs to be around people her age, with someone she can trust. Giselle could assist you in the start of your endeavor, or as little as you see fit. Maintaining your dream, which is a wonderful plan in my estimation, by the by. As you both get along well, with her sense of humor and all," he added teasingly, "I'd like you to watch after her."

"What if my vision and my friendship don't interest Giselle?" Not to mention they were not of the same age. Elspeth was twelve years Giselle's senior.

"Then this conversation could all be moot. No matter what happens, the funds are yours alone. It is not an appendix for your assistance." He snorted. "Believe me. I would much rather you had the money than any of my kin. All I ask is that you keep my family from harming or damaging Giselle personally or to her spirit."

The Colonel clasped her hand again. "I'm an intentional bachelor, Elspeth, and can't even begin to understand the deep emotions of the heart, no matter the gender of the parties involved. I realize it is considered wrong by so many, most heathens in their own rights. However, I have witnessed your subtle interventions when the family has attacked or insulted Giselle. If anything were to happen to either Preston or me, who would be there for her?" Elspeth felt the gentle squeeze of his hand. "Even if she doesn't share the depth of your feelings, could you ever purposely let harm come to her?"

"No, sir, I could not," she said simply. Elspeth doubted Giselle shared the emotions Elspeth had for the beautiful woman. What normal woman would have such feelings for another woman? So far, it appeared Giselle viewed her only as a stiff and formal—as well as homely—nurse merely being polite to the ward of her employer. "I will attempt to honor your proposition, Colonel. However, I must add my hope your concerns are simply a matter of overwrought nerves."

He barked a short laugh, picked up the reins, and

headed the buggy back toward the mansion. "As do I, dear. Just because I have already lived a long life, doesn't mean I'm prepared to give in easily or give up yet. However, I've learned never to underestimate the power of greed."

****

Doctor Edwin Merrick opened the door to his new office suite in the Bradbury Building, built beside the Daniels & Fisher Tower in downtown Denver, with an exciting flourish. Life moved at an impressive pace for him these last few years, and he hoped it never slowed or stopped. He never expected the prestigious position at the City Hospital, even if through the courtesy of the esteemed and wealthy Colonel Reginald Gardiner; and now he had an opportunity to conduct research and make a substantial name for himself.

As he walked through the suite of offices, Edwin made a mental note to hire someone for the front, have more furniture brought in for his own office to complement the oak desk, and make sure the area for the laboratory was fully stocked with supplies. He walked to the lone desk and picked up the phone, noting the connection active. With a long-term strategy started, Edwin only needed to discharge and complete the short-term plan. An objective his wife, Astoria, and he worked out at the beginning of their marriage six years ago.

Edwin sat on the desk corner and rang up the local pharmacy. He placed an order for the cyanide of potassium and an order for a popular digestive compound.

The clerk at the end of the line, stuttered, "Are you certain, Doctor, you need four five-grain capsules of cyanide of potassium?"

"Is there a problem?" Edwin asked harshly. The pharmacy manager never questioned his requests, yet some wet-behind-the-ears clerk intended to query an order? "Are you presuming to know my needs, challenge me about an order?" Edwin let his voice drop an octave. "Maybe you should have the owner contact me upon his return. He and I need to discuss how you're more qualified than I and, as such, able to challenge a doctor's order—my order."

"Well, no, Doctor Merrick," the clerk stammered, "I only needed to clarify, making certain I heard your request correctly."

"All right, then. I'll let the matter go. This time," Edwin conceded with a haughty sniff. Once he confirmed delivery for the next day, Edwin took one more turn around his office suite, locked up, and left to make it home in time to take Astoria to dinner.

Life was good, and about to get better.

At least better for him.

Chapter Two

October 1909

Giselle Sanders loved days like this, a beautiful late afternoon, with minimal clouds dotting the clear blue skies. A day cool enough to be comfortable and warm enough not to require too many layers. As luck would have it, October was one of the better months for good weather in Colorado, although the weather could still be haphazard. Having spent a wonderful day with school friends from college, and a recent acquaintance, Giselle was now enthusiastic to get home to her uncle—a relative so distant as to share little to no blood—and hear all the stories of his day. She knew Uncle Preston embellished these accounts to keep from sounding stuffy to her ears, which only made Giselle love the sixty-three-year-old all the more.

For the last week, Preston Muir had been low-spirited. She hoped everything was all right at the bank, where he worked as director; and, as the financial manager of Mrs. Gardiner's affairs, the woman whose home she walked toward now. If Preston weren't the dear-to-her-heart man he was, Giselle would not have willingly consented to live in a house, grand as it was, with the constant reminder she was the poor orphan relation living off their largess, and at twenty-two. Her cousin, Lilly Gardiner, might be the only near relative to show her any affection. Lilly, however, lived in New York City. The younger Gardiner children, Charles, eighteen and too busy for a nanny, Susan and Blanche, seven and six respectively and loved everyone, and Rosiland, named after her mother and thus spoiled and temperamental with entitlement, each accepting of her presence and what it could do for them.

She was grateful for the roof over her head. How many young women could boast living in the grand Gardiner home at the top of the highest hill in Maple Woods? Even now, after her time in residence, Giselle strode the winding walk and could still marvel at the beauty of the maples, elms, and pines on the multi-acre estate. Meticulously edged lawns hugged the paved drive, another sign of privilege. Built of brownish-red brick and sandstone, the home itself had more than twenty rooms within three stories, including a library—her favorite room—a music room, and a third-floor ballroom with an additional staircase and opposite that, the staff quarters, where she roomed.

Although, to most who passed by, it was a hodgepodge of mismatched shapes of design, Giselle thought it a welcomed sight where she could feel safe in the presence of two older men constantly disrespected by blood relations. As she made her way up the stairs, flanked by columns and pediment, Giselle spotted her uncle sitting on the long porch, Colonel Gardiner in the chair beside him.

Making her way toward them, she smiled when both men rose in greeting. "Ellie, honey," said Preston, bending for his usual hug. "Reginald and I were just commenting on the day being the most beautiful thing we've seen in our miserable old lives, and here you appear to prove our statement wrong."

Blushing at the compliment, Giselle grinned and said, "I know you're teasing, Uncle, but I thank you nonetheless."

"I do believe Preston has the right of it, young lady." Reginald shifted himself and raised his arms to his waist level. "And where is this uncle's hug?"

"I didn't wish to ruin your reputation, sir, in the event any of the family should witness it." Giselle immediately gave the requested embrace, before she stepped back to be an even distance before them. Though Preston was her favorite, and her original benefactor, she loved both men deeply. The foremost reason is that without Reginald's assistance and persistence, Preston never would have persevered to become her guardian officially. He was a single man, after all.

Reginald grunted. "They would think it a trick of the sun."

"Or a deteriorating brain," Preston clarified, "and reason to lock you away and lose the key."

With a loud guffaw, Reginald added, "Only after they emptied my vaults."

Giselle shook her head sadly, knowing both spoke the truth, whether couched in banter or not. As a savvy entrepreneur, Reginald Gardiner had amassed a healthy sum and purchased their current home for his brother, now deceased, and family. His fortune the size of which the family worked diligently to deplete in the numerous shops on Sixteenth Street. "More the fools are they, uncles. I have seldom heard kind words from them toward anyone, so please don't take it personally."

"Enough of such talk," Preston said. "Did you have a good time today?"

"Yes, it was wonderful. A gift to be introduced by Elspeth to her acquaintances, and one of which I'll always be grateful. I do wonder, deares, rather than an act from her own kind heart toward thet uncles, if you forced Elspeth's intervention merely as a desperate means to clear me out of Uncle Reginald's library resident orphan." She smiled shyly at the oldest man, as she moved off to his side, bending close to both men's ears. "Uncle Reginald seems in good spirits, too. Did today's buggy ride with Nurse Keillor work this wonder? You have heightened color in these cheeks of yours." She quickly placed a kiss on his cheek before she rushed to stand beside Preston.

Giselle knew Elspeth Keillor to be a skillful nurse, hired as an in-house nurse for Reginald after a relatively minor household accident had injured his shoulder. Yet, she was a curious wonder for Giselle. As sharp as Elspeth was, to most people, she lacked the one skill thought the most important—open emotional warmth. Giselle, however, knew Elspeth's company brought color to Reginald's cheeks, along with the fresh air and the sunshine from their lengthy jaunts down the country roads, which he wouldn't be making without Elspeth's insistence. The nurse cared a great deal about her charge, though if the family knew just how much then they would immediately dismiss her, so Elspeth never let on. Giselle, who also benefited from Elspeth's presence, would never provide the ammunition to the hateful people who would use it against the woman.

Reginald growled at her. "I should throw you over my knee—"

Preston broke into a loud laugh. "Ha-ho, because you're too close to the truth, Ellie."

After she received a playful wink from Reginald, Giselle moved the conversation to other topics. She couldn't guess how long they had been conversing before Nurse Keillor stiffly made her way across the porch. With a barely perceptible nod and grin in Giselle's direction, Elspeth gave her full attention to Reginald. "It's time to retire to your room, Colonel." Giselle always smiled at the title given to both older men. An honorarium title of the time, and not for a stint in any military service.

Rolling his eyes, Reginald growled, "Fiddlesticks. You two had best not have too much fun at dinner. I expect a full accounting of the conversation I'm missing first thing tomorrow." Mumbling, he dutifully marched into the house, followed by Elspeth.

"Guess I should wash up before dinner," said Preston as he stood and offered an arm to Giselle. "Shall we, young lady?"

Giselle warmly smiled as she laid her hand on the offered arm. "If only I could meet someone as wonderful as you, Uncle Preston."

"Oh, posh, Ellie," he said softly. "I'm not ready to lose you, I'm afraid. Should a young man come calling too soon, I will scowl fiercely and promptly boot him out the door. I'm sure Reginald would agree with me, too."

With a playful giggle, she stated, "No need, Uncle Preston. We'll just sic Aunt Rosie on him."

Chapter Three

Preston apparently managed to beat Giselle to the dining room and started on his meal. Everyone knew Preston hated eating alone, so when Elspeth passed by the door, she heard, "Ah, Nurse Keillor. Would you mind joining me?"

"Where is Miss Saunders?" she asked. The room was large, with a mahogany table and eight chairs, the two at each end with arms. Preston and Reginald usually occupied these. Next to the large window was a built-in open hutch. And, across from it, and near the entry to the kitchen, a buffet table. In the far corner, now behind Elspeth, was a scroll-worked china hutch. Some members of the house did not approve of Elspeth's appearance at the family dinner table. Yet, Preston and Reginald both commanded the family to be accommodating, or eat meals in their rooms, stating, "We men enjoy her company."

"She should be down after a bit," Preston answered. As if cued, Giselle rushed into the room and sat down opposite Elspeth. "Glad to see you, Nurse. I do beg your pardon, Uncle, but one of the children needed assistance with their studies." Immediately, the cook materialized and placed a plate in front of her and Giselle.

Elspeth harrumphed as Preston gently patted Giselle's hand. "Don't know what those children will do when you find a husband. The family won't feel the loss until it's too late."

As if an omen, Mrs. Rosalind Gardiner, Rosie to all, and her third oldest and namesake, arrived home. "You cannot imagine the day I've had." Rosie sighed as she heavily sat in the chair at the far end of the table.

"Rosalind be a dear, and ring cook. Ah, there you are," Rosie exclaimed as the cook came from the kitchen with two more plates. "Withering down to nothing, I'm so famished."

Giselle noticeably bit her bottom lip to stop the laugh in response to Elspeth's raised eyebrow. Both knew it would take quite a few missed meals before Rosie Gardiner wasted away. Rosie (those closest to her referred to her as full-figured) was indeed a heavy-set woman. "Was it a good shopping day, Cousin?" Giselle asked of Rosalind.

Elspeth listened dispassionately to the ramblings of the Gardiner women as they complained about their shopping expedition. Of course, the salespersons were too slow and rude, taking advantage because of jealousy due to the loftier station and plumper purses of the Gardiner's.

She was about to excuse herself from the table, as her meal was quickly consumed during the ramblings, when she heard Preston whisper, "Oh, dear." Elspeth considered it might be his sensitive stomach acting up, as the present company—except Giselle—tended to give her indigestion, too.

As Elspeth stood, Preston reached for his water glass. She hesitated, noticed the water sloshing to the table in his violently shaking hand. "What do you reckon has overcome me, Miss Keillor?" he asked. She shifted closer to his side, startled when Preston latched almost painfully to her arm. "I don't want to be sick, my dear," he said with a hastily applied smile and shaky laugh. She caught his nervous glance toward Giselle, and realized even in his pain and panic, he worried about alarming his ward. "You best provide me a speedy recovery."

Elspeth gave what she hoped would be an assuring nod, then assisted him to stand from the table. "Let's get started then, sir. Please excuse us," she said to the others at the table. She hadn't missed that no one other than Giselle seemed concerned with the turn of events and returned to consuming their meals as if this matter was an annoyance. Immediately, Elspeth gave a silent prayer of thanks Giselle wasn't biologically part of this horrid family.

"Please, let me help you," Giselle said, a quiver in her voice. She supported Preston on the opposite side of Elspeth. As they slowly left the dining room with Preston between them, Giselle demanded of Rosie, "Contact Dr. Trent immediately."

Elspeth grew more concerned with Preston's condition by the moment. "We won't be able to get him safely upstairs. Let's take him to the couch in the library." Together, they half-carried him and Elspeth noted Preston was nearly slathered in sweat. Preston's right leg gave out. Both women struggled not to lose their balance, which would result in all three crashing to the floor. They managed to get Preston to the couch and in a reclining position, where Elspeth gently tucked a pillow beneath his head, as Giselle removed his shoes.

"Miss Saunders," Elspeth said, trying to get Giselle's attention. "Maybe—"

Fear-filled eyes met hers. "Please, don't ask me to leave him," Giselle whispered.

"I've called the doctor. Rosalind is notifying Edwin and Astoria," Rosie announced as she loudly entered the library.

Much as Elspeth didn't wish the older woman's presence at this time, asking her to leave would prove more uncomfortable. Most certainly, retribution would occur later if she considered voicing such a request. Elspeth didn't mind so much for herself, rudeness was part of the job for her position. But she wouldn't provide a reason for them to mistreat Giselle—any worse than usual.

Giselle dropped to her knees beside the couch and held

Preston's right hand tightly in her own. His left hand shakily scrubbed at his face. "Sorry, Ellie, honey. I don't want to burden you, dear, but I'm feeling rather dreadfully."

"Oh, Uncle, you could never be a burden," Giselle announced tearfully.

"You've been such a light in my life," Preston told her.

Elspeth silently prayed the doctor would arrive soon. Preston's voice was getting thicker. His ordinarily ruddy color grew redder, speedily darkening to a near purple shade.

She couldn't keep up the formality considering this horrible situation. "Giselle," Elspeth said, a hand placed on Giselle's trembling shoulder. When the younger woman pulled her gaze from Preston and looked up at her, Elspeth said, "I'd like to take his vitals. But the Colonel hasn't eaten yet."

Shaking her head, Giselle said, "I'm not leaving Uncle Preston like this."

"Please," Elspeth softly pleaded, bending close to Giselle's ear. "The Colonel will panic if he isn't given this news from someone he trusts. His condition will suffer if he doesn't eat when the stress of this matter hits. I'd rather he learned of the circumstances from you." Giselle didn't appear ready to budge. "I won't leave your uncle's side before the doctor arrives. I promise." The panic on Giselle's face nearly broke her heart. The fact her gut intuition signaled this matter would not end well, had Elspeth needing Giselle as far away from this room as possible.

With apparent reluctance, Giselle nodded, clearly, her duty to Reginald winning out. After a final squeeze to Preston's hand, she stood and left the library with pain etched on her face.

Luckily, as Elspeth heard Giselle's footsteps climbing the stairs, Doctor Trent arrived. Elspeth would have been more relieved by his arrival if Edwin and Astoria Merrick weren't directly behind him. Luckily, Rosalind hadn't joined the others in the room.

"What have we, Nurse?" Trent asked as he placed his black medical bag on a side table near the end of the couch. Elspeth locked away her concern for Preston, and Giselle, and put on her nurses face as she explained the succession of events since dinner and concluded with Preston's vitals.

"Sounds like apoplexy." Edwin Merrick insinuated himself into the conversation and inserted himself between Dr. Trent and Elsbeth while removing his suit jacket and rolling up his shirtsleeves. "We'll need to bleed him."

Curling her fingers into fists until her short nails bit into the flesh of her palm, Elspeth carefully said, "I don't believe bleeding is necessary. Maybe you should examine the patient before jumping to a diagnosis?" Merrick sniffed derisively. Elspeth believed—knew—Edwin Merrick was an idiot. Despite his credentials, she refused to call Merrick a doctor. It was almost 1910, and men still believed themselves superior and that a woman's thoughts and opinions were nothing more than drivel.

Merrick opened Trent's bag and pulled out a scalpel and a rolled length of tubing.

She turned to the older man. "Doctor Trent, please?"

"Nurse…" Trent raised a questioning eyebrow.

"Keillor."

Trent nodded. "Nurse Keillor. You should know the best way to handle apoplexy is with bleeding."

"Yes, that's all very well, Dr. Trent. However, the patient hasn't even been examined by either of you. How can you possibly know the symptoms are the results of a cerebral hemorrhage? What if it's something else entirely?"

"Are you saying we don't know our business, nurse?" Merrick asked, stressing her title with sarcasm. "Maybe you should see to the ladies and let doctors handle this matter." He turned and sliced an incision on the inside of Preston's right arm."

"Yes, dear," Trent said. "We can call you should we need you."

She bit her tongue, literally. The copper taste filled her mouth. They didn't need Elspeth. Astoria and Rosie watched zealously from the room's corner. Trent placed a hand on her arm and gave a small push until Elspeth had no other option but to back away from the couch. She moved to where the women were, but refused to engage them in conversation or eye contact. Elspeth hadn't broken her promise to Giselle, as she had stayed until the doctor arrived, yet she felt herself about to break her promise to Giselle anyway. No. The situation would not end well.

Trent stood at the end of the couch. He stared between Merrick and Preston with a perplexed expression. Elspeth wondered if he reconsidered letting the younger doctor take control of the situation. A gusher of vomit spewed from Preston, just then.

"Damn," Merrick snapped. "Nurse, get over here." Reluctantly, Elspeth did as commanded until she stood at the head of the couch. Pointing to the blood-filled jar, Merrick said, "Switch that out."

"I believe you've bled him enough." She flicked her gaze toward Trent. "I beg you, sir, stop this atrocity." Everyone was tense and on edge. Elspeth worried most about how far Doctor Trent would let Merrick take this despicable bleeding process.

Pulling a handkerchief from his trouser pocket, Trent shook his head as he mopped at the sweat beading on his forehead. "Go ahead and take care of that, nurse. This won't be much longer."

That was the crux of the matter. Was Merrick merely incompetent, or intent on murdering Preston? Questioning Merrick's performance was one matter, and Elspeth had no problem living with his dislike of her, as there was no love lost between them. Doctor Trent was another matter. He held a considerable amount of respect among his peers and the community. One didn't go against a man of his position, even with her being in the right. The mere hint of her impropriety would not go well for Elspeth or her career. Her plans for a nursing home would never see the light of day.

Nevertheless, what was she to do? If this bleeding continued, surely Preston would die. Maybe, if she gave both men a chance to consider what they were doing, they'd stop. If they hadn't stopped by the time she returned, Elspeth would do what she must to intervene. Despite her misgivings, Elspeth switched out the jars and left the room with Preston's blood to do as she was commanded.

****

Merrick watched every drop of blood with a macabre sense of glee as it dripped from the tubing and plopped into the glass jar. The exhilaration of emotions he always felt when others were mere putty in his grand machinations, and experiments thrummed through him. Preston currently fell into both categories. He stood in the way of Merrick's plans and seeing how this bleeding played out fascinated him. The experiment had its downside, too. The labored guttural sounds from Preston were getting on Merrick's nerves. Why couldn't the man die quietly?

Edwin became annoyed with the waiting. He hadn't expected this to take so long. Not that he hadn't had his fair share of setbacks. Only a couple of years ago, an incident led to a hearing before the Board of police commissioners. He had tested the waters, so to speak, in experimentation with a situation that got away from him. As the official police surgeon, patients—of a less desirable nature, namely poor—were brought to him for medical examination. Edwin's opportunities for experimentation became limitless. Until, that is, the arrival of a mousy miscreant, Jane Goode, claiming excessive abuse at the hands of her husband.

During the examination, Edwin had used a mustard-oil concoction on her genitals. Her screams became so unbearable, Edwin had left the room until Jane could be more compliant—and quiet. In his absence, Jane saw fit to crawl well over a block before a policeman came to her aid. She pressed charges against Edwin. He had explained merely attempting to counteract her drugged stupor. The allegations of cruelty against him was a bit excessive, too, not to mention trumped up by his political enemies jealous of his professional success. No matter his denials and offers of supportive claims otherwise, Edwin had been fired from his post as a police surgeon.

Dire as the situation seemed at the time, Edwin discovered a ray of hope. The matter led him to his wife, Astoria. It was during the formal dinner at the Governor's home when Edwin realized there truly existed someone for everyone. Astoria had asked him directly about Jane Goode. Edwin prepared to lie or to spout the same malarkey he'd given at his inquiry, but the charming woman—though decidedly dull—raised an eyebrow and said, "The truth Dr. Merrick, no matter how gruesome." So, he told Astoria, not even trying to hide his excitement in the telling. After all, they'd already fired him for the event, so the matter already used against him. Edwin considered Astoria using the telling to defame his character and, in the aftermath, might put him in a bad light with current patients, titillating to the curious woman. However, it would be the word of a highly sensitive female aristocrat too shocked to hear or repeat his rendering correctly.

As an unexpected result, Astoria Gardiner gave a wicked grin and said, "Oh, we shall get along famously." After five years of marriage, Edwin regaled his wife with precise details of specific examinations; and, Astoria held the presence of mind to assure Edwin never went too far.

The bitchy nurse returned to the room. "Are we just about done with this procedure? Shall I call an ambulance?" She moved to the back of the couch and took Preston's free hand in her left, two fingers from her right hand to the soft flesh of his wrist.

Merrick snapped, "Do you not see the patient's ruddy coloring? His pressure is still too high."

Trent's voice held a hint of uneasiness. "Muir's face has always been ruddy, Merrick. Why do you think the neighborhood children believe him to be Santa Claus without a beard?"

"We give the matter a little more time," Merrick said, his tone firm. He was the attending physician, after all, as the authority from being a member of the family.

"We wouldn't want to bleed him to death mistakenly." Trent took a hesitant step forward.

Merrick wanted to snicker openly, knew the old man wrestled with the idea of interrupting a fellow doctor, thus suggesting possible unsuitability. You don't call out a fellow doctor before the patient and family. Not that anyone present would be heartbroken by Preston's death. Well, maybe the noisy nurse, but only because she'd have to explain her lack of assistance to the Colonel.

His beloved Astoria stepped closer and held Preston's jaw. Even now, Astoria realized when he needed reining in. "My dearest, I believe you should quit. Doctor Trent thinks you've bled him enough."

As she had done since the moment they met, Astoria grew concerned for his welfare, wanted to protect him. He couldn't do anything but her will. "Very well," Merrick said. He removed the tubing and bandaged the incision.

Preston's eyes popped open so suddenly, Merrick's hand stilled, and he pulled back. The older man focused on the nurse, her expression giving nothing of her feelings as to this event away. "Look after Ellie. Remind her I...I love...her." The nurse nodded solemnly.

With those words, Merrick realized his efforts weren't in vain. Preston went into a brief seizure, gasped, and died. The family linchpin was no more.

"I'll make arrangements to have Muir taken away," Trent said, then darted from the room. Did the old buzzard believe distancing himself precluded his culpability?

Merrick saw the look of disgust the nurse—whatever her name—pointedly flashed at him. He ignored it. There were other important matters of concern now. "As soon as you've some leisure time, Nurse," he addressed, though loath to acknowledge her position, "I'd have a private word with you."

"We've nothing to discuss." So, the nurse would be a bitch to the end.

Merrick turned to his wife. "Astoria, dear, please take your mother away and get her some tea. We don't wish to compromise her delicate constitution with all this drama. I'll join you in a few moments." He'd not wait for compliance. The nurse would hear him out.

Once the room cleared, where only the nurse, he, and the corpse remained, Merrick said, "Isn't this awful?" He tried to interject a tone of commiseration. He offered a few words about Preston Muir's many excellent qualities, which didn't appear to win her to his side. Merrick smiled and got to the point. "I would like you to do something for me tomorrow. Now, I am not a businessman, but I can be, in a pinch." He put his hands into his trouser pockets, hoping for a less formidable appearance. No sense being off-putting, he thought. "Now that this esteemed man is gone," Muir's position was as the administrator of Colonel Gardiner's will, "I want you—as you have some influence with the old man—to suggest me in Muir's stead. Colonel Gardiner will be making a new will in a few days. We wouldn't want the family represented by someone without knowledge or understanding of our family quirks."

The nurse had the audacity to glare—at him.

"I don't suppose you would," she said inflexibly.

He realized, only when the movement caught his attention, she still held the older man's hand. She gave a small squeeze, released it, and took a small step away from the couch. If Merrick didn't know better, he'd characterize her movement as unsteady. Was there more to the haughty, and homely, nurse than he had gleaned in their short meetings? No, it was only a product of his exhausted brain. Either way, the woman unsettled him. "Doctor Trent and I will take care of matters from here. You should probably see to Colonel Gardiner."

Without a word, she pivoted on her heel and left the room in her stiff gait.

Merrick stood and stared after her for a moment. Nurse Keillor hadn't been a consideration when he'd initially mapped his plans. Maybe the time had come to make a few modifications to his campaign.

Chapter Four

The waiting, the not knowing, was killing Giselle. She shuddered and gave a soft whimper when she realized what she'd thought. She wanted Elspeth to rush into the room and tell her Uncle Preston would be all right. The more time that passed, the less likely that would occur. Giselle had no allusions about how the situation would end. Edwin was a horrible man and a most incompetent doctor. Not that Giselle had any proof to corroborate her belief, but anyone with his personality couldn't be decent. Yes, a good part of her estimation revolved on the simple fact Edwin gave her the willies. She also knew the limits of being a nurse—and female—restricted Elspeth's assistance with Uncle Preston's care.

"Come away from the window, Ellie," Reginald said softly from the bed. She turned to him, looking so frail since she'd told him of the happening's downstairs. He'd seldom acted or looked his eighty-two years. Until now.

The lap-tray with his supper lay untouched on the bed beside him. Giselle inclined her head in its direction. "You need to eat. This could be a while, and I wouldn't want to upset Nurse Keillor by not conducting the easy task she presented me." Most young women, family or no, wouldn't be alone with a male of any age, let alone one abed. There was a level of trust built since Giselle first came to be part of the life of both Reginald and Preston. She loved them deeply, implicitly, and trusted them more than anyone.

Well, she modified internally, Giselle trusted Elspeth, though she couldn't explain why. The nurse was polite, even helped with taunts about her origins. Mostly, she never talked or looked down on Giselle. And it wasn't as though she missed the glances Elspeth cast her way, even if she couldn't quite identify the implication behind the gazes. More than that, both her uncles adored the nurse, which told Giselle all she needed to know.

"Not so hungry, Ellie. And I know Elspeth will understand, given the situation." Away from family, he never referred to the nurse formally. Reginald shifted, rearranged the pillows behind him, and cleared his throat. "Come here," he said, patting the side of the bed near his hip. She complied. "I want only the best for you, as does Preston. However, without an apparent cause for concern or proof, we have become concerned with the changes in the household." When she started to speak, he shook his head. "Much as it pains me to admit this, Preston and I can't protect you from the Gardiners or the Merricks."

"Why would—" A chill raced up her spine. Despite Reginald sounding overly dramatic, a part of Giselle accepted he wasn't.

"Promise me, no matter what happens from this moment forward, if you need something, someone to talk to," he paused, stared directly into her eyes, "someone to trust, you will turn to Elspeth. She cares for you, Ellie, and will make certain no harm comes to you."

Giselle wasn't sure why he stressed the word "cares" to her. But the emphasis seemed essential to him. It was a matter she'd probe later. Indeed, she preferred Elspeth's company above those who supposedly shared her blood lineage. "We cannot expect anything of her after she is discharged of her duties, Uncle Reginald."

Reginald squeezed his eyes closed, inhaling. "Please, Ellie. Promise, whatever happens, you rely on Elspeth. That if you place your trust in anyone, it be her. Do whatever she asks of you, okay?"

She furrowed her brow, confused by his intensity on a

matter that didn't exist. What did he know which he had yet to share with her? "Uncle—"

A quick, sharp knock sounded at the door before it was pushed open. As Elspeth entered, with unshed tears in her eyes, and the difficulty the nurse had keeping her stoic expression, made Giselle jump from the bed. She grasped the lap-tray, turned her back on Reginald and Elspeth, and placed the tray on the table. The table sat before the room's window, with curtains currently drawn against the waning daylight. Two chairs were on either side, and a hurricane lamp rested unlit on a dark blue doily at the table's center.

When Elspeth spoke, Giselle heard the tremor in her voice. Tears fell as she listened, knowing already what would be shared. "Colonel, I regret," Elspeth's voice broke. She inhaled deeply. "Despite the attentions of Doctor Trent and Merrick, Colonel Muir has passed away."

Although Giselle suspected that very announcement, hearing the words spoken aloud broke the dam of reserve she could no longer hold. Giselle's legs buckled beneath her, and she dropped to the floor with her dress pooling around her, sobs joined the tears raining down her face. Lost in grief, she barely heard the groan from Reginald in response to the news. Hours or seconds could have transpired before she felt strong hands gently pull her to her feet. Elspeth. The nurse nudged her toward the chair, but Giselle didn't want to sit. Instead, she turned around, flung her arms around Elspeth's neck, and wept into her shoulder. Giselle, even in her despair, felt Elspeth stiffen in surprise. Moments passed before Elspeth wrapped her arms around Giselle, and pulled her closer. Elspeth's supportive embrace provided warmth and comfort.

"Elspeth," Reginald said. "You should take Giselle to her room. She needs rest and privacy after this news."

Giselle felt Elspeth nod. "I'll be back to check on you

once she's settled."

"No, stay with Ellie. I doubt anything more will transpire this night, so see to her. Ellie needs you."

For a second, Giselle felt the need to remind them she was neither deaf nor a child, but Reginald was right. She didn't want to be alone right now. So, when Elspeth broke the comforting embrace, placed a hand on her shoulder, Giselle followed obediently. Until she noticed the look of anguish on Reginald's face. She ran to the bed, threw her arms around him, her face buried in his neck, and whispered, "He loved you, as do I. Uncle would want us to carry on. We're here for each other, okay?" When she felt the dampening of tears on her face, Giselle pulled back only slightly. Reginald would not want either her or Elspeth to witness his emotional breakdown, which was not far from the surface. "I'll be back in the morning." Feeling his nod, she turned away and let Elspeth lead her from the room.

As only Preston's ward, and since four of Rosie's six children and the real family occupied the second-floor bedrooms, the third-floor staff quarters were where Giselle roomed. She didn't mind. Giselle was glad to be removed from the majority of the chaos that was the Gardiner family.

Inside her room, Giselle moved toward the four-poster bed, grasped a smooth bedpost with both hands, and paused. She didn't—couldn't—turn to look at Elspeth, afraid of what her next words would inspire as a reaction. Disgust? Pity? "Would you stay with me until I fall asleep? I don't—"

A trembling hand lightly rested on her shoulder. Why was Elspeth unsteady? Belatedly she realized Elspeth might have come to care for her uncle as more than a friend. "Get changed, and I'll turn down the bed."

Giselle walked behind the three-panel changing screen

and proceeded to get ready for bed. When she finished, she stepped back into the open. Elspeth had turned down the bed, and placed a straight back chair nearby, which she currently sat upon, her back to Giselle. Giselle suppressed a small grin. Elspeth, ever dutiful and considerate, no matter the circumstances. And, Giselle thought, despite her rigid exterior, Elspeth's body had been warm and calming while she'd held her. She knew the odd thought was inappropriate, but Giselle couldn't help herself. There was something about Elspeth Keillor that called to Giselle's soul.

She must have made more noise than intended because Elspeth turned to her. "Can I get you anything? Tea? A book? A pill to assist with sleep?"

"I'm fine, thank you," she said. "I just—" Giselle knew there was an age difference between them, but Giselle didn't want to appear childish to Elspeth. Regardless of what her head reasoned, her mouth had other ideas. "You probably view me as behaving like an infant." She crossed the floor, and climbed into bed, quickly jerking the covers on top of her.

Elspeth stood, moved closer, and stopped Giselle's movements. "No, I do not. I see a caring young woman who just lost her loving uncle. You have reason to behave and grieve any way you wish." The nurse was back in the forefront, not that the persona was far from sight at any given moment, but Giselle had glimpsed the emotions Elspeth kept reigned in for everyone but the Colonel and Reginald and Giselle. Knowing this brought a small sense of pride to her. Elspeth meticulously drew the covers around Giselle. "Rest. I'll remain as long as you have need of me. You'll need refreshing. The next couple of days won't be easy for you. Especially in this house."

The grimace on Elspeth's face lead her to believe the comment wasn't meant to be said aloud. She grinned up at

Elspeth. "They are quite trying." Before she could move away, Giselle clasped one of Elspeth's hands in hers. She grew still as Giselle held the steady, warm hand, the slight tremble in evidence on her own. She didn't want to let go, confused as to why she felt that way, but recognized Elspeth's discomfort, which she still reigned in. All except the darkening of her grey eyes, now resembling a thundercloud. "Thank you. Uncle Preston could be trying at times, but you always treated him with respect."

Elspeth nodded. Giselle let her extricate her hand from Giselle's own and return to the chair. "Colonel Muir was a good man. I could do no less." She deeply inhaled and exhaled as Giselle gazed at her. Yes, there was undoubtedly more to the enigmatic woman than Giselle first glimpsed. "You should try to sleep." With a comforting smile, Elspeth focused on the closed bedroom door.

With Elspeth's focus elsewhere, it was easier for Giselle to study the nurse, though part of her felt guilty for doing so, Preston's death mere hours ago. The nurse was thin but sturdy, her eyes grey, hair dark brown, with a full mouth and square jawline. Elspeth's narrow face was sharper with her hair pulled into a tight bun. Most would and had referred to the woman as severe and homely. Giselle disagreed. Although Elspeth was no great beauty, she had a softness about her. No, she thought, softness wasn't correct. A tenderness to Elspeth, which someone would have to look for to find. It was there, hidden in the depths of her stormy, grey gaze and hidden with the relaxing of her lips when she was amused, in the caring warmth of her long fingers as they held Giselle's hand.

Giselle squeezed her eyes shut. She needed to rest, not focus on her confused reaction to the woman who offered comfort. There would be time enough for that later. At least, Giselle hoped so.

****

The Merricks returned to their home in Denver. A home bought as a wedding gift by Reginald Gardiner when he and Astoria returned to the Denver area. The house was two-and-a-half stories made of stone and shingles, both blocky and stable. Reginald purchased it complete with furnishings, with a single check for twelve thousand dollars. The couple appreciated his gesture, but the action reflected Colonel Gardiner's disdain of Edwin's ability to provide for himself and his wife. And, maybe, to assure them a place away from the Gardiner home?

Safely inside, Astoria walked straight to the master bedroom. Edwin dutifully followed. He knew his wife desired to discuss this evening's events without the household staff overhearing. Once the door closed, she turned toward him, her features giving none of her feelings away. "You exceeded the limits this evening, Carson. Dr. Trent could become suspicious. When Trent suggested you desist, that should have been the end of it." Astoria scowled at him. "You take too many chances with an... inquisitive nature." His wife, of course, referred to the previous charges levied against him, and others only they were privy to. Astoria had an irregular interest in the painful afflictions of others. Her only consolation was that it does not happen in her home, or to her.

Edwin moved closer, placed his hands on her waist. She'd used his middle name, so he knew his wife wasn't overly upset with him. "I did what was medically acceptable within the situation. There will be no repercussions, dearest Tori."

"We need to help mother, get you positioned as

Reginald's executor. That will not happen if there is even a hint of impropriety," Astoria sternly stated. "Too much is at stake."

As she yanked the gloves off her hands, Edwin removed the wool cape from her shoulders and tossed it on the settee. He didn't want to upset his wife, but the uncalled for criticism wounded. Not that he'd acknowledge it. His plans were proceeding as expected. Of course, it didn't hurt to have Muir out of the way. He smirked. And such a terrible way to leave his earthly coils. "I'll return to the mansion in the morning, Tori, make certain everyone is well. Now would be the perfect time to institute the purified water into the family's kitchen. Wouldn't want any terrible ailments assaulting your family, would we?"

Astoria gazed at him with one eyebrow raised. "Then, I shall go with you. This is a traumatic time for them, considering tonight's events."

Events. Yes, one of many moving toward their future.

Chapter Five

Elspeth was not happy about Merrick's return this morning. Not that she witnessed their arrival or laid eyes upon them. But Edwin had a way of making his presence known and heard. And from the shiver running up her spine at his voice, his presence was felt. The occupants of the home were relatively sullen with the death of Colonel Preston Muir. The funeral home came for the body last night, while she broke the news to Reginald and dear Giselle. The rest of the family wasted no time in deciding arrangements for the funeral, stating the need to cause as little disruption as possible on the Gardiner children.

For her, it allowed hope that the loss would be easier for Giselle to handle if they didn't draw out the funeral. The Gardiner's certainly wouldn't want to extend the process any more than necessary.

"Why the sudden scowl, Elspeth?" Reginald asked. He had copies of all the local papers strewn across the bed's top, and one clutched loosely in his hands. A knock sounding on the door saved her from responding. "So, he wishes to be seen, as well as heard."

She grinned at Reginald on her way to the door. Elspeth opened it only because a prolonged response would assure Edwin entered anyway and groused as he did so. Better the visit is on the Colonel's terms. She sent a silent prayer Giselle wouldn't choose this time to visit Reginald. Elspeth blamed Preston's death on Merrick and imagined Giselle did as well. The Colonel certainly did, and vocally said as much to her.

Without acknowledging her presence, Edwin strode to the closest side of the bed. She walked around and stood next to Reginald on the far side. "How are you, Colonel, on this fine day?"

Reginald's face flamed, and Elspeth shifted closer. He shook his head at her, effectively halting any response she intended. "Fine day?" Reginald growled. "My best friend is dead, boy. Under your care, I might add. How can you see the day as anything but abysmal?"

Edwin replied, "The perceived disrespect was my attempt to cheer you up, sir." Elspeth didn't believe the remark. Reginald's continued scowl suggested he didn't either. Edwin removed a prescription box, an inch and quarter square, from his inside jacket pocket. Merrick said, "I've today's medication." He removed a white capsule and held it out for her. She took the pill and placed it on the bedside table.

"He'll be sure to take this later." Elspeth raised an eyebrow at Edwin, then pointed to the box already in their possession. "Any reason for this pill over his current medication?" She caught the flash of irritation before Edwin could hide it.

"Trying a different brand to see if the results of the Colonel's recovery are improved." Merrick glanced at the lone pill, then back to Reginald. He cleared his throat. "I should return downstairs, leave you to your grief." He walked to the door, grasped the knob, and turned back to her. "How is Muir's niece doing? Should I check on her?"

Elspeth stiffened. No way was she allowing this monster anywhere near Giselle. He couldn't even address, or possibly remember, her Christian name. "Miss Saunders is resting." She hoped Giselle didn't make a showing and discount Elspeth's defense of her.

He nodded and opened the door. "Should you need me, I'll be here. Due to Preston's popularity, and to avoid too much disruption, the funeral will be tomorrow. Astoria and I shall remain overnight to attend."

"Oh, joy," Elspeth mumbled, once the door closed behind Merrick.

Despite the dispiriting situation, Reginald snorted. "Not an admirer of the esteemed doctor?"

If anyone else asked, Elspeth would have prevaricated. "His ego allows room for only him to admire himself. And, please, sir. Let us not insult legitimate doctors by adding Edwin to their ranks."

"True enough." Reginald frowned. "I suppose I should start putting affairs into order, now Preston—"

Elspeth hated seeing the proud man forced to hold back his emotions from the view of anyone. "We could use fresh coffee, Colonel. I'll fetch some straight away." She cleared her throat. "I should check on Miss Saunders as well, see if she needs anything."

The corner of his lip curled even as the rest of his features were a picture of anguish. Elspeth rushed out of the room to afford the older man his privacy. It also hadn't gone unnoticed that she now brought Giselle under her wing just as Reginald had wanted.

****

Hesitant to intrude, but with a need to assure herself Giselle was unharmed, Elspeth gave two swift taps to the door with the knuckle of her pointer finger. Much as she wanted to do her duty to the beautiful young woman, Elspeth knew any signs of Giselle's pain would have Elspeth acting quite inappropriately. It already took all she could muster to share any space and not fawn over her, pull Giselle into her embrace, and promise anything. Promise everything.

This visit is a bad idea, she reprimanded herself. Also,

not part of her duties in this household, even if it were her duty as a human being. Berating herself for uncharacteristic actions, Elspeth turned on her heel and made for the stairs.

"Nurse Keillor?" A pause. "Elspeth?"

The voice, hoarse from crying, followed her down the hall. Inhaling deeply with hopes to focus her own emotions, she turned. What Elspeth saw, even as she expected the sight, propelled her toward Giselle, who stood in a nightdress and wavered in the bedroom's doorway. "I wanted to see how you were faring, see if you needed something."

Giselle indicated they enter her room, and Elspeth quickly complied.

The door closed behind them, and Giselle leaned wearily against it for a few moments. Then, she straightened, extended a hand toward a wing-backed chair near the window. "Please, sit a moment."

Her better judgment demanded a hasty retreat, maintain her professional distance. One glimpse of Giselle's red, puffy, cry-swollen eyes and Giselle's withered posture was Elspeth's complete undoing. She clenched her hands on her lap, willed them not to reach forward and pull Giselle into her arms. "Can I bring you anything?" Giselle shook her head. "You should keep a little sustenance in your stomach for strength. I could also bring tea or coffee if you prefer."

"I only need time to process that Uncle Preston is truly gone. It's harder than I expected it to be."

Unlike the rooms of the floor below them, with large spaces and even larger furniture, the third-floor rooms were intended for the live-in staff and only sufficient enough in size not to be claustrophobic, and the furniture modest and basic. This room contained a bed with a wrought iron frame painted white and light blue, presently unmade, the quilt a solid sky-blue color., There was an armoire against the wall opposite the bed and the chair by the window which was smaller than the windows on the two floors below. Giselle moved to the end of her bed and clutched the metal top in her left hand as if it was the only thing keeping her upright. Elspeth suspected it just might be the case.

She had to say—do—something. Remind herself of her position in the household before she did anything she could regret later. "It's no consolation at this time, Giselle, but I truly am sorry for your loss. Preston was under-appreciated in this household." Giselle gave her a barely visible nod in response. "I want to extend—"

Giselle's shoulders shook violently in her attempt to staunch her emotions. Elspeth didn't think, just responded. Rising from the chair, Elspeth swiftly moved to Giselle and wrapped her arms around her. The action broke the reserve the younger woman attempted to maintain. Heart-wrenching sobs broke free, and Giselle trembled against her as she released her pain at the loss of the one person, other than Reginald, in this vast house that cared for, protected, and loved Giselle with all his heart.

Elspeth couldn't say how long she held Giselle, feeling her warmth, her soft breasts pressed into Elspeth's, and the fact the embrace felt so wonderful, so right. But it wasn't right. At least not the right time. The young woman was in mourning. She hadn't forgotten her duty to Reginald, who probably wondered where his coffee had gone, but couldn't let Giselle suffer alone. There was no need to inquire whether other family members had come to offer condolences or support to Giselle. The answer was obvious. Elspeth could also imagine all the fear that would accompany the loss of Preston.

Her conversation with Reginald two months earlier niggled at the back of her mind. Who would be there for

Giselle? How soon before she was tossed from this household, that could well afford to support her indefinitely. There was nothing Elspeth could do at this time to assist Giselle, and both of them would need to rely more heavily on the support of Colonel Gardiner.

Giselle became more compliant in Elspeth's arms, effectively pulling her from her thoughts. There would be time for proper plans later. Elspeth realized Giselle was about to nod off; her strength depleted from loss and no sleep. Nudging Giselle backward, Elspeth gently held her until her bottom met the mattress, then lowered her to the pillows.

"I'm sorry," Giselle mumbled.

"Shush. You've nothing to be sorry for," Elspeth softly said. She pulled the comforter over Giselle and tucked it close under her chin. "Rest now. I'll check on you later." Before she could consider it or curb her impulse, Elspeth leaned down and placed a light kiss upon Giselle's forehead. She silently chided herself even as a slow smile tugged at Giselle's perfect lips.

****

Leaving Giselle to her much needed sleep, Elspeth rushed down the stairs to prepare Reginald's coffee. She hoped to avoid bumping into the Merrick's but found her prayers unanswered. As she walked into the kitchen, Edwin was placing a five-gallon jug of water on the counter, *Youthful Fountain* printed on the front. The oddity gave her pause.

"Ah, Keillor," Edwin said. She bristled at the informal acknowledgment to her entrance, expecting it was probably in retaliation for her refusal to call him a doctor.

"What do you think of the new addition?"

Elspeth bit back the cynical remark dancing on the tip of her tongue. It would do her no good to offend him, especially with Mrs. Gardiner and Astoria in the corner of the room looking on. "I don't see the need."

"Neither do I," Rosie said. "But if you think it's best, Edwin, I'll defer to you."

Astoria glared at her mother. "Edwin only wishes the best for our family, Mother."

Edwin finished his task, turned to them as if prepared to address a classroom. "This is double-distilled drinking water. We need the best and safest to be consumed by our loved ones. Don't we, dearest?" He flashed a smile full of gleaming white teeth. "With the death of poor Preston, I must assist with the many tasks resulting from the family tragedy."

His concern for the family didn't explain the necessity for bottled water. Unlike so many homes, the Gardiner's had the benefit of indoor plumbing and modern toilet facilities on all three floors, and one off the kitchen for the staff. One viable water source present in the mansion was provided by a deep cistern, complete with a charcoal filter and fed by rainwater, professionally cleaned each year. Second, for washing and other household uses, was the clear, untreated faucet water provided by purchase from the city.

Walking around him, Elspeth purposefully avoided Edwin and his addition, filled the percolator from the cistern faucet, and added coffee grounds before placing it on the stove to heat. She expected Edwin to comment, but instead, he sniffed rudely and asked, "Has the Colonel taken his medicine?"

Hackles up, Elspeth said, "Not before I left, but I'm certain he'll do so. His medication hasn't changed—"

"No, no. Same medication, only a different supplier. I

wanted to switch to them as their charges are more feasible for the average person," Edwin said.

Rosie scoffed. "Money isn't a problem for us, Edwin."

"Of course not, Mother Gardiner. But I need to consider all my patients. If this new pill works as well as the other, I can recommend providing for those from lesser circumstances."

"And you would use Colonel Gardiner as your guinea pig?" Elspeth decided then to take the pill from Reginald as soon as she returned to the room. She didn't believe the older man any more worthy than more impoverished people who might seek treatment from Edwin. Still, something about the sudden testing of new medicine the day after losing Preston worried her. Elspeth focused on the percolator, shrugged negligently, and said, "But I see your reasoning." Elspeth hoped to assure Edwin she held no doubts or fears concerning the pill he'd left for Reginald.

"Enough of this, Mother." Astoria left her place by Rosie's side and strode to the kitchen door. Rosie obediently followed. "We'll be in Mother's sitting room, Carson."

"I'll join you shortly, dearest," he said. "I'd like to have another check on Colonel Gardiner." He wrinkled his brow. "I should have a look-see on Muir's girl, too."

The words made her heart thump in panic. Elspeth wrestled with her need to defend Giselle openly. She, in absolutely no way, wanted him anywhere near Giselle. Not that she believed Edwin should be near anyone in the capacity of a doctor. Elspeth couldn't bear the thought of him touching Giselle, even if clinically. But any outward expression of protection would go badly for them both. "I've just come from checking on her, on Colonel Gardiner's request, and she's resting," Elspeth said stiffly.

Edwin shrugged negligently. "Of course, maybe

later."

Elspeth would be sure to prevent him from seeing Giselle, at least not without her in attendance. She'd have to find a way to inform Giselle of his intent, warn her of the concerns Elspeth had with Edwin. Was she wrong about him? Could her dislike of the man be clouding Elspeth's judgment? She hadn't any proof of his incompetence, though he displayed a perfect exhibit with Preston. But if Dr. Trent hadn't seen fit to intervene, Elspeth would find no agreement from him.

"I believe your coffee is ready," Edwin said, pointing to the stove. "Get your tray together, and I'll follow you up presently." Elspeth nodded, less than pleased with the prospect, but relieved to be engaged in one battle at a time. It hadn't escaped her that Edwin didn't even pretend a show of courtesy and offer to carry the tray for her.

She shook her head as he left the room. And why should Edwin suddenly show any manners which might prove him respectful? Wouldn't want to overtax the delicate hands of a man of his profession, even if Elspeth believed in her heart Edwin was unsuited as a doctor. Edwin and his disingenuousness were more suited to the less savory side of life work that she believed to border on criminal.

Her nerves were suddenly more on edge than the previous day. Elspeth wasn't clairvoyant by any stretch of the imagination, but a sudden flush of dread coursed through her, and she shuddered. Why did the feeling foretell events were about to get direr?

Elspeth needed to separate her professional self from this situation. She would share her thoughts with Reginald, who had, after all, first brought up the suggestion that not all was right in the Gardiner mansion.

****

Astoria strode into the sitting room, the place her mother occupied religiously when at home. She waited until her mother took her seat, and pulled off her gloves as she sank onto the couch next to Rosie's chair. A tea service, like the one that snooty nurse was using, sat on the rollaway cart between them. "Is that still warm?" she asked.

Rosie nodded. "Coffee, however. Still interested?"

"Of course. Anything warm and wet." Astoria took the cup offered and remained silent until she'd taken a few sips. "When the funeral's over, we need to move on." She snickered. "Can't believe after all we've done for that child that he hadn't seen fit to show a bit of gratitude for our endeavors."

Rosie leaned forward to pat Astoria sympathetically. "There wasn't much to leave. She'll have enough to finish her schooling and a dowry for her future husband."

Astoria rolled her eyes. She despised the need to spell the obvious out. Her mother was supposed to be more sympathetic to her oldest daughter's point of view. "What about your funds? Or Reginald's? There are monies we shouldn't allow to go to street children we don't even know. Wasn't it bad enough he sunk so much into that ridiculous park? The old cuss wanted to assure that he wouldn't be forgotten. By next year, no one will remember him. It will be, 'Gardiner Park named after who?' Reginald can't have much longer. You need to convince Uncle Reginald to make Edwin his executor before it's too late. Before more squandering of family monies."

"You sound a little bitter, dear. It's not like we'll be left destitute. Besides, I should object. Don't you believe one of your uncles, on my side, of course, would be better suited to the task?"

"That isn't the point. Our money should remain in our family." Astoria wasn't getting through to her mother. Why should it be easy? Astoria's father had left Rosalind Gardiner a fortune. She needed a different approach. Astoria pulled a tissue from her pocket, dabbed her eyes, and turned away from her mother. "I thought you'd forgiven Edwin."

Rosie chuckled. "What has that to do with anything? Of course, I have."

Rosie's words would have meant more if Rosie's tone held more conviction.

Astoria didn't return her gaze to her mother. She shook her head. "You wouldn't think so, the way you are intentionally missing my point."

"Fine, dear. Please explain it to me," Rosie said, shifting in her chair uncomfortably. "Help me understand."

It wasn't easy to hide her smirk of satisfaction, but Astoria managed. She twisted back to her mother and decided to spread the petition on thick. "My beloved Edwin also wishes to create a legacy. He can't do it on his salary. We need more funds for him to study the horrid diseases plaguing so many. His brilliance can live on long after he is gone."

"I'm more than happy to provide the capital necessary." Rosie wrinkled her brow in confusion. "If his focus is on this study, how can he expect to do it while encumbered with the business as executor of the family monies?"

Astoria ground her teeth. Of all the times to apply reason, why did her mother pick today? "Because he's trying to consider the best interests of this family."

Rosie remained silent for a long while. After

excruciatingly long moments, she said, "If you believe it best, dear, I'll have a word with Reginald."

Hallelujah. "Thank you, Mother. You won't regret it."

Chapter Six

Edwin followed Elspeth closely as she shouldered open Reginald's door, and carried the tray inside. What she saw nearly had her dropping her burden, but from a professional habit—and she abhorred for Edwin to witness her upset—allowed her to bring it safely to the dresser's top. She raced to the Colonel's side, while Edwin stood in the doorway.

Reginald was violently shaking; the comforter kept his arms and legs from flailing too much, and he made guttural sounds. Was he trying to speak? His skin was dreadfully pale. There was a bluish tint suggesting cyanosis. Elspeth wiped a gooey white substance oozing from his between his clenched teeth. "Colonel." She spoke, hoping to catch his focus. Elspeth had no way to talk Reginald through this, mostly because he had no control over what was happening to his body. Reginald's gaze turned to her and mouthed "medicine."

Without moving, Elspeth glanced to the top of the nightstand. The pill Edwin left wasn't there. She squeezed her eyes tight, furious, and distressed, since her intention was to destroy that particular pill and continue with his usual medication was no longer an option. A good two or three minutes passed, and Edwin still stood in the doorway. "Have you any intention of attending the patient?" She twisted toward Edwin long enough to glare.

"Yes, of course. I'll get my bag," Edwin said before finally moving away.

Once Edwin left, Elspeth leaned closer. "I'm so sorry, Colonel. I should have removed the pill before I left. I'm—" She bit her bottom lip between her teeth.

Reginald's mumbles were nearly incoherent, and each hard-pressed due to the quivering. "Ellie...please..." Elspeth nodded. Even in distress like this, Reginald thought of the young woman. A tear slid from her eye, too strong to be held back. Would Giselle be the next victim of whatever was happening in this house? She couldn't take any chances. Edwin had a plan, and Elspeth didn't feel confident enough to fight him.

"Don't...fight...Edwin on anything," Reginald managed to get out. He fell back on the bed, and the shaking limbs minimized slightly. "Always...Ellie." A single tear also fell from Reginald's eye. Elspeth quickly wiped his and hers away. She wouldn't allow anyone to view the Colonel as less than formidable and hoped she portrayed the same. "Watch...back...too."

She would have said more, but Edwin rushed into the room then. Oh, now he shows immediacy, she thought bitterly. "Was he able to talk?" Edwin asked.

"No, just the incoherent muttering," Elspeth said. Afraid he'll identify you as his executioner? she wanted to ask, but remained resolutely silent. She and Reginald understood what was happening, their silent accord in place for whatever happened next.

And it didn't take long.

This time, there was no Dr. Trent. There were no other family members to witness. The only positive point for Elspeth was Giselle wouldn't know what transpired in this room until either the Colonel's miraculous recovery or his death, at Edwin's hands. Edwin removed and filled a syringe.

"What is that?" she asked, her heart hammering in her chest. She couldn't stop this charade without physically attacking Edwin. Damn her career. A man's life was in the balance. But as she moved to perform that very function, Reginald grunted loudly.

"Strychnine," Edwin said, unaware of the silent conversation happening in the room. "He'll need another in fifteen minutes.

When Elspeth glanced in Reginald's direction, he gave a nearly infinitesimal shake of his head. Please, she pleaded with her eyes. Let me save you. Reginald glanced at the ceiling. At first, she believed it was from the fluid Edwin injected in his arm. Then Elspeth understood. Reginald reminded her of Giselle, one floor above. A moment's hesitation, forcing herself to blink back tears, before Elspeth inhaled deeply and took a step back. She needed to focus on something other than Reginald possibly dying in the next few minutes. Well, probably, if Edwin was giving strychnine, as the drug would stimulate the pulse. "Why? His pulse is already racing. If you'd—"

"Must I again remind you of your place, nurse?"

Elspeth bristled. "No, of course not."

Edwin straightened. "Maybe a review of your capabilities is in order." There it was. The threat she expected, but still sent a chill through her. He glanced at his pocket watch. "Make certain he gets another injection in thirteen minutes."

"No." She'd not physically stop Edwin, but Elspeth would not take any part of it either. "If you think this is the best course of action, I leave you to it. For the Colonel's sake, I will remain and assist him as best I can through this. Do as you will to me personally, I don't care." Elspeth cared very much. But in no way would she put the wrong medicine in Reginald. If Edwin followed through with his threat, she could lose all hope of ever opening her care facility. Would James be able to come to her rescue? She would need to talk to her brother. These events were not something she could keep to herself. Not with Giselle's life possibly in the balance.

Elspeth expected more fight and bluster from Edwin.

Instead, he said, "Fine. But I'll not forget your reluctance to provide the services we hired you to do."

"I was hired to care for Colonel Gardiner. You and Dr. Trent are to provide diagnosis and medications." She tried to keep the belligerence from tone but couldn't quite manage. Keep burying your career, Keillor, she chided herself. "If you'd like, I could go call Dr. Trent, get his opinion. Maybe he should be available to assist you as with Colonel Muir."

"That won't be necessary." Edwin scowled. He tilted his head in Reginald's direction. "He's gone into a coma." There was a knock at the door. "Come in," Edwin all but shouted.

Astoria, her usual pinched faced plastered on perfectly, entered the room with Colonel Gardiner's lawyer, Bernard Dailey. "Mr. Dailey is here to see— Oh, dear."

Edwin put on his solicitous expression. "I'm sorry, my dear. The nurse and I found poor Reginald in ill health when we arrived earlier." Elspeth nearly snorted. This charade obviously for Dailey's benefit. She was certain Edwin would have already explained things when he went for his bag. "We're trying to rectify the matter, but I'm afraid his already ill health and the death of Muir has been too big a strain on him."

Dailey stared at the man in bed, pale and unmoving, and asked, "Is he dead?"

Edwin dropped his head. Elspeth knew he didn't want the Colonel to survive. "Not yet, and we can only hope he'll recover successfully."

The lawyer nodded solemnly. "I shall wait if you don't mind. See how events transpire." Another glance at Reginald and he rushed out of the room.

"Will it be much longer?" Astoria asked. The words were solicitous, but Elspeth's ears heard the underlying pleasure of expectation.

With a quick pat to her hand, Edwin said, "No, I shouldn't think so. Maybe you should prepare your mother for the inevitable."

Astoria gave a quick nod. "Of course." She turned and walked out of the room. Elspeth was sure she noted a small smile lift the corner of her lip.

Elspeth's attention focused on Astoria's exit, so she missed Edwin deliver the final injection. She only became aware when Edwin pulled the needle from Reginald's arm and replaced it in his bag.

Edwin moved around the bed and plopped into the seat she'd occupied earlier. Had it only been a little over an hour ago? "Take a walk, Keillor. I'll look after the old man for a bit."

Elspeth balked for a second time this morning, both at the command and in the tone it was given. She didn't want to leave Reginald but knew there was nothing she could do to help him. Not anymore. In her heart, Elspeth gave her final farewell to the cantankerous man she came to love.

But Edwin wouldn't be able to sit and revel over his handiwork. With her hand on the doorknob, Reginald's breathing slowed as it softened. In less than a minute, his breath stopped altogether.

Edwin huffed. "That's it then." Yes, Elspeth thought dismally. You've accomplished your goal. Another great man has died by your miserable hands.

Again, Elspeth believed, painful as it would be, she needed to be the person to break the news to an already grieving young woman.

****

Edwin was leaving Reginald's room when Astoria returned. She noticed Bernard Dailey sitting rigidly on the settee at the end of the hall. Bernard stood and ambled over to them.

"Mrs. Merrick," he said with a nod of acknowledgment. "The Colonel, Doctor?"

"Deceased, I'm afraid," Edwin said. She wanted to slap her husband for sounding so jovial about it. Why wouldn't he learn to apply more empathic emotions to a situation? He didn't have to feel them, which Astoria knew he couldn't. Her six-foot, masculine built husband, with his strong chin and deep-set eyes, sometimes hidden behind his spectacles, was a sadist. A quality that initially drew her to him. Well, if she were honest with herself, Astoria was more drawn to his childlike demeanor, his malleability. A gift most were unaware of his having, in spades.

"Between his recent health issues, and the loss of his cousin yesterday," Astoria said, putting a small catch into her breath, "who also stood as his best friend. It proved too hard on him."

"My condolences to the family," Bernard said. "I shall set the steps in motion to have the will read. I'll let the family know when a time is set, which is agreeable to Colonel Gardiner's executor." He took a step toward the staircase.

"Wait," Astoria said, a hand to his arm. "I don't understand. With Preston gone, the Gardiner estate has no executor."

"Oh, yes, he does. Effective since last week." Bernard placed his hands in his coat pocket. At over six-foot-five and bone-thin, the action made him appear as a haphazardly packed bag of sticks. "Colonel Muir had relinquished his duties. He'd been talking of retiring. Consequently, Colonel Gardiner required a new executor.

He selected and concluded all the necessary signatures and filings early last week." With his job done, Bernard continued his departure.

Astoria was too surprised to stop him. Not that they could say any more at this point. Alone, she spun around and pushed Edwin back into Reginald's room, shutting the door behind her. "Do you know what I have accomplished this morning?" she asked, releasing her fury in clipped words. Edwin stared at her in confusion. Probably wondering if this were a trick question. "I managed to convince Mother to talk to Reginald."

Edwin crossed his arms over his chest. "Guess that's not necessary now."

She glanced toward the bed at Reginald's corpse. "If you hadn't been so hurried in your plans, Mother could have talked Uncle into making you the executor. You know how he always gave in to Mother's insistent whine and cajoling. Now it's too late." Astoria further emphasized her displeasure but pounding her fist against Edwin's chest.

"But not all is lost, dearest." Edwin yanked her into his arms with a vice-like grip to her arms. He roughly pressed his mouth to hers in a demanding kiss, followed with a bite to her lower lip just short of drawing blood. "I'm not yet finished securing our future."

Astoria let him drag and push her onto the bottom of the large bed. Edwin jerked up the layers of her dress, pulled down her underdrawers, and released himself from his trousers.

Chapter Seven

Giselle tugged the woolen cape tighter, more out of nerves than to stave off any chill. She expected this day would arrive, but never suspected it so soon. She had hoped to spend so many more years with her uncle. Now, two days after his death, she and most of Maple Woods were in attendance of his funeral. Giselle was proud of her uncle, but no more so than to learn how important the people of Maple Woods believed him to be, proven by the closing of schools in remembrance. She glanced at the carnation covered coffin, another symbol of love. Anyone who walked the same streets, or even had a passing acquaintance with him, recognized the flower that rested on his lapel every day.

Preston would have loved the service and the many people who spoke of him fondly. He would also be heartbroken to learn Uncle Reginald followed only a day behind. Giselle hoped heaven had a porch and chairs for the two men to relax upon, able to converse freely without the family listening.

She glanced at all those who surrounded the coffin and hovered about the hole that would be his body's final resting place. The Gardiner's, Merrick's, and many local politicians and bank employees who worked with Preston over so many years were here. Giselle had wanted—needed—Elspeth by her side, but Edwin managed to force her to the back. But not before Elspeth gave her a supportive nod. Giselle knew she would not be too far, would rush to her side should she need her.

The reverend seemed to drone on forever. Not that she didn't want the best for Preston, but she was tired of listening to the feigned sobs and sniffles from the Gardiner's, from Astoria. None of them had any real love for her uncle. And, if she were honest with herself, Giselle believed Edwin entirely responsible for his death. Just as she suspected he was accountable for Reginald's death yesterday morning. It broke her heart. Two great men brought down in such horrible manners.

Would she be next? It wasn't like the family held any great feeling for her. Giselle was expendable. She'd also taken Elspeth's words to heart. Don't trust or take anything from Edwin. If possible, only imbibe what she prepared on her own. Elspeth would probably have shared more, but Astoria interrupted, saying Elspeth was needed to provide information about Reginald's death. Reluctantly, it seemed, Elspeth had left the room. Left Giselle to the horror's only her vivid imagination could produce.

The reverend droned on.

"Into the warmth of the earth,

Followed by our sadness and our memories,

May you rest in peace, feeling fulfilled, with our love."

All the surrounding mourners responded, "May the Lord embrace you."

Giselle's lips moved, but she couldn't be sure she spoke aloud.

"May the truth that sets us free," the reverend started solemnly.

And the hope that never dies,

And the love that casts out fear,

Be with us now,

Until day breaks,

And the shadows flee away."

The reverend glanced at the family, closing the bible held in his hands. "We have been blessed by life. Go in peace. Amen."

A collective, "Amen," reverberated from the crowd. With the final word, the crowd unhurriedly dispersed, many giving Giselle a hug or handshake in commiseration of a shared loss.

Behind her, Giselle heard Rosie ask, "We're leaving, Giselle. Are you ready?"

She shook her head. "No, I'll find another way home. I'd like to stay for a while longer."

Rosie sniffed. "As you wish. Mind the weather, child. Wouldn't want you sick next."

The comment was probably innocent enough, but a cold shiver ran down her back. "I'll be mindful, Mrs. Gardiner." Quicker than the non-family mourners, the Gardiner's and the Merrick's were gone.

She was alone with Uncle Preston's coffin. Off to the side, Giselle noted the men with shovels, ready to conclude the coffin's final placement, but they didn't appear too hurried as they hadn't moved from where they stood. Maybe they knew Preston Muir and understood the extent of her loss.

"What should I do next?" Giselle asked the carnation draped coffin. "I believe the mansion may be unsafe for me. I'm sure I can deal with things on my own. What about the children? Who will help with their lessons?"

Movement from the corner of her eye brought her attention to the left. Nurse Keillor had remained. Elspeth. She turned back to Preston's coffin. "Thank you, Uncle, for always listening, for always responding, and for always providing. I will love you forever. Love you until we meet again."

****

Elspeth watched the service, then as the Gardiners and the Merricks slowly returned to their waiting vehicles. She watched the events from beside a tree, off to the left. A large number of people were present, offering a farewell to an honored and appreciated man. She suspected a few were here for the notoriety brought by associating oneself with the fame of being a rich and prominent man in Maple Woods. Elspeth also understood most were here because of the great admiration they held for the man.

As nearly all the crowd dispersed with the final amen, then the exit of the family, Elspeth noted none took charge of Giselle. She remained by the gravesite, alone on more levels than the obvious. She was about to go to Giselle when a deep, softly spoken voice said, "Let me drive you both back." No surprise that her brother—half-brother in truth—came to offer his support to her.

She didn't need to turn to him. He would understand Elspeth's need to keep an ever-watchful eye on Giselle. "She'll soon have to do this again for Colonel Gardiner. He died yesterday."

"You care deeply for this young woman?" he asked, though it sounded more like a statement of fact. There was, and never had been, recrimination in his tone. Elspeth briefly twisted her head to him before she returned her gaze to Giselle. James Campbell, physician, and bacteriologist was younger than Elspeth by two years. He was an addition when Elspeth's mother couldn't take the loneliness after her father passed away. Maybe it was because they were so young when they became a family, or maybe because James was always a giving and caring child, they had blended into a healthy sibling relationship. Even when James became a handsome, highly sought-after bachelor and she was considered the homely spinster sister. "What can I do to help?"

She shook her head. "Other than providing the ride, I don't think there's anything you can do. Giselle lost both the men who gave her love, shared laughter and heartache. Who will be there for her now?"

James pressed a hand to the small of her back, lending his strength to her. "She has you, dearest. You are by far the better knight than I."

"I'm not family, James. What can I do?" Assured that Giselle would not leave her position any time soon by posture and the far-away expression, Elspeth faced her brother and heaved a sigh. James would never scoff at her emotions or when she boldly spoke her opinions. Now she needed to share her fears. "There's something wicked going on in that house, and I fear Giselle might be the next unexplained death."

"They were both old men, so their passing is not considered suspicious." He raised an eyebrow that Elspeth recognized from childhood. He would play the devil's advocate.

"Age was no matter against orneriness, which both had in spades. Preston had many a good year left in him despite any medical condition he had presently. Reginald not as many years, but his recovery was improved." Elspeth shook her head. "Timing is suspicious given Colonel Gardiner was noted to be in the process of changing his will. Colonel Muir is his executor."

"And?"

"And," Elspeth said sharply, but only for his ears. "Edwin Merrick is involved."

James smirked. "Your affection for the man is showing."

Elspeth snorted softly. "Honestly, James, I've tried to mask it, but he just makes my skin crawl. I can't explain it, and I don't believe it has unnaturally influenced my belief in his culpability in the matter." She turned her attention back on Giselle. "After she buries Colonel Gardiner, I'd like to have some of your time to talk about the night of Muir's death, and Gardiner's yesterday morning."

"Time I will always find for you." He cleared his throat. "You truly believe their death's wrongful?" Elspeth nodded. "Then we should find the time sooner rather than later. Will you be able to keep an eye on your young lady until we can make that happen?"

"I certainly hope so. Giselle needs to be willing to accept my intrusion into her privacy." Elspeth took a step forward when Giselle shifted away from Preston's gravesite. "She's ready."

James moved with her. Softly, he said, "Do what you can. We'll find a way to insinuate me into the picture so I can do some snooping of my own."

"Thank you."

"Not necessary," James said. "I'd like to see how strong the pull is."

Elspeth paused. "Pull?"

His smile was too bright for the cemetery, and she would have reprimanded him for it, but didn't want Giselle to see and question her later. "Yes, the pull on your heartstring in her hand."

Giselle saved her from responding. "Thank you, Nurse Keillor, for staying behind with me," Giselle said. A small smile of gratitude graced her lips.

"Elspeth," she said as correction. "And this is my brother, Dr. James Campbell."

"Pleasure to meet you, Dr. Campbell," Giselle said, extending her hand.

"James, to you. For the record, the pleasure is entirely mine." Elspeth's heart warmed at the blush suffusing Giselle's cheek. Then a thought quickly cooled. Was the blush because he offered the informality of his given name, or because she appreciated the attention of her brother? She knew James wouldn't take any infatuation further since he knew her feelings. They never suffered from that particular sibling rivalry. But Giselle was a beautiful young woman and James what a woman like Giselle would be looking to have in her future. In her forever.

Pushing the depressing thought aside, Elspeth said, "James has offered to take us back to the mansion."

James clasped his hands behind his back, and said, "I'd prefer you ladies allowed me to take you to dinner first. After all, how often can I brag about the company provided by two beautiful women?"

"At least you're partially correct with her," Elspeth mumbled.

Her words weren't soft enough. Giselle placed her hand on Elspeth's arm and leaned closer. "Beauty is manifested in many ways, Elspeth. Don't discount your own." Elspeth's step faltered, and Giselle smiled at her while her grip tightened.

James barked a laugh. "Oh, I like this girl." Yes, so do I—entirely too much, Elspeth thought. "Off we go, then," James said, as he escorted them to his car.

Spending more time with Giselle was sure to be a blessing and a curse. Would she be able to sit through a meal in public without making a fool of herself? Without Giselle suspecting the depth of Elspeth's feeling for her? Or would James, willingly or not, conquer Giselle's heart?

****

Giselle felt awful to be enjoying herself. She frowned. Part of her reasoned Preston understood life must go on in his absence, but Giselle still felt she dishonored his memory.

"Enough of that," James said from across the table.

Had she missed something? "Excuse me?"

"Believing you're doing Colonel Muir a disservice," James said. "He would want you to have some time to get your thoughts and feelings together. Especially as you are doing so with others who also appreciated him."

A warm hand covered hers, and Giselle nearly gasped. The touch infused Giselle with feelings of comfort, trust, and strength. Elspeth's hand gave hers a comforting squeeze. "We can leave if you'd be more comfortable." She tilted her head in James' direction and quirked a smile. "He can afford to pay whether we eat the meal or not."

"We couldn't put him out after being so kind." Giselle leaned closer to Elspeth but kept her voice where James would hear, and said in feigned shock, "It wouldn't do to upset him before we gained our ride back." They laughed, but the changes to Elspeth were what snagged Giselle's attention.

Laughter darkened her grey eyes while softening Elspeth's features. She hadn't lied earlier. Elspeth wasn't a conventional beauty, but Giselle saw the depth of her beautiful spirit. Here was a woman who may not show it on the outside but would give her heart and soul to someone she cared for. Giselle wondered if Elspeth had ever done so. What type of person would snag Elspeth's heart?

More importantly, which gender? Having spent some time as a child around her older cousin Lilly, Giselle learned the heart didn't always choose the opposite gender. Or, in Lilly's case, while attracted to the same gender, her heart stayed fickle, and was never wholly given. Of course, Lilly may have settled down by now. It wasn't a subject they could discuss. They'd shared correspondence when Lilly first moved away. They suspected, after the first few letters arrived for Giselle mangled and opened, the letters were read before they were given to Giselle. She'd passed on the information and since then, Lilly hadn't written. The loss of her friendship had proven difficult in the beginning.

Giselle shook the memory, and pulled her attention back to the conversation.

"Assault my affections all you like, ladies. It won't keep me from my duty to you," James said playfully.

"It was your purse that we laid siege to, dear brother."

Giselle smiled, joining in their banter. "I doubt at your age that any number of someones haven't played with your heart. And had the favor returned."

James placed a hand over his alleged offended organ. "Strike at my age and my ability not to be toyed with, or the—" He put a finger to his lip and stared upward, feigning deep thought. "Hard to defend myself when I can't tease with the right word. Toyed with or the toy-er doesn't work."

"I'm sorry." Giselle blushed, her face warm. She hadn't intended to bring age into the conversation. He appeared to be the same age as Elspeth, and Giselle never viewed her as old. "I shouldn't have said that."

"Why ever not?" Elspeth asked. Was she masking hurt from the remark? "Playful teasing is acceptable among friends. And, you're correct, James has broken a few hearts, and had his broken several times, too. Impossible to avoid when you're such a pretty boy, and now so as a man," Elspeth said, patting his cheek playfully for emphasis. "Much to our mother's chagrin, James has yet to settle down in his dotage, and provide her grandchildren."

"What about you, Elspeth?" Giselle asked in a near whisper. "Don't you wish to provide grandchildren?"

Elspeth flushed. "My career leaves me little time. Besides, I can't continue the family name as James can.

Certain duties aren't as pressing for me." Giselle felt she'd wounded Elspeth in some way. Should she press further? Drop the topic? Or ask again when they were in a private place?

"What about you, Giselle? Children?" James frowned. "That's an indelicate conversation after your recent losses. You're in mourning. My apologies."

"Nothing to apologize for," Giselle said. After all, she's the one who muddled a perfect evening with her words. Maybe, she could use this opportunity to get a better idea about expectations in Elspeth's ideal partner. "I need to finish school. Then, I hope to find employment suitable for my business degree." She shrugged. "Honestly, I don't need children of my own. But I would like to have someone to share my life with, who can appreciate me for myself. I don't see myself draped on a man's arm so that he can show off his prowess."

The waiter came to clear the dinner plates. Another inquired if dessert was in order, or maybe a dessert wine? They declined, and he topped off the glasses they already had before moving away. Giselle took a sip and continued, "I would need someone who can treat me like a prized possession without being a possession. Someone who can share a couch or a room with me and not feel a need to fill the silence. Someone who believes laughter and positive words are the best medicine."

James raised an eyebrow. "Sounds very much like someone already at the table." Oh goodness, Giselle thought. I hope he doesn't mean himself. James raised his glass as if in toast, but his gaze was fixed on Elspeth. "Am I right, dearest sister?"

Giselle noticed Elspeth turned a dark, but charming, shade of red. Could he intend— Did a light just flicker in the tunnel of her future? Giselle smiled.

Chapter Eight

With her usual modulated gait, Elspeth walked into Rosie's sitting room. She expected to see at least one Merrick present, but neither was there. Mrs. Rosalind Gardiner was short at five-foot-three, with thick grey hair always pulled up on top of her head. The best description for her was round, from her body type to her bulbous nose. She wasn't a bad woman, overall, but a product of the time and massive bank account. Plus, the woman was easier to deal with when not influenced by either Astoria or Edwin.

Elspeth anticipated and dreaded this day in equal measure. She had no problem leaving the mansion, probably wouldn't look back under other circumstances. But that was when Preston and Reginald lived. Now, she feared for Giselle's safety, wanted to be close by to protect her better. "You wished to see me, ma'am?"

Rosie shifted in her seat, one hand on the arm of her chair, the other resting limply on her lap. "As I'm sure you're aware, with Reginald passed on, your services are no longer required."

"I am." What else could she say?

"The events of the last couple of weeks have raised frustrations and been emotionally trying. That said, I wanted to take this opportunity to bring up the matter of Edwin." Elspeth stiffened. She hoped it wasn't obvious. Rosie hadn't noticed or would have addressed it. Instead, she said, "We have no issue with your work during your time here. However, before you leave us today, I would warn you that Edwin has a bit of temper. I can't control him, so now you're leaving this house, I don't know what he will do."

So, Rosie expected Elspeth to leave today, probably as soon as this conversation concluded. "I understand." What else could she say? Marching orders were given to her and topped with a warning. Not that it was needed. Elspeth didn't doubt Edwin would try to sabotage her career. She would worry more if it were Dr. Trent. Edwin? He didn't have the teeth, no matter what he and his ego believed, to disparage her with more than words. "If there's nothing else, I'll pack my belongings and be out of the house before nightfall."

"Very well," Rosie said. "Should you need a reference—"

"That's not necessary, Mrs. Gardiner." Elspeth didn't wish to burn bridges; however, now, Giselle's well-being was in question. She wanted to be able to come back without being barred from the mansion. "I appreciate the offer. And the opportunity to work in your lovely home." Even if it did border on dangerous, she thought. Not that she'd admit the feelings aloud to anyone but James and Giselle. But Giselle suffered from the same opinions of the danger, right?

Rosie preened from her chair. "Thank you, Nurse. As per usual, your funds will be deposited directly into your account. Good luck."

Elspeth turned and left. She was more than ready to exit this place. Her only regret being Elspeth couldn't take Giselle with her. Of course, she couldn't know how Giselle would view the offer, even if Elspeth's destination were ready for company, let alone long-term guests.

She noticed Giselle's beauty, who wouldn't, and tender heart from the moment she met her. During Elspeth's extended stay as a live-in nurse to Colonel Gardiner, her affections for the Giselle grew. How could her appreciation not increase when Giselle spent quality time with both Colonels? Elspeth had to interact or be considered rude. Granted, she wasn't the most expressive person herself. Giselle never dismissed Elspeth, like so many wealthy and entitled, and attempted to include her in the teasing of the older men.

The problem was Elspeth couldn't control her infatuation, her attraction to Giselle. Until Reginald's request during the buggy ride. When he asked her to look after Giselle, hinting more could come of the arrangement, Elspeth was unable to think of little else. Then, with the loss of both men, one hug of support, Elspeth's heart became lost in all that was Giselle.

After sharing a relaxing and enjoyable dinner with Giselle and James, Elspeth had spent the moments wondering if she could ever be more than a friend to the young woman. James further confused the situation with his comment. Had Giselle understood his underlying meaning? Was she disgusted by it? Would Elspeth lose Giselle's budding friendship?

Enough, she scolded herself. Elspeth needed to pack and vacate the premises. She hoped Giselle would come to see her off. Should Elspeth find Giselle to say goodbye?

Goodness, infatuation was too complicated.

****

Giselle found Elspeth, finally, walking up the stairs for the third floor, having searched as unobtrusively as possible. She was glad to find the woman alone. She didn't want the family to learn Giselle purposely sought her out.

"Elspeth."

She turned and gave Giselle a wry smile. "I'm preparing to pack. Would you like to join me?" Elspeth stared beyond Giselle and down the staircase. "I could tell you more about the book we were discussing with Colonel Gardiner before I go."

"Of course, I was hoping you would," Giselle said. She moved up the stairs after Elspeth, who started walking again. She suspected Elspeth wanted to forestall later questions of her, or at least give her a topic if questioned by the family later.

Elspeth's room was at the opposite end of the same floor as hers, the layout the same, as was the size. The difference made by the furniture. Preston upgraded Giselle's, but this room's furniture, fundamental and reliable, lacked all personality. Elspeth pulled a carpetbag from beside the armoire, placed it on the bed, and opened it. She then proceeded to remove items from the armoire and dropped them into the suitcase, all without once looking at Giselle. The idea she had somehow displeased Elspeth saddened her.

"Have I upset you?" she asked.

Back turned to her, Elspeth said, "No, of course not." She quickly glanced over her shoulder. "I'm expected to leave immediately. Goodness knows I have no wish to be here if the Merrick's come by."

Giselle could understand. She didn't fully believe her but couldn't put her feelings into words. Would this be the last Giselle ever encountered Elspeth? She at least wanted to share her fears. "I think the Colonels were murdered," she said. Elspeth's back stiffened, but she didn't move for many moments.

Finally, Elspeth heaved a sigh. Dropping her head, Elspeth said, "I do too, but can't prove it." She turned to her, and Giselle saw a parade of emotions flicker across Elspeth's face. "I have no reason to stay, have already been dismissed, so I can't provide you protection."

"I don't need protection," Giselle said, surprised at her protest.

Elspeth smiled sadly. "Of course. My apologies if you took offense." She stepped toward Giselle, seemed to rethink her actions, then moved to the other side of the bed. She removed a few items from the small drawer of the nightstand.

"Should I talk to someone about my fears?" Giselle asked. "I mean if he—"

"No," Elspeth all but yelled. "Don't do anything, Giselle. You can't put yourself in danger." She quickly came back around the bed and clasped Giselle's hands. Elspeth squeezed her eyes shut for a moment, then focused on her. "I want you to move away. I can't provide you anything as fine as this, but you'd be safe. Please, consider leaving here." Elspeth released one hand and pulled a piece of paper from a hidden pocket at her waist and held it out to Giselle. "This is my address. You're welcome anytime. For as long as you wish."

Giselle accepted the paper. "I appreciate the offer but can't leave the children right now."

"I suspected as much. Sometimes you're too caring for your own good," Elspeth said. "The offer is always open." With a squeeze to the hand she still held, Elspeth said, "It's a lot to ask of you but don't trust the food or drink. Make your own and take it to your room or even the library. Go out if you must. Don't let anything you consume out of your sight. If you get as much as a headache, don't take any medicine from Edwin. Please."

"Do you think I'm next?" Giselle asked, the word difficult to release over the lump of fear in her throat. She carried the same worries.

Elspeth nodded. "I plan to have a conversation with James and recommend he check into the matter."

"It can't be safe for him if he does that," she said. Who knew where Edwin would stop in whatever diabolical plan he devised?

"James can acquire information by talking business. He'll be fine. You are the one I worry about." Giselle then grew aware of their still joined hand, of Elspeth's thumb brushing soft circles to the top. If she looked down, or in any way made Elspeth aware of her actions, it would embarrass Elspeth. Not to mention the soft comfort the small gesture provided to Giselle would cease. "I'll keep in contact so you know what is going on. The offer is open. You'll always have a place with me. I could even find another place for you if my company doesn't suit you."

Before Elspeth could release her hand, Giselle tugged and brought her into an embrace. There was warmth and comfort when they'd hugged after Uncle Preston's death. She felt the same this time too. But there was something else, something Giselle couldn't put her finger on. Something deeper, through to her soul. Until this moment, when she was about to lose daily contact with Elspeth, Giselle realized how much Elspeth meant to her peace of mind, to her feelings of safety, belonging, cherished.

Elspeth pulled away slowly, turned and secured her carpetbag, then faced her. "Never doubt your importance to me. My offer has nothing to do with politeness, and everything to do with how much I care for you, Giselle." Elspeth's face held sadness, even as it reddened in a flush. "Stay safe," Elspeth said. She caressed Giselle's cheek. An explosion of emotions raced through Giselle. What were these confusing emotions? This was more than friendship, wasn't it?

Giselle felt tears welling in her eyes. She tried to force them back, but knew she failed when Elspeth brushed the pad of her thumb across the cheek she held in her hand. "I'm going to miss you, Elspeth."

"And I will miss you." Elspeth gave a wry smile. "Please don't let it be for too long."

She could do nothing but nod. Anything else would

have her breaking down and throwing herself into Elspeth's arms again. Elspeth left the room first, Giselle following as far as her room. There appeared to be a silent understanding; this would be where they parted company. She stared after Elspeth as she made her way down the staircase. Once out of sight, Giselle rushed into her room, threw herself across the bed, and let the tears flow freely.

Was it because she was all alone now? Ready to latch on to anyone who showed the slightest positive attention for her? Or, had Elspeth become such a secure constant in her life, alongside Uncle's Preston and Reginald, that Giselle hadn't noticed when Elspeth became more? But how much more and what did it mean? She felt drawn to Elspeth in ways she didn't understand. Found herself looking at the older woman in ways no one else appeared to see her. Found herself looking at Elspeth in ways a friend should not. What would Elspeth think of her if she suspected even a hint of what Giselle felt when they were in the same room?

The memory of Elspeth's flushed face at dinner, James's words, brought Giselle into a sitting position. Could it be possible? Might James have confirmed Elspeth could be more to her than just a friend? Giselle grinned, but it quickly disappeared. How did one go about getting a stoic, solid woman to admit similar feelings? Did they share the same attraction? Giselle fell back onto her bed. Why was this so hard to work out? No wonder the Colonels had remained bachelors.

Chapter Nine

The family estate consisted of a three-story, square brick structure with more rooms than any one family should fill, set in the middle of twenty acres. The original intention of the design was to resemble the plantation homes in the south. Why building this type of model on the outskirts of Denver, Elspeth would never know. There were probably journals or such in the massive family library, but she didn't care. At least not enough to seek out the answers at this time. She had a plan. And, with the contribution to her funds before the death of Colonel Gardiner, Elspeth would be able to transform the rundown structure to the facility of her dreams.

Elspeth managed to clean a single room, one she intended as her permanent set of chambers. She planned the area for sleeping, entertainment, and office space. There was also a room for at least one guest in her new home. Elspeth hoped to offer that chamber to Giselle, wanting to invite Giselle to join her in this new venture.

In the living room of the suite, she pulled the dust cover from a small couch and plopped down with a low groan. She startled when a voice said, "Long day, dear?" James entered from the door she'd left open to the suite of rooms. "I'm sorry. I should have made more noise when entering."

She shrugged. "I should have locked the doors."

"Ah, not necessarily a prohibitive act against a brother with a key."

"Then, I shall add lock changing to the list of things to do." Elspeth smiled at James as he sat beside her. "What brings you here tonight?"

James slapped a hand to his chest. "Does a sibling need a reason to visit his sister?" He tapped a palm to her leg twice. "Needed to make certain you were doing okay after leaving a beautiful, auburn-haired young lady behind."

Tears of frustration filled her eyes. She turned away from him. "That was the hardest thing I've done, James." Her voice broke, and then she inhaled deeply. James pointedly ignored her turmoil. He'd never make light of her emotions. At least, not since they were teens and he'd laughed at her tears when she'd refused to talk or interact with him for nearly three months. Elspeth perfected her impenetrable walls during that period. "I invited her to come here. I'm scared for her. She's so sweet, so trusting."

"Did you share your concerns with her?"

She nodded. "Giselle came to me while I packed. She shared her suspicions of Edwin murdering her uncles." Elspeth managed to get her emotions mostly under control, and twisted to face him. "This will sound like something out of one of those gothic novels, but I believe Edwin is attempting to remove anyone between him and the Gardiner fortune. No sooner does Colonel Gardiner mention changing his will, both he and Colonel Muir are dead."

James frowned. "Then Miss Saunders should be safe, shouldn't she? Is she in receipt of a fortune?"

"Not that Edwin can get his hands on. But I don't know what his grand scheme entails. It isn't a secret that Giselle is less than impressed with him, especially after Muir's death." Elspeth shook her head. "There's no love lost between us, so I wouldn't be surprised if Edwin took his frustrations out on her. Especially as she no longer has anyone to defend her. Did I tell you Edwin wanted me to talk Colonel Gardiner into making him the executor for the family?"

"What did you tell him?" James asked.

"I glared at him and walked away."

James snorted. "I've been the recipient of one of those glares. Bet he wet himself."

"Be nice." Elspeth lightly slapped his shoulder, then stood. "James, I can't prove it, even with Dr. Trent present, Edwin killed Preston, and the next day, Reginald." She paced in front of him as she conveyed the events that she witnessed surrounding both deaths. "Reginald knew what was happening to him and wouldn't let me stop it. I believe he thought my intervention would make me a target too."

James asked, "What do you need from me?"

Elspeth shrugged. "There isn't anything you can do in terms of an investigation. But, would you consider meeting with him? I'd like to learn about your impressions. Just because I think he's a slug doesn't mean you will."

James was silent for so long, Elspeth expected him to decline her request, surprised when he didn't. "You're right. We've no proof of his perfidy. But I can determine if he requires some watching." He stood and halted her pacing by placing his hands on her shoulders. "Watch yourself. Keep this place locked, especially when you're here alone. Lock changing is a good idea." He released her shoulders. "We'll keep your young lady safe, too."

"She's not my young lady, James." He raised a questioning eyebrow. Elspeth ignored it. "However, I did promise, at Colonel Gardiner's specific request to look out for her."

"See that you do," James said. His tone feigned reprimand. "Now. Show me around this mausoleum and explain your plans." Three-quarters of an hour later, James walked to the front door with Elspeth following. "I'm proud of you. With the few changes I noted, use them or not, you will have a wonderful business here."

"Thank you, James. Your opinion means a lot to me. I hope you consider offering your services and time, for a fee, of course," she added with a smile. "With your assistance and our old home, we can bring life and laughter back within these walls."

"When does the construction crew begin the repairs and modifications?"

"They'll start next week. I'll be certain to contact the foreman about the changes we discussed tonight." She crossed her arms over her chest. "The schedule isn't as quick as I'd like, but that is probably due to my impatience. It will be into the new year before the work will be complete."

"That could work to your advantage. Plenty of time to work on your business plan and get your personal life in order."

"What's wrong with my personal life?" she asked, more defensively than intended. They both knew she understood what he meant. The image of Giselle flashed in her mind.

"Add contacting the telephone company to your list of immediate things to do."

She smirked. "Why, so you can call before you scare the wits out of a woman?"

James's smile beamed, nearly wicked. He leaned down and kissed her forehead. "To call a certain young lady to make sure she's well and hearty. And to repeat your invitation as many times as necessary until she agrees."

"That could backfire, James. Scare her into staying away."

He shrugged. "Or, place Giselle safely under this roof. With someone who has only her best interest in mind."

"It would be best if she could contact me, to talk or visit, when best suits her." Elspeth reached up and bussed a kiss to his cheek. "Thank you for stopping by. You always manage to lift my spirits."

"What are little brothers for?"

"Teasing, mostly."

"Too true, too true. Okay. I leave you to your rest, remodeling, and planning. I'll let you know what happens with Merrick."

"You think he'll agree to meet with you?" she asked.

"If he's as you perceive him," James said, opening the door. "He'll jump at the opportunity to toot his own horn." He stepped outside. "Sleep tight. And lock this behind me."

As James strode away, Elspeth closed and locked the door, having secured the building during her tour with James. She made her way to her suite of rooms. Elspeth closed and locked the suite door, and made her way to her bedroom, glad she'd cleaned the room and placed fresh sheets on the bed.

A rush of loneliness filled her. Elspeth, used to her solitude, suddenly felt alone. But there was only one person she wanted to share in her privacy, share in her life. About a quarter-hour later, Elspeth turned out the light, climbed into bed, and closed her eyes. "Good night, Giselle," she whispered into the dark. "May you keep safe."

****

Only James' love for his sister would force him to share space with this man. He'd heard mutterings about Edwin around various medical facilities over the years. He conducted further digging after his talk with Elspeth and conceded, with much reluctance, to dinner with Dr. Edwin

Merrick.

James spoke with one of the nurses Edwin previously worked with before she married and quit her career for the job of raising children. He trusted her opinion and wasn't surprised with her comment that Merrick has a snap-on, snap-off personality, manifested before his eyes. Edwin's emotional responses did just that. He would seem incapable of animated reaction one moment and then snap, he would show a reaction. It wouldn't take long before he clicked back off as if nothing short of torture would get him to respond with any form of real sensitivity.

"So, what do you see yourself doing in the future?" James asked. "Continuing your medical career?"

"No, no," Edwin replied, his features impassive as he sipped his wine. "I'd like to set up a laboratory for the study of disease bacteria. You of all people understand the fascination, being a noted bacteriologist, in how something so minute as bacteria can have such devastating repercussions on living organisms." Edwin's sudden grin was almost sinister before it disappeared quickly.

"Such as human organisms?" James asked.

"Exactly."

Before he could consider it, James proposed, "If you were to come by my laboratory, I could provide you an assortment of germ species. A starter collection if you will." A chill ran up James' spine. Did he just offer to give potentially lethal specimens to a possible murderer? He consoled himself with the knowledge that ingratiating himself to Edwin could provide the opportunity to check in with and discern Edwin's real intent without raising suspicion.

This time, James knew Edwin's grin held a disturbing purpose. The first time any honest emotion lit Merrick's eyes. And it shone dark and creepy. "I'd appreciate that, James. I could get some glass tubes of sterile culture jelly together. It would be a great beginning to my study."

"No problem, Merrick. We inquisitive minds must bond together."

Edwin smiled emptily. "Glad you see it that way. Most would worry about infringements on their work."

James waved a hand dismissively. "Nonsense. I doubt our studies will follow the same lines. Even similarities can be productive."

"Quite so."

Making headway with their dinner bonding, James decided the time came to change the topic closer to home. At least for Edwin. Closer to the reason he agreed to entertain him. "Terrible business about Colonels Gardiner and Muir. Not surprising, though," he added when Edwin scowled. "Quite a few years on them. A shame to lose both so close together. Must be quite trying on the family, to bury the men right after one another."

Edwin stared at him for so long, James believed he overstepped their new alleged friendship. Would Edwin become suspicious of his motives for dinner? "Yes. I do what I can for the family, but you can't rush the mourning process. This has taken a toll on my dear wife. It's equally disappointing to be so close to the holidays."

"Ah, yes. Thanksgiving is just around the corner, isn't it?" James topped their glasses from the bottle resting on ice in the bucket beside the table. "Having to decide whether or not to celebrate must be a difficult one."

Edwin frowned. "What do you mean?"

"Double-edged sword, my man." He could almost see the wheels turning in Edwin's head. Was he calculating what he may have missed? "On the one hand, being thankful for those loved ones alive and well in your life." James shrugged negligently. "On the other, does it appear disrespectful to be celebrating so soon after the family members you've lost."

"Disrespectful, how?"

"Well," James said, drawing out the word. "Celebrating Thanksgiving is kind of an acknowledgment that says I'm thankful it wasn't me, doesn't it?"

"Hadn't thought of that," Edwin said, his voice a mere whisper. There was a long silence between them. James only meant to change the subject so as not to alert the other man to his inquiry's real intention. But a strange expression crossed Edwin's face, one James couldn't quite identify. Finally, Edwin sat straighter in his chair, with palms pressed to the table. He realized Edwin intended to take his leave. "Thank you, James, for dinner. Lovely time." Edwin stood, and his expression blanked. "I'll be by for those specimens. I appreciate your assistance." Edwin's voice dropped again as if in preoccupation. "Need to talk to my wife." He held out his hand, which James shook and noted Edwin's sweaty palm before Edwin spun on his heel and left.

James sat confused for a moment as he stared after the departing Edwin. While Edwin's reactions proved a bit off, they were far from nefarious. Instead, they could be explained as an earnest man's distraction in thought about reveling in a holiday too early. He now understood Elspeth's dilemma. Nothing Edwin did outwardly proved him to be anything but odd. However, there was something James couldn't quite put his finger on that led him to believe, as did his sister, wickedness lurked within Edwin Merrick. He and Elspeth were usually rather good at judging character. He doubted they were too off the mark on this matter.

He managed to sign off on the check, added a substantial tip, and took his leave of the restaurant for a destination he'd intended to leave for tomorrow. James needed to talk to Elspeth while the dinner was fresh in his mind. He hurried to his car and drove directly toward his rock of rational thinking. Directly toward Elspeth.

****

"Well?" Elspeth said, holding the door open for James to enter. "How did things go with Merrick?" James came in, and she noted his preoccupation. "Whatever is wrong with you, James?"

"S'why I'm here. I'm not certain." James followed her inside, waited for her to sit on the couch and joined her, his brow furrowing deeper. "It's the strangest thing, being prepared to maintain an open mind about the fellow and finding I have no more of an explanation for Edwin Merrick than anyone else."

"I don't understand," Elspeth said. She'd only seen James this distracted with a problematic prognosis on a patient he cared for deeply. Her brother cared about all his patients, naturally, but some had burrowed into his heart.

He stared directly into her gaze. "There's a feeling deep in my bones when I was with him that all is not right, beyond his being simply an oddball. A feeling which shouts the man has embraced the darker side of curiosity. And there are records to prove it, records confirming Edwin conducted himself just shy of torture on his less fortunate patients." Elspeth watched as his gaze shifted away from her and she tried to prepare herself for his next words. "I may have agreed to help in the next steps of whatever deed he has planned."

"Help how?" she asked. "What aren't you saying, James? Has he murdered before, or only tortured people?"

James leaned against the back of the couch. "If Edwin has murdered, there's no sign of it on record. There is, however, a record of a complaint by a who…ah…a woman of the evening. She managed to get away from Edwin and find a constable to alert. It seems Edwin placed mustard-oil on her genitals." Elspeth winced at the cruelty of it, and the pain that the poor woman must have suffered. James's next words confirmed her thoughts. "She couldn't walk, couldn't stand. The woman dragged herself from the building until she located a constable." She held back the playful teasing customary with her little brother. She held back the smile when James couldn't say whore but had no difficulty speaking of very personal human parts.

"I'm not surprised," she said. Elspeth remembered Edwin's expression as he stared down at the form of Preston in pain, watched as increased amounts of blood drained into the jar. She knew he'd have removed every drop if Astoria hadn't stopped him. If there hadn't been witnesses, well. Not that Edwin had appeared aware of their presence. Like a hammer to her head, Elspeth registered James' other statement. "What do you mean you may have agreed to help him?"

"He asked for specimens for study and," he lifted one shoulder. "I agreed to provide them from my laboratory. He'll be by sometime this week."

Elspeth leaned back and turned her gaze to the large window behind the desk a few feet away. She understood the vagaries associated with medicine and research. James would look foolish if he denied the assistance to a fellow doctor. He also couldn't take back an offer freely given. Did that put Giselle in further danger? She was doing a poor job of protecting the young woman. How was she supposed to—

"Elspeth?" James placed a hand on her thigh. "Are you alright?" Genuine concern clouded his gaze.

"Yes, fine," she said, though they both knew she lied.

"You're worried about Giselle, aren't you?"

She snorted. "Like I have a right to anymore." Elspeth

told him about her conversation months earlier with Colonel Gardiner. "I owe it to the Colonel to keep my word, James. But how am I to do so when I no longer have reason to be at the house."

James shifted closer. "It's more than that, and you know it. You owe it more to yourself than to the Colonel. Giselle already has your heart."

Elspeth jumped from the couch and paced. "Damn, is it that obvious? She must be disgusted." Although, Giselle wouldn't have embraced her during their goodbye if she were appalled by Elspeth, would she?

James snorted. "I seriously doubt that." He stood from the couch and walked to her, forcing her to cease her pacing. Placing his hands on her shoulders, he said, "I saw the looks from both of you, at dinner, when neither of you thought anyone was watching. Giselle may not understand what she feels for you, but basic friendship is not what I saw."

She shook her head. "She's so young, James." And so beautiful and smart and kind, Elspeth wanted to add, but had no reason to acknowledge or list all Giselle's apparent attributes. She trusted very few people in her life, some having broken the faith she'd given, along with her heart for one woman. Isolating herself from people hadn't been too hard for her. Her naturally severe appearance, along with her speak-only-when-it-serves personality, made it difficult for others to attempt to get inside her emotional barriers. Any person who worked at it managed to win the accomplishment. Giselle never had to work for it. Giselle had only to look at her and smile.

"In age, maybe. But inside the adorable young woman is an intelligent old soul. How are you going to know if you don't try?"

Elspeth raised her hands above her head and groaned in exasperation. "What do you propose, oh smarty britches brother? I stand before her and announce my intentions to ravish her sometime in the nearest future?"

"Oh, ha-ha, this is rich." James plopped back on the couch and slapped his hands loudly on his thighs in three rapid successions. He gazed at her for so long, as if he could see through to her psyche. After tense minutes, all of them hers, tone serious, he said, "This is stronger than your feelings for Maddie, isn't it?"

She sucked in a surprised breath. Did James remember her last lover? But they'd barely met each other, and Elspeth hadn't been as forthcoming with sharing all of herself with him then. "How did you know? You met her once, maybe twice."

"Give me credit, big sister. Much as you'll hate to hear this, it was in your eyes. The way you gazed at her as if you'd been given a miracle." James cleared his throat. "But the same intensity was never returned, hon. Not that I don't doubt she cared for you in her own way."

Elspeth nodded, walked to the desk, and leaned against it, afraid if she sat beside James, all the pain would return. Yes, she loved her brother, but crying wasn't something she looked forward to sharing with him. "I know she loved me. But love wasn't enough for her." Madeline Brewster, now Jenkins, had been her lover in nursing school. While Elspeth conceived plans for a future together, Maddie had been biding her time until the right man—rich enough—came along. Maddie believed a woman could never follow her heart in romance. That kind of affection was for passing the time until a woman's destiny was adequately fulfilled. Women were made for men and to keep their household, birth and raise their children, until death parted them. Elspeth had been hurt, but didn't regret her time with Maddie, or her decision. What were Giselle's feeling on the topic? she wondered, then said as much. "Giselle may view her future much as

Maddie did."

James shrugged. "Possible, but doubtful." He tapped the side of his nose. "The answer is elementary, my dear. If you give her a reason to visit," he said, head tilted to the side.

"Giselle knows she has a place here," Elspeth said. She pushed off the desk and walked toward him. "She's been through so much, James, which makes her vulnerable. I don't wish to add to the burdens already on her."

"Well, think about it," James said as he rose. "I need to go home and get some rest. In the morning, maybe, I'll have come to grips with whatever has me so disturbed about Merrick." He walked through the suite door and toward the front door where he stopped so suddenly Elspeth literally slammed into his back. "We're so blind, Mairi." He spun toward her. His excitement palpable in his expression and use of her middle name, which he preferred. "She's about to graduate with a business degree. Why not have her assist? At least until she can find full-time employment. She could help with cataloging the construction costs, cost of supplies and equipment. Make her feel useful."

"I don't know, James." Elspeth dropped her head. It was a good suggestion, but would Giselle believe herself only an employee? Would that be so bad if it meant she was safe under Elspeth's roof? If it was only the two of them, how long before Giselle realized how deeply Elspeth cared for her? She could very well frighten Giselle and lose her completely.

James tucked a finger under her chin, and said, "Offer. Whether you share an attachment of the heart or not, Giselle will be safe. I know her safety is important to you, right now. Baby steps, Mairi." He leaned down, planted a quick kiss to her forehead, and walked outside. "The rest will come in time," he said, waving over his shoulder as he walked to his car.

Elspeth closed and secured the door. She locked the suite's outer door and returned to the couch, her head in turmoil. Merrick was a dangerous man. Murdering two prominent men in Maple Woods was daring. James was right. Elspeth had to try to get Giselle away from the Gardiner house. If Giselle proved to be no more than a good friend when all was said and done, so be it. Would Elspeth be able to keep her from suspecting how deep her feelings went for Giselle? Would she be able to maintain distance with Giselle nearby, alone together? Elspeth had to do it. Giselle's safety depended on it.

She threw her head back against the couch with a thud and groaned. "I just have to assure my eyes aren't tattling on me."

Chapter Ten

Giselle left Blanche and Susan Gardiner's room, where she'd been working with them on their homework. A few minutes ago, Charles , the oldest and only Gardiner son, had come home feeling ill and asked if she'd let the cook know he wouldn't be eating dinner. "Would you like me to have the doctor brought in?" she asked.

Charles shook his head and trudged to his bedroom door. "Nah, I just need to rest."

"Alright, then." She watched him enter and close the door behind him. Giselle wondered what virus might be going around since the youngest girls had been cranky and unable to concentrate fully. Giselle shook her head to clear it, then went downstairs to the kitchen. She'd pass Charles's message along, and warm up some of the soup she'd prepared yesterday. Soup and a good book would be the perfect way to relax tonight. Other than her intermittent interactions with the children, Giselle had no wish to spend any time with the older members of the family.

There was unique comfort to a kitchen, especially this one, when the cook was baking. "Oh, Lottie, supper smells wonderful."

Lottie Kaplan was a large, heavy-boned, and round woman. She stood close to six-foot, with blonde hair quickly fading to grey. Sparkly blue eyes, set in a pale face above rosy cheekbones, flicked Giselle's way, before returning focus on the pie crust dough she was rolling. "But, you won't be eating any?"

"It's not your—"

"I know, child. And with your Uncles dead—" Lottie

winced. "I'm sorry."

But Lottie didn't finish her thoughts. Edwin pushed the kitchen door open, hard enough to slam it into the wall with a loud bang. "Ah, Giselle. Will you be joining us for dinner?" He waggled a finger in her direction. "I think you're avoiding us."

Giselle straightened, doing her best not to flee his presence. "I was just telling Lottie to bring..." Damn. She didn't want Edwin to check on Charles, check on anyone.

"Bring...a tray? To whom?" Was that a gleam of glee in his eyes? Was he expecting illness? "Someone ill?"

"No, nothing like that," Giselle said. "Charles is tired." She started to move to the refrigerator for her soup but stopped. The bowl had been unattended; she couldn't eat it now. Edwin had no problems entering the kitchen, and Lottie wasn't here all the time. She'd have to come back later when the family was busy. "I have studies and papers to complete," Giselle said, realizing she'd have to brush past Edwin if she left the way she entered since he still stood in the doorway. Giselle stepped in the direction of the servant's staircase instead.

Only for that exit to be blocked by Edwin. "What's the hurry?" He grabbed her elbow, his grip painful, his glare vicious. "Did that witch of a nurse say something to you?"

Startled, Giselle jerked her arm from his grip. "What?" Why would he say such a thing if he weren't genuinely guilty of misdeeds?

"Why are you avoiding us?" Edwin asked, teeth grit.

She took a step back, closer to Lottie. The sad thing about rich people and servants, the former never seemed aware of the latter. Her presence made Giselle feel better, nonetheless. Giselle hoped the glare she directed at him reflected the angry fire she felt. "I just buried two of the most important men in my life. I'm in the last months of my degree. I believe I'm entitled to a little time alone to mourn while I work at the one thing which made them proud of me."

Edwin took a small step back, holding his hands in front of him as if warding off an attack, his vehemence of a moment ago vanished behind a facade of unexpected shock. "I only meant this is a time to be with family, to let us support you."

"Uncle Preston was my family." Giselle shook her head. He'd never understand. To so many of his ilk, the family was the same as a commodity. "I'd like to go to my room now, if you don't mind."

"Before you go, you should know that I've come to ask the cook," he stabbed a finger in Lottie's direction, "and Mother Gardiner if we can delay Thanksgiving a day or two. Whatever we decide, I think it would be considerate of you to join us for at least that meal."

Giselle refused to provide an answer. She wouldn't, but he needn't know that now. Instead, she harrumphed and walked toward the servant's stairs. "Good night, Lottie." So as not to be too rude, she glanced at him. "Edwin."

"We're here if you need us," Edwin said. "We need each other, family, I mean."

She didn't reply; she just went straight to her room. Giselle hadn't realized how unnerved the interaction had affected her until closing her door and turning the key in the lock, and realized she was trembling. What was Edwin doing? Why would he possibly need a reason to change the day of a holiday meal? Would he want to move Christmas next? More important, why so adamant about her presence at the family table? A table no longer his except for visits. A shiver ran up her spine. He and Astoria never visited this frequently before, so why now?

A knock sounded at her door, and Giselle hesitated,

worried that Edwin had followed her. "Miss Giselle," Lottie's voice whispered through the wood. "It's just me." Giselle unlocked the door and pulled it open. Lottie stood with a linen-covered tray. "I know you've been careful, Miss Giselle, but I can't see you going without food. When I noticed you'd gone without lunch," Lottie bowed her head, "and Miss Astoria and Doc Merrick was here, I couldn't let you miss supper, too." Lottie stepped into the room. "Now I hope you're trusting me, Miss, I didn't make any of the meal here," she said, taking the tray to the small table.

Giselle felt guilty, believing she may have insulted the woman. "Lottie, I hope you know it's not your cooking I'm wary of."

"I know that Miss or you'd be avoiding me too. After both the Colonel's, I'd be purdy suspicious of things in this house myself. So, my oldest girl, she cooks at that place a few blocks from here, brung this over on her way home." Her eyes gleamed with mischief. "Doc Merrick ain't been anywhere near it. Came after he stormed outta the kitchen."

"Thank you, Lottie. You needn't have gone through the trouble for me." Giselle felt warmed from Lottie's consideration. "Please, thank your daughter for me."

Lottie beamed a smile. "It's our pleasure, Miss." Her smile disappeared and her tone grew somber. "Don't tell anyone I've said this, but I'm scared of what's been happening. Please be careful." Her voice lowered, and Giselle would have missed her words if they hadn't been so close. "I know I'm being disrespectful and can lose my job. But, them Merrick's? Well." Lottie scrunched up her nose. "He's a hard one to take kindly to. And I've been around Miss Astoria since she's been a little girl." Giselle had only been with the family for a few years. "We both know she's a mean one."

"No one will hear of your concerns from me, Lottie. Please, look after yourself, too." Giselle stood on tiptoes and kissed her cheek. "Things are bound to change soon."

Lottie nodded as she moved into the hallway. "Yes, Miss. But which side will the changing land? Good or bad?" With those words, Lottie made her way toward the servant's stairs, and Giselle closed and locked her door again.

At the table, she lifted the linen napkin to reveal a teapot and cup, a small plate with a wedge of blueberry pie. There was another folded linen napkin under her utensils. Finally, a plate containing mashed potatoes and gravy, roast beef, and string beans with bacon lay before her. Giselle smiled, sitting to enjoy the meal. It was a heartwarming blessing with such caring people in her orbit. If only…

If only, Giselle thought, I could walk down the hall and share today's events with Elspeth. Of course, if Elspeth was in the house, Edwin would think twice about confronting Giselle as he did. He'd been careful around Uncle Preston and Uncle Reginald. She had no one to go to now.

Giselle nearly lost her appetite. Lottie, and her daughter, had gone through so much trouble to assure she ate tonight. She couldn't disappoint them. And, wishing wouldn't accomplish anything. So, she devoured the meal, surprised at how famished she was, not aware of it until the first mouthful was consumed.

What would Elspeth think of Edwin's actions in the kitchen? Giselle wished she'd dared to slug him for his name-calling.

She missed Elspeth, wondered if she missed her at all. Why would she? Giselle groused. A successful nurse, smart, and mature, miss the company of a mere child? Giselle remembered how much she'd enjoyed the dinner she shared with her and James. It was the most relaxed she'd felt in a long time. That's all it was to them, right? Politeness for the girl who had just buried her uncle.

The warmth and feelings of safety Giselle felt when hugging Elspeth goodbye were real. Elspeth gave Giselle her address, said it wasn't due to social politeness. She wouldn't have done that if she hadn't expected Giselle to accept the offer and visit. Elspeth wasn't one to feign offers, pretend courtesy that she didn't feel. Was she? Maybe Giselle didn't know Elspeth at all.

There was one way to find out. Giselle would have to visit Elspeth. It was the polite thing to do. Then, maybe, she'd be able to discern Elspeth's true motives in her offer to Giselle. Possibly, Giselle would be able to understand what she felt for the stoic and charming woman.

****

"Really, Mother, is this a time to go gallivanting around the country?" Astoria whined so loud Giselle heard her from the library. Rosie planned this trip with her friend's ages ago. Even Giselle remembered, and she'd only known about it from overhearing the discussion. Why the sudden need for her mother? Giselle snickered quietly. The Merrick's were perfect for each other, as both brought her to shudders. Both were as bad as spoiled children.

"It's only for a week, Astoria. What possible reason would compel me to cancel at the last moment?"

"What if something were to happen?"

Rosie sniffed loudly. "Then it shall happen whether I'm here or there. Is there something you aren't telling me?"

"Nothing," Astoria said, her tone defensive. "Can't a

daughter want to spend time with her mother?"

"We just spent Thanksgiving together." There was a long stretch of silence before Rosie spoke again, her voice higher in pitch. "Astoria, are you with child?" Her excitement at the prospect keen in her tone.

Astoria replied with an unkind tone. "Ick, gawd no, Mother."

"Well, you don't have to sound so appalled by the idea. I thought you loved Edwin. Don't you want to have his progeny?" Please say no, Giselle silently pleaded. The thought of a child raised by Astoria and Edwin was frightening to her. And probably not any better a hope for the child either. "Since the prospect isn't in the immediate future, I see no reason to delay this trip."

"Argh. You're just difficult," Astoria yelled.

Giselle heard the battering clack of heels as Astoria stomped down the hallway, then the entry door slammed. Giselle blessed the fact the library was farthest from the entrance, and she wouldn't have to watch Astoria and her temper tantrum. Or get caught and suffer the slicing whip of Astoria's tongue. When she heard another set of heels, Giselle worried she might not come out of this day entirely unscathed. She all but shoved the book into her nose to hide behind it. Yes, because that's not obvious, Giselle chided herself.

"Oh, Giselle, dear," Rosie said from the doorway. "Studying?"

"Yes, ma'am." Rosie appeared too distracted to detect her lie. "Need to focus before school closes for the Christmas holiday." She lowered the book, placed her finger as a bookmark, and closed it.

"Ah, yes, of course."

Because her concerned inquiries hadn't ended well previously, Giselle hesitated to probe further into Rosie's real state of mind. Rosie appeared to be wrestling with her inner thoughts. "Are you all right, Mrs. Gardiner? Can I get you anything?"

She may have overstepped again when Rosie scowled, and Giselle believed a scolding would follow. Surprisingly, Rosie stepped fully into the room, paused, and then sat in a chair across from Giselle. "I'm fine. Thank you." They both knew there was no way for Giselle not to overhear the conversation with Astoria. Rosie didn't reprimand her or do the socially polite thing by avoiding the topic. "I don't understand why she is so upset. This trip was planned for some time now."

"Yes," Giselle said, adding a smile intending to relax Rosie. "I remember how excited you and your friends were when planning it. You'll have a wonderful time, I'm certain." Giselle dropped the closed book beside her on the seat, removing her finger after noting the page she'd stopped on. Still, Rosie's expression didn't alter. "Are you considering canceling, after all? Your friends will be disappointed." It wouldn't be surprising for Rosie to cave under the pressure of her oldest daughter's whims and pouts.

"No, no, nothing of the sort. I'll leave tonight, as planned." Rosie clasped her hands on her lap. "Have you thought about your future, Giselle? Not that I don't appreciate your visit or the help you've provided the children while here." And there it was, as Giselle expected. Rosie couldn't take her frustration out on Astoria, so why not shift it to the orphan who no longer had a benefactor.

Okay. Might as well cut to the heart of the matter. "Am I to be gone before you return from Chicago?" she asked.

"Oh, heavens, no." Rosie smiled graciously. And again, they would both know her meaning was false and openly ignore it. "The children would like to have you here for the holidays, of course."

"Thank you." Giselle wasn't sure what or why she should be thankful, other than not wishing to ignore politeness. Rosie seldom paid attention to those in her house, so Giselle's presence couldn't have been a burden. She dealt with her children to remind them they had a parent, but other than Astoria, and occasionally with Rosalind, Rosie rarely interacted with them. Other than holiday meals, the children ate in the upstairs playroom. If Giselle were to hazard a guess, Astoria or Edwin had a hand in this decision. Maybe both.

"Think nothing of it, dear," Rosie graciously said as she rose from her chair. "Well, I have packing to do so will get to it. Enjoy your evening, Giselle."

Giselle quietly snickered when Rosie left the room. Think nothing of it. Other than you must find other accommodations. Enjoy your evening, even though I've added to your strained emotions by booting you from the only home you've known for a decade and a half. There was no way she'd get more studying done today. She picked up her book and made her way to her room.

With the door firmly shut and locked behind her, Giselle threw herself on top of the bed. The action was becoming a horrible habit recently. Part of her expected this outcome, but not quite so soon. She had hoped her residency wouldn't become an issue until after she'd graduated. Another part of her reveled in the notion she'd not have to put up with the Gardiners, and the Merricks, for much longer.

But where would she go? Giselle hadn't wanted to dip into the funds, gracious as they were, left to her by Uncle Preston. At least not so soon. She'd made no plans further than graduation, believing time on her side. Giselle wished Elspeth were here so—

Giselle sat up. A smile spread across her face, merely

thinking of the nurse, growing when she remembered the offer Elspeth gave before she left. Would it be wrong to accept? They were friends, after all. Giselle would do what she needed to earn her way. Had Elspeth meant the offer? Or was it a polite comment which she never expected to be accepted despite her protestation otherwise? Giselle hoped the latter wasn't the case. She didn't wish to be a burden, but she enjoyed the older woman's company. Moreover, Giselle liked the idea of an opportunity to interact without any of the Gardiners looking on with disdain.

She needed to pay a visit to Elspeth. A call that wasn't entirely to beg for help, a roof over her head. Giselle genuinely was intrigued about what Elspeth did in the short period of their separation.

Giselle was also so very curious to know if away from nursing duties at the Gardiner mansion did Elspeth wear something other than the severe black cotton dresses.

****

Astoria barged into her sister's room. She was livid. "Whatever do you mean by canceling on me, Rosalind? I thought you would appreciate my taking time for you." She shot a glare at Rosalind, propped up in bed, three overstuffed pillows behind her. Truth be told, her sister did look slightly pasty, more so than usual, and her hair looked atrocious, lank, oily, and disheveled. Rosalind clutched a handkerchief in her fist, dabbing at her reddened nose intermittently. "Couldn't you try?"

"I did try," Rosalind whined. "I can't do it. I'm too sick."

"Too sick?" Astoria frowned. She sat on the bed beside Rosalind and brushed at the fabric distractedly.

Was it just Rosalind who was sick? Other than Rosalind, Astoria had three more siblings in the house.

"Yes, feeling awful." Rosalind shifted, lifting herself a little higher on the pillows. "Not as bad as Charles, but not well at all. I did mean to go. Would have been nice, with Mother in Chicago, just us sisters."

Astoria patted Rosalind's leg. "Sorry I was harsh with you. You know how I hate changes to plans."

"I understand."

"How are the little ones? Are they feeling okay?" Astoria hoped Rosalind would know one way or the other as she had no intention of stepping foot into the nursery.

Rosalind gave a small shrug. "They seemed fine when they came to visit earlier."

"Really, Rosalind, why do you indulge them?" Astoria wasn't able and unwilling to hide her lip curling in a sneer.

A chuckle escaped Rosalind. "Because they're our siblings, silly. And they're simply adorable."

"They're loud, too energetic, and small." Astoria managed to conceal the shiver of disgust from Rosalind. No need for her younger sister to question her responses to the little children; two, Blanche and Susan, born after she'd left home. She remembered their mother's excitement when hoping Astoria was pregnant. Astoria wished that she could share her dislike for even the thought. There wouldn't be children in her future; she'd make sure. After all, her husband was a doctor. He may want children, not that they'd discussed it since she diverted the topic whenever broached. But Edwin had doctor friends she could rely on, for money or favors, to assist in ridding any…accidents.

Rosalind wiped at her nose. "Do you think this is the flu? Are the children vulnerable with their visits? I would so hate for them to get ill. Christmas is just weeks away."

"I'm sure they'll be fine. I'll have Edwin stop by and

have a look at all of you." Astoria stood. She had to have a long talk with her husband. Astoria leaned over and kissed Rosalind's forehead and moved toward the door, where she paused. "How is Giselle feeling?"

"Don't know. Giselle's been rather reclusive since Uncle Preston died." Rosalind questioningly stared at her sister for a moment. "To be expected, isn't it? Since he was her guardian and all."

Astoria huffed. "We shared more blood with him than she does, and we aren't all morose. But what should we expect from an interloper?"

"It's not like Giselle had any say in the course of her life, Astoria. We should be more understanding of the emotional trials this is placing on her."

"You be as understanding as you like. I see no need." The sooner the upstart was removed from the house, the better. One question stuck in her mind. If Giselle spent time with Astoria's siblings to tutor them, how had she not shown symptoms of illness? "Giselle will be gone soon enough, and no longer a Gardiner problem. Good night, Rosalind." As she closed the door behind her, Astoria heard Rosalind mumble, "I like her."

Astoria pushed those words out of her mind. She had more pressing matters than to concern herself with Giselle. She was certain Mother had spoken to Giselle before she left. Soon the young woman would not be a problem. And life in this house would proceed as expected. The way she intended they should.

Chapter Eleven

The early November days were getting colder. Elspeth didn't mind. Cooler days tended to keep people at home, warm in the comforts of their own homes. More importantly, since the deaths in the Gardiner home, Elspeth only worried about the well-being of one family member there. James, the other one holding a place in her heart, updated her with his status daily. She hadn't intended to sound paranoid, but he was all the family left to her.

Elspeth often worried about Giselle, but had no way of knowing how she faired. Elspeth missed watching the way the young woman interacted with the Colonels, missed the smiles she encouraged from them—from herself.

Elspeth wondered if Reginald scowled down on her for not doing more to keep her promise. There was nothing she could do if Giselle weren't receptive, right? Elspeth couldn't expect to force her protection on Giselle. It wasn't like she didn't have enough of her own worries.

Currently, she needed to focus on the resurrection of this old house, not focus on dark green eyes, beautiful auburn hair, and a long neck that begged for slow, tender kisses, gentle caresses. Attention Elspeth wanted to be the person to provide. Giselle, it appeared, didn't feel the same since she'd never made contact. She needed to put Giselle out of her mind. Friendship didn't seem meant to be for them. Torturing herself wasn't helping her put Giselle out of her mind or her heart.

Thoughts of Giselle didn't help the room get painted either. Above her, the noises of hammers, stomping feet, exuberant male voices mixed with boisterous laughter and other sounds associated with construction filtered down to her.

She climbed the step ladder, paintbrush in one hand, paint bucket in the other. At the top, Elspeth placed the bucket on the ladder shelf, dipped the brush in the paint until saturated, and swiped the excess off on the sides. Elspeth raised her arm and was then startled by the voice behind her.

"An accomplished nurse and a painter." Elspeth turned to see Giselle standing six feet away from the ladder. Giselle giggled. "Can you do carpentry, too?" Giselle was gorgeous. She dressed simply today, as tended to be her custom, in a black skirt and long-sleeved, dark grey shirt with a beautiful lace pattern. Draped across her arm was a black, wool cape, mourning clothes without overdoing it with an all-black attire. Adorning her head sat a wide-brimmed hat of black with tiny white flowers. Elspeth wanted so badly to pull Giselle into her arms, partly because she looked so adorable, mostly because Elspeth realized with one glance how empty she'd been until Giselle stood before her.

Instead, she laid the paintbrush on the shelf and took slow, deliberate steps down. Her whole body trembled. Any faster and she would miss a rung and fall. Elspeth reigned in her excitement by the time her feet were firmly on the floor, cloaked in her expected, reserved persona. "Carpentry? In a pinch, if needed, I guess. To what do I owe this visit?"

Elspeth loathed herself when Giselle's features became crestfallen. "I'm sorry," Giselle said, backing away. "I needed—"

Before Giselle could entirely turn away, Elspeth was there to halt Giselle with a firm hand on her arm. She put as much regret into her voice to assure Giselle of her sincerity. "I'm the one who should apologize." When

Giselle raised her gaze to meet hers, the brimming tears were Elspeth's undoing. Elspeth yanked Giselle into a hug and Giselle tensed against her. "I'm sorry. I never meant to— I've missed you." Giselle relaxed into the embrace, burying her face into Elspeth's neck, which smashed the hat's brim into Elspeth's chest. After a few moments, Elspeth realized her neck and shoulder were dampening. Giselle was crying. Crap. "What do you need? I'll give you anything."

Giselle gave a watery chuckle, while she pushed her away to arm's length. "Anything, huh?"

"Please, just ask it of me." Great, Elspeth winced, I sound like an idiot. Impulsively, Elspeth reached over and brushed the tears from Giselle's cheek with the pad of her thumb. "What's wrong? What did those vile people do to you?"

"Goodness. You don't care for them, do you?" Giselle removed her hat and tossed it onto the end table by the couch.

"No," Elspeth said. "I liked your uncles a great deal, and probably more than I should have in my job. But I don't like the others, the adults anyway. They didn't appreciate the woman you are, Giselle." She winced. Again, she said words that proved her unable to handle this situation well. "It's probably best I shut up now." Giselle smiled at her, and it was a wonderous thing. "Can I get—"

There was a knock. Elspeth glanced up to see the contractor in the suite's doorway. She'd focused on Giselle and hadn't heard when the workmen had ceased from above. "We're finished for the day. Would you like me to lock up behind us?"

"Yes, please. I'll see you tomorrow, Andrew."

"Will do, ma'am. Tomorrow it is," Andrew said, as he tapped his fingers to the bill of his cap as he nodded.

Elspeth waited until she heard the retreating footsteps

and the click of the turned lock. Now it was just the two of them. She needed to get her bearings, her focus. More importantly, Elspeth wanted to keep Giselle here for as long as she could. "Um." Would Giselle be interested in her work? Maybe she'd find it interesting enough to want to participate in a combined future. Or maybe only interested in the present work. "May I show you around?"

"I would love that, thank you." The tears had dried, replaced with a sparkle which gleamed in Giselle's eyes. Elspeth took that as a positive sign. Elspeth clasped Giselle's arm, this time to guide rather than stop. She showed Giselle both floors, explained her intended plans as she had with James. When they returned to Elspeth's suite, Giselle pointed to the ladder. "I should probably go; let you finish."

"No," Elspeth said, probably too quickly. "Sit down and relax, we'll talk. Just let me cap the bucket. It's too late to save the brush."

"I'm sorry."

"Don't be. I've others." When finished, Elspeth returned to the couch and sat beside Giselle. "Despite my earlier rudeness, I'm genuinely happy you came by. Please, don't let it interfere with sharing the true purpose of this visit."

Giselle squirmed, paying too much attention to the rearrangement of her skirt as she brushed away imaginary lint. "Uh...I uh..."

Elspeth reached over and took Giselle's hand in hers. "You can say anything, ask anything. No need to fear me." She raised an eyebrow. "No matter how daunting I tend to appear, or sound. I can be brusque, I know."

"You're too hard on yourself." Giselle inhaled deeply. Her features hinted at her hesitation. She seemed to have marshaled her courage to press on. "Mrs. Gardiner's given me until after the Christmas holiday to move out."

She gritted her teeth to keep from yelling. Elspeth barely managed to get her inner seething controlled. She didn't want Giselle to misinterpret the reaction as directed at her. "How gracious of her to wait until the children's school year concluded."

"I still have another semester, after then, before I graduate. I wonder if—" Giselle cleared her throat. "Is your offer still available for a place to live?"

Elspeth refused to hold back the smile straining for release on her lips. She stood, tugged Giselle with her. "Come with me." Giselle put up no resistance as she strode to a door on the right. Elspeth pushed the door open, a hint of fresh paint wafted toward them. Inside held a bare, medium-sized, four-poster bed of cherry wood against one wall, night tables on each side, a large armoire opposite. On the wall between the bed and dresser, and below the ceiling by about six inches, were four stained glass windows over an etch-paned French door. On the right of the outside door rested a roll-top desk, opened to display the stacked compartments, shelves, drawers, and nooks, also of cherry wood. "The door opens onto the shared patio," she told Giselle.

"Who shares the patio," Giselle asked in hushed tones as she stepped across the threshold.

"I do. My room is on the other side of the combined parlor and office. I should probably move the office things to my room, but I like the idea of distancing myself from work, even by only a few feet and a door. Eventually, I'll have a separate room added if none is available when everything is up and running. Don't want to detract from my availability to provide housing." Elspeth didn't know why she rambled, other than not wanting Giselle to believe her uncivilized for her need of organization, or lack of it. She wanted Giselle to view her in a positive light. Elspeth drew Giselle entirely into the room and pointed to a door beside the armoire. "There's a washroom with tub, sink, and a small vanity area."

Giselle slowly spun in a circle. "This is so lovely, Elspeth." The tender tone Giselle used to speak her name had Elspeth's heart pounding a tad bit faster. Then Giselle gazed at her with a mischievous glint in her eye. "Even with the fresh paint smell."

Elspeth flushed. She prepared for a glare of distaste for what she was about to admit. "I wasn't able to air out the room as long as I intended. Took longer to bring the furniture in than I'd accounted for timewise. Otherwise, there would be bedding and drapes hung."

"You did this all on your own?" Giselle asked. Her tone held surprise, not disfavor, and a hint of irritation, which was unexpected until she fisted her hands on her hips and spoke again. "By yourself? You should have had assistance. Or, maybe," Giselle said, frowning, her tone an octave higher, "hired men to do it. What if you'd hurt yourself?"

Did Giselle truly focus on the concern about her safety? Well, they were sort of friends. "Andrew assisted with the armoire. That was a bit much for me alone."

Shaking her head, Giselle chuckled. "You're amazing." No, I'm not, Elspeth silently responded, though pleased with the compliment. Because of whom it came from, she knew the words weren't idol praise. "The more layers of you I peel away, Elspeth, the more remarkable you are to behold."

Stunned, and face aflame, Elspeth suffered a moment of speechlessness, which caused her to fiddle with one of her shirt buttons. She swallowed the lump of emotion building in her throat. "Um, well, this is your room. Let me know what changes you wish made, and I can take care of it for you. I've new bedding, but if it doesn't suit you, we can purchase something that does. There's a young seamstress I know. Her grandmother was under my care once. She'll come in when you're ready to select material colors and fit the drapes. Andrew plans to install the rods in the next day or two."

"This is already an imposition, Elspeth. You shouldn't have to go through any more inconvenience on my behalf."

"It's not. I've been preparing since I left my duties at the Gardiner house."

"You knew I would need a place?"

Elspeth shook her head. "I suspected it was a distinct possibility."

"Why would you do this for me?" Giselle straightened, hands still on her hips.

"Because we're friends," Elspeth said. "I care about what happens to you."

"Is it so you can foist me upon James?"

Elspeth felt the color drain from her face. "No. I mean, I hadn't...hadn't intended—" She was going to suffocate from the disappointment in Giselle believing that was a possibility. Is that a goal Giselle would find pleasurable? "Would you want me to?"

"Certainly not." Giselle lowered her defensive pose and stepped closer. Too close since Elspeth could feel her body's warmth, smell the floral scent of honeysuckle, stare into eyes the color of emeralds. She bit back a groan when Giselle stopped the hand that nervously twisted the button of her shirt. Lifting onto her toes, Giselle placed a kiss on her cheek. "Thank you for the room. I don't need anything special, Elspeth. The security, the safety you offer is more than I hoped. I don't know how or when I'll sufficiently be able to repay you."

"That isn't necessary."

Giselle dipped her head. "For me, it is."

"I understand." Elspeth did. Giselle may be young, but she was proud, independent. "If you could see your way to helping with the accounts, I would be appreciative. I very much dislike the business part of my venture." In time, she hoped Giselle would join her permanently. Elspeth stepped away from Giselle and went to the desk, opened one of the drawers, and pulled out a ring with three keys. She handed them to Giselle. "One is for the front door, one for the suite door and the last is for this room. I hadn't time to mark them, but you can sort them out. I'm usually here, and the building's unlocked."

"That's not a safe habit," Giselle said, staring at the keys.

Elspeth noted the tears had returned and panicked. "What did I do wrong?"

With a sniff, she swiped the tears away with the back of her hand, then Giselle smiled up at her. "You've done so much right. How do I possibly deserve your friendship?"

"You deserve so much more, Giselle."

"I should probably return to the Gardiners place. Charles hasn't felt well lately, and I need to check on the children before bed." Giselle appeared ready to say more but didn't. She walked to the bedroom's door, and Elspeth followed her out, all the way to the front door, which Elspeth automatically unlocked for her. Elspeth wanted to ask more about Charles but reminded herself it wasn't her place. "Good night, Elspeth. Thank you for everything."

"You're welcome."

"My next visit," Giselle said saucily, "I'll have to thank you properly."

Elspeth, too stunned to respond, stared after her, vaguely aware Giselle was chuckling.

Chapter Twelve

The amusement Giselle felt from the shocked expression she'd left Elspeth with carried her the entire way home. She couldn't seem, not that she wished to, to erase the happy feeling from teasing Elspeth. Her boldness should stun her, but Giselle received so much information from tonight's interactions she refused to feel bad about it. If she'd read her reactions correctly, Elspeth didn't want her to have an infatuation with James. And she may be young but was not entirely stupid. Heavens, most girls her age were already married and raising children.

Elspeth's body, and her heart, enjoyed the simple kiss, the touch when Giselle removed Elspeth's hand from nervously working the button. The sympathetic hug when she'd first arrived. Could it lead to more than friendship? Giselle sincerely hoped so. Something about the tall, solemn nurse made Giselle's heart pound rapidly, made her warm from head to toe. Made Giselle feel safe in her presence.

Concern quickly dashed the excellent mood. The moment Giselle entered the house, ten-year-old Blanche ran toward her and wrapped her arms around Giselle's waist. "What's wrong?" she asked, kneeling, so they were eye level.

"Charles is getting sicker. Momma's not here, and I don't know what to do." Blanche began to cry.

"Where's your nanny?" Giselle removed her cape, hat, and gloves as she ascended the stairs to the second floor. Blanche's response when she didn't want to lie was a double shoulder shrug, and she suspected that was the reply. Blanche followed her until they reached the room Blanche shared with her seven-year-old sister, Susan. "You wait in here while I check on Charles. I'll be right back." Giselle made a quick stop to her room to deposit her outerwear. She placed the ring of keys Elspeth gave her on the table by the window. The presence of the keys reminded Giselle of her future possibilities and she smiled. First things first, she told herself. Need to see to whatever upset Blanche so severely. She returned to the second floor.

Then she was at Charles's door, knocking. "Charles? May I come in?" Giselle heard a grunt and took that as acceptance, whether he intended so or not. Charles lay on his side, facing the window, although the drapes were closed. He was a thin, eighteen-year-old with the Gardiner brown hair and little to set him aside as anything but average, indistinguishable or memorable. His face was pale, body curled into a near-fetal position. Giselle walked into the room but stopped at the foot of the bed. "Is there anything I can get for you?"

His head shifted enough to reflect movement, if not an actual shake for a positive or negative response. "No. Probably nothing wrong," he said, his voice raspy. Right, she thought, because young men didn't get sick. "Hear Rosalind's sick, too. Cook has been tending to us."

That wouldn't usually be surprising. Rosalind, at sixteen, tended toward hypochondria for tidbits of her mother's attention. Considering the lethal events lately and Charles's illness, this time may be a legitimate cause for suspicion. The situation became worrisome to her, so close on the heels of the Colonels' deaths. "All right, Charles. I'll leave you to your rest."

Giselle peeked in on the two girls and explained everything would be okay. Then she made her way to the kitchen. It was after quitting time for Lottie, not that time factored into the cook's schedule, and Giselle hoped tonight was one of those times. Mostly because she needed a friendly face in a situation Giselle believed would get worse before it got better.

"What in the blue blazes is going on, Giselle?" Lottie asked when she entered the kitchen. She wiped at the counter hard enough to remove the grain.

"Why are you still here?" Giselle took the cleaning rag from her.

Lottie *tsk*ed. "The nanny stormed out, waving her hands about a death house. I couldn't leave the children alone. So, I waited until you came back." Her eyes sparkled more than usual. "Were you being courted?"

Giselle shook her head. "You're a romantic, Lottie." She never lied to Lottie and didn't intend to do so now, not entirely anyway. Besides, it wouldn't be long before Lottie knew this truth. "I visited with Nurse Keillor. Mrs. Gardiner gave me until Christmas to leave. Elspeth offered me a place to live. I've accepted it."

"Nice woman that Elspeth, I like her." Lottie crossed her arms over her generous chest. "Wish she could have stayed."

Yes, Giselle liked her, too, though probably more than she should; and, undoubtedly, more than society considered acceptable. Giselle groaned inwardly. She'd too much time lately to dwell on her feelings and the past. "There was nothing left for her to do," Giselle said. "Well, maybe now there's something." They both sighed. "I should call Dr. Trent. I don't have a good feeling about the outcome of this situation." Why did she feel the house's occupant's were dominos in a game Edwin played?

Less than thirty minutes later, Dr. Trent arrived at the house. Giselle met him at the door and explained what she knew of the situation. He proceeded to Charles's room, assuring he'd examine Rosalind after, while Lottie stayed with Giselle in the library. Both knew, since they were considered merely the hired help, Dr. Trent would summon them if they were needed. What they hadn't expected was the arrival of the Merrick's. Again. Features displaying more glee than the situation warranted, Edwin strode directly to the second floor. Astoria stopped at the threshold of the library. "I'll be in mother's sitting room," she announced before she turned on her heel and stomped away.

"This makes me feel better," Giselle said quietly. Lottie hadn't missed her sarcasm and tittered, replying, "Devil's spawn, the both of them."

Short of an hour later, they heard the heavy tread of the two doctors on the stairs, then the hall. "I'll return in the morning," Dr. Trent's voice. "I'll put in the request for additional help soon as I get home." Giselle and Lottie shared a glance, both understanding the situation was more direr than they expected.

"My wife and I will be here," came Edwin's reply. "There's a private sitting room behind Mother Gardiner's parlor. We'll move in there to be present for any aid we can provide our family." Too afraid to use a room on the children's floor, Edwin? she silently inquired.

Giselle took Lottie's hand and tugged. With Edwin occupied, the two made their way to the kitchen, Lottie was the first to speak. "I better take my leave before he puts me to work."

"Or confines you to the house, for your safety, of course," Giselle said. "Be safe. I'll see you tomorrow."

Lottie hesitated, and bit her bottom lip. "I don't feel right leaving you alone with him. With either of them if I'm honest."

"I'll take the back way to my room and lock the door." She pulled Lottie into a quick hug. "Hurry now." As soon as Lottie left, Giselle locked the door and ran up the servant's stairs to her room, where she did as she told Lottie she would, and locked the door behind her. The idea of needing to bolt her bedroom in her own home had her shuddering.

She inhaled deeply. Maybe a little light reading was in order to calm her nerves. Her gaze fell on Elspeth's keys, and an involuntary smile grew. Giselle allowed it to remain. A little more time. That was all she needed. Time would lead her to a whole new set of adventures. Preferably, with a particular dark and tall nurse. She could be patient. Giselle believed her future experiences would well be worth it.

****

Today was the third day since Giselle initially called Dr. Trent to the Gardiner home for Charles. The doctor hadn't said much to her. Nothing since Trent contacted Edwin. She didn't know it was due to her being a woman or the fact she hadn't carried the bloodline and was considered more staff than family. However, her concern remained only for the children, so she ignored the slight, whether intended or not.

As her room was on the servant floor, Giselle made herself known to the three nurses hired to provide care to the children. First, Helen Paige, a gorgeous 5'4" blonde with a round face, heart-shaped lips, and delicate nose. Her personality exuded her honest kindness. Second, Carol Newman, a woman as heavy as she was short, she barely surpassed five-foot. Everything about her emitted plain, from her mousy blonde bob hair cut, her dull brown eyes, and a personality that screamed I'm-here-but-don't-want-to-be. Third, Nora Hunter, a woman who brought Elspeth to mind in looks but not attitude. Nora stood close to six-foot, with raven hair pulled into a severe bun, obsidian eyes, clear olive complexion, with thin pursed lips, but an exotic beauty, nonetheless. She displayed the same stoic bearing as Elspeth, yet there was no spark.

Each nurse was assigned a room. Nora cared for Rosalind, Carol tended to Charles, and Helen looked after Blanche and Susan, who started to show signs of illness the previous night. Dr. Trent made a daily visit but left most of the management to Edwin, which caused all the civilized and structured nursing to change.

A commotion in hallway brought Giselle to her door, which she opened only fragmentally, not even a full gap, when she heard Edwin's voice. The three nurses stood by the doorway to the room that had last been Elspeth's, which Helen now occupied. Nora and Carol had their backs to her, but Helen and Edwin faced forward.

"But it's standard practice in cases like this, for our assignment to be to a single patient," Helen said.

Merrick smirked. "As long as you work in this house, you'll follow the direction of the doctor, which is me. And I say, you will share duties with all the children, and with sixteen-hour shifts." Goodness, Giselle reflected, did Edwin want the nurses to quit? Because he certainly pushed them toward that end. More reason to distrust his motives.

Nora stiffened her back. For a moment, Giselle believed the woman would physically launch herself at him. Much to Giselle's dismay, she did nothing other than speak in even, measured tones. "Your schedule will sacrifice our continuity of care, and leave only eight hours for sleep, let alone time to spend with our own families."

"And make record keeping a mess," Carol stated blandly. "We better get properly paid." Giselle realized her initial impression of Carol hadn't been wrong.

Merrick stood unwavering in his expectations. "There will be no changes in my requirements. If they don't meet with your approval, I'm sure we can find nurses willing to replace you." He shoved his hands into his trouser pockets and rocked back and forth on his heels. "Am I to conclude my terms are acceptable?" They all nodded. "Very good. Enjoy your evening. I'll expect you to begin in the morning."

Giselle quickly closed the gap in her door until Edwin stomped down the stairs. The nurses spoke in hushed tones, as Giselle joined them. "I don't mean to intrude but I wanted to let you know I'll assist in any way I can." Carol snorted, walked to her room, and slammed the door behind her.

"Thank you, Giselle," Helen said, smiling. "We wouldn't want you getting ill, too."

"Can you keep that prick away from us?" Nora asked.

Helen's face flushed. "Nora, your language."

"What?" Nora lowered her voice. "He hasn't a good reputation, you know. There are rumors." Giselle wasn't surprised to hear this. She still believed Edwin was instrumental in Reginald and Uncle Preston's deaths. But he couldn't possibly be so heinous as to murder children, could he? Nora tilted her head in Giselle's direction when she said, "Not that I know anything for certain."

Giselle believed there might be a fire inside Nora Hunter after all. "For the record, I don't care for either of the Merrick's. I'm the interloper, as I'm sure you'll hear or have heard during your stay at work. Nothing said to me will be repeated." At least not to anyone but Elspeth. "I hope you'll conduct the same courtesy on my behalf."

Both agreed and then retired to their respective rooms, each needing a full night's rest to adequately deal with Edwin Merrick and the illness of the children.

As she lay in bed later, Giselle reflected on the numerous times Elspeth Keillor came to mind since her visit three days ago. Even to the point where she compared

Nora to her. Although there were similarities, even with seeing a bit of spark in Nora, she didn't get the same feeling of comfort or safety as she did with Elspeth. That had to foretell something, right? It wouldn't be long now when she'd find out one way or the other.

Chapter Thirteen

"What the hell is going on?" Rosie Gardiner yelled down the hall to no one in particular. "Who are you people?"

Giselle thought the answer was obvious but understood what Rosie wanted. The circumstances certainly couldn't be the welcome home she'd expected, though Giselle assumed Astoria would leave word for her mother at the station. Three nurses bustled around the second-floor hallway with arm's full of towels, trays, and bedpans. Doctor's Trent and Merrick made their way in and out of the various rooms dispensing pills. Rosie's home mirrored a hospital. "Mrs. Gardiner, please, allow me to get you some tea. You are certain to be parched after the train ride." Rosie turned to her with a confused expression, which quickly reflected hostility. Giselle didn't want to be the recipient of her anger, hoped she could deflect it. "Astoria is here. I'm certain she'll make herself available to answer any specific questions until Dr. Trent has an opportunity to do so."

"Very well," Rosie said. The mention of her oldest seemed to calm her somewhat. Giselle waited until Rosie was seated before leaving long enough to alert Lottie of the need for tea. Astoria was in the room and explaining by the time she returned. "Good afternoon, Astoria. Lottie will be in with tea momentarily. I'll leave you to your reunion."

Giselle turned to leave, Lottie simultaneously entered with the tea cart, when Rosie stopped her with a bark of her name. "You're still a resident in this house. Stay until I have a complete and proper understanding of the situation."

Thank you for the reminder. It can't happen soon enough, Giselle told herself. "Yes, ma'am," she said, noting the sympathetic glance from Lottie as she left the parlor. Astoria proceeded to explain the reason for the nurses and the current medical state of the children. The room grew quiet when she finished until Astoria turned to direct a glare at Giselle.

Astoria smirked. "When is your move supposed to happen?" she asked as if the change of topic was for her mother's benefit.

Giselle recognized it for what it was. A twist of the knife. They would see it as a hardship, maybe a reason to beg for assistance. She took comfort in the fact the proposition was an emotional relief. "Your mother asked me to stay until school lets out for Christmas." She silently questioned Astoria's motives. Would it be easier to murder the children if Giselle weren't here as a witness?

"It's not like they'll be returning before then," Astoria snipped. She glared at her mother.

"Enough, Astoria." Rosie passed her daughter a cup of tea. "Family needs to stick together during this time." She raised her hand to forestall Astoria's retort. "Giselle can communicate with the children, understand them. Until evidence provided otherwise, she will continue to assist as she can."

"Of course, Mother. Your heart has always been too big. I worry people take advantage of you for it."

Giselle refrained from rolling her eyes—barely. She sat in a chair, with *fleur-de-lis* brocade, placed as far from the women while still being in the same room. She recognized her presence gave the impression of solidarity, though none Giselle could expect to receive. Had she been an acceptable participant in their unity, wouldn't she also have earned a cup of tea? Not that she wanted one, or to prolong this discussion any longer than necessary.

Rosie turned her attention onto Giselle. "I'd like you to keep the spirits of the children high. I will require you to assist the nurses where needed or to share their concerns when essential. We can forego their schooling needs as a priority for the time being."

"Of course," she said. "Will that be all?"

"Yes. I'll let you know if your situation changes."

She stood to leave. Again, her departure halted, this time by the entrance of Trent and Edwin. Edwin entered the room and stopped beside her chair. "Mother Gardiner. Glad to see you. You were sorely missed."

Giselle attempted to move around him, but Edwin merely shifted with her, sure to block escape. "Excuse me," she said, making another attempt before her temper rose.

"What's the hurry?" Edwin asked.

"Carson," Astoria said, her voice hard. "Let the child go."

"Tori, honey, she's far from a child. I'd say Giselle here is Preston's greatest accomplishment." Edwin finished the statement by clamping an arm across her shoulder. Giselle stiffened. His touch made her skin crawl, and she hated his mention of her uncle. "She's quite the young lady."

"May I please be excused, Mrs. Gardiner?" Giselle hoped her voice didn't sound as frightened as she felt. "I still have schoolwork of my own to finish."

Rosie waved her hand in the air. "Yes, yes. Edwin let her go and come sit with your wife."

"Certainly, Mother Gardiner." Edwin chuckled. It turned into a laugh that followed Giselle as she left the room and hurried up the stairs. Her heart didn't even begin to slow to normal until, once in her room, she locked the door. Thirty seconds later, Giselle slid the back of a chair under the doorknob. There was no such thing as overreacting where Edwin was concerned.

****

Edwin closed the door to Charles's room when he noticed one of the nurses returning from dinner. He was glad when Rosie agreed the nurses should eat in the kitchen, as staff should, not the family's dining room. "Ah, nurse," Edwin said, his expression relaxed. He enjoyed the power he held over these wretched women. His only wish was for them to be more amenable, especially to a man who was their better. Proper groveling from them couldn't hurt either, he thought. This one, Hunter, reminded him of the last one. The one who worked her wiles on Reginald. "I've given Charles his pill. The boy needed an intestinal antiseptic. I'm concerned with his fluctuating pulse. I'll need to keep track through the evening."

"Yes, Doctor," Nurse Hunter said simply.

"I'll be downstairs if you need me."

"Yes, Doctor."

The nurse's tone was polite, concise, but Edwin had the impression she intended sarcasm. Should he call her on it? Edwin shrugged, then twisted a knot of tension from his neck. Maybe he was overly sensitive. This entire situation proved frustrating. It was one thing to deal with patients and then walk away. This matter insisted he be more personable because it involved family.

He went downstairs to the room he shared with his wife. Rosie offered them the use of Preston or Reginald's bedroom, but they declined. Edwin explained he didn't wish to see his wife fall to whatever brought the rest of the family to confinement. In truth, he enjoyed the unexpected privacy provided by the barrier of Rosie's parlor, which no one breached without permission.

Edwin entered the parlor and planted a quick kiss to Rosie's cheek. "Need anything, Mother?" he asked. Rosie responded with a negative. "Fine. Must have a word with Astoria, but then I'll return and give you the day's update."

Rosie wanly smiled up at him. "Thank you, Edwin. Take your time." Ah, finally, an accommodating woman.

Astoria sat rigidly in the chair as he entered their temporary quarters. He'd told her to go home, but she insisted it would look bad if she abandoned her family in their time of need. The sick were her siblings, after all. Edwin knew his wife loved him, in her way, and had his best interest at heart. But Edwin also suspected she didn't trust him enough to leave him to his own devices. That would be the real reason she remained.

"What's the status, Carson?"

"I wanted to check on you before I shared the report with your mother."

"Status?" she asked, her teeth clenched.

"Should be over by the end of the year." Edwin reasoned her attitude was a result of a house of severe illness. He didn't expect she would turn her tense emotions on him. "Are you all right, Tori, dear?"

Rather than answer his question, she posed one of her own. "Are all precautions and arrangements in place?"

"Of course, Tori, honey," he said. He kneeled before her and clasped her hands in his. "This is important to us. I would never let you down." Her glare indicated she still fostered anger in her heart. "What has you upset, dearest?"

A long moment of silence. Finally, Astoria's expression softened. She brought her hand up to his cheek. "Never mind me, Carson. Having nearly my entire family so gravely ill is just so fractious."

Edwin leaned forward and touched his lips to her

forehead. "I've accounted for every contingency. You have nothing to cause you to worry. If you'd prefer to go home, no one will fault you for considering your safety. Even Rosie would be supportive."

"I will stay." Astoria rose.

Edwin pulled her into his arms, cradled her head on his shoulder. "Won't be long now. We will get through this." He drew back. Flashed a smile and gave a wink. "Let's go give your mother her nightly update." Play the situation down just a little bit, he thought. After all, he wouldn't want her knowing how severe the matter is until it's too late.

****

When Giselle knocked on Charles's door, a frenzied Nora answered. She would have laughed had the woman's expression not looked so dire. "Nora? Are you okay?" she asked.

Nora peeked into the hallway behind Giselle, grabbed her arm below the elbow, and tugged her into the room. Her usual tight bun showed some of her stress, a few locks of hair released, and brushed her collar. Giselle noted a three-fold screen had been placed beside the bed to hide Charles from anyone entering the room. "Look, Giselle, I'm out of line here, I know. But at my wits end."

"Talk to me," she said. "Trust me, I can be discrete, even if I can't help with anything."

"Granted, I'm only a nurse—"

"I trust nurses before most doctors," she said honestly. Nurses spent more time with patients than any doctor.

Nora gave her a weak smile. "Dr. Merrick instructed me to give Charles a morphine shot. Then, he ordered a hot-water enema." Nora winced. "It's unnecessarily cruel, but, well..." she shrugged.

"He's the doctor. I understand." And she did. It was embedded into the female psyche to always defer to the male. A concept passed down from mothers onto daughters. Personally, Giselle appreciated that more women were leaving those perceptions behind. Maybe a day would come where women were viewed as equals. Sadly, it probably wouldn't be in her lifetime. She was fortunate to be raised by two gentlemen a bit more open-minded. "I assume you followed the order."

"I did, and it was horrible." Nora wrung her hands. "His legs went so rigid. The bowels failed to discharge most of the fluid. Charles is in more discomfort than earlier. The doctor may have made him worse." Giselle noticed the tears building in Nora's eyes. "And I'm the one who did it to him."

Giselle rested her hand on Nora's clenched fists, to still them before she broke a knuckle. "Trust me. It would have been worse for you to go against Edwin openly."

"What should I do?" Nora asked in a rough whisper.

"Nothing. Your job is at risk, immediately and in the future." Giselle gave a wry grin. "The penalty for me will be less severe. I'm going to call Dr. Trent. You continue to do the best you can."

Giselle placed the call and returned to the second floor. She sat on the alcove's settee at the end of the hall. She couldn't have been there for more than ten minutes when the doorbell, followed by footsteps announced Trent's arrival. A surprised and annoyed Edwin followed the older man to Charles's room. Giselle expected Edwin to reprimand her for her involvement in Trent's appearance, but the doctor gave nothing away.

"Merrick, calm yourself," Trent said wearily. "You have three nurses and four sick children. I would think you'd appreciate my checking in and relieving you of your burden for even a moment." Was Dr. Trent just as tired of Edwin and his shenanigans as the rest of them? Astoria and Rosie, because of her daughter, appeared to be the only ones who held Edwin in a favorable light. "I didn't have time to forewarn you of my decision to stop by. Get over yourself, man."

They entered Charles's room, and Giselle couldn't hear if Edwin responded or not. She gave them a chance to focus on the sick patient before carefully making her way to the door, which was fully open, the screen two feet away from the entrance. With caution, Giselle moved close enough to watch through the slim gap where the screens joined.

"Damn it all," Trent said, his flustered gaze darted from the watch he held in his left hand to where his fingers rest on Charles's wrist. "Pulse is too quick. I can't make an accurate count."

Edwin pushed his glasses up his nose. "Has to be meningitis. It is a by-product of typhoid fever, after all. The city is rife with it, now."

Trent's expression reflected his disagreement, whether with the inference or the medical conclusion, it wasn't clear. He said nothing to discredit Edwin's claim, so there was no way for Giselle to discern his intent. "The boy's in pain. Give him a hypodermic of morphine while I check on the other children."

Giselle stepped clear of the door and strode away so it looked like she'd recently come down the hall. "Dr. Trent, sir. So good to see you this evening," she said when he exited the room, Nurse Hunter behind him.

"Ms. Saunders. Please tell me you are free of this radical germ afflicting the rest of the family?" he said, taking a hand in his. He gave a quick squeeze.

"Yes, thank you."

"How are you managing after Preston's loss?"

She flinched at the mention of her uncle, but knew he meant to be solicitous and not hurtful. "Better, but grateful for the time I did have with him. His memory makes each day easier."

Trent patted the hand he still clasped. "If you ever needed anything…"

"Thank you, sir. I'll keep you in mind." She glanced over his shoulder, wondering about Edwin and what he might be doing.

One last squeeze, and he released her hand. "See that you do. Now, if you'll pardon me, I must check on the children." He turned to Nora. "Stay with the boy. I'll call you if I need you." Nora nodded and returned to Charles's room while Trent moved on to Rosalind's.

Giselle took this opportunity to hover outside Charles's room, back to the screen, and her vantage point to watch Merrick. Nora sat in a chair pulled close to the head of the bed, her hand on Charles' pulse. On the opposite side, Merrick sat.

Thirty minutes later, Trent returned and gave Giselle a wink as he passed her position behind the screen. "How's the boy doing, Nurse?"

"Not well, Doctor. His pulse is erratic."

Trent shook his head. "Won't be long now, I'm afraid."

Much as it pained her, Giselle agreed. Charles's chest seemed to slow in his inhales, less productive in their job on the exhales. How could the family bear another death? How could she?

"He's gone," Edwin said. His tone held as much inflection as if he said the newspaper had arrived.

Nora glowered at Merrick. "He's still breathing, Doctor."

Trent moved closer to the bed, placed his finger on the

pulse of Charles's neck, and was silent for a few moments. A clipped shake of his head. "He's slipped away."

Giselle's heart broke. Charles was only eighteen and should have been able to fight longer. She twisted to leave for her room but paused when Edwin spoke.

Edwin sighed noticeably. "And no progeny to carry on the name or to inherit." Giselle frowned. Why would he say such a thing, the insufferable bastard? Realization struck. Charles's share of Uncle Reginald's estate would revert to the sisters—one of which was Mrs. Edwin Carson Merrick.

Was this proof Edwin was intentionally killing off the Gardiner's? For the Colonel's estate? Were the Gardiner girls next? Giselle needed to talk to someone, share her fears. There was only one person she trusted this theory to, one person who would understand her misgivings.

She desperately needed to talk to Elspeth.

Chapter Fourteen

Giselle left the kitchen and her visit with Lottie and headed for the front of the house. She intended to take a walk, try to organize her thoughts before her impromptu visit to Elspeth and her need to share her concerns. She'd made it as far as the parlor when Rosie called out to her. Giselle hoped the interruption would be quick, so she didn't remove her wool cape. The evening was coming, and she didn't want to lose the daylight. Giselle did remove her gloves, her grip tighter than necessary in anticipation of another negative encounter. The gloves would provide a diversion should Rosie trigger Giselle's need to choke her.

In the parlor, Giselle noted Rosie wasn't alone. Carol sat on the sofa, looking as unhappy as usual. "Giselle. Nurse Newman has informed me she is leaving our service."

She turned in Carol's direction. "I'm sorry to hear that. Is everything all right?"

The round woman harrumphed. "I can't keep up with his schedule or his impossible demands," Carol said. "It's offensive. We are nurses. Educated women, not slaves, to indulge his exacting whims."

Rosie sniffed indignantly. The effect lost with her red, swollen eyes from crying. She may not have shed a tear for Preston or Reginald, but she did love her son. "He is a doctor, after all." Giselle bit her lip to curb the snarky remark she wanted to make. Carol wasn't as inclined to hold her tongue or her opinion.

"Yes, professionally." Carol smirked. "He's not as respectable as other doctors, such as Trent. Or others I've found working with a pleasure. Your son-in-law is a tyrant."

Giselle had enough. She may feel the same, but further upsetting Rosie wouldn't achieve anything. And, she wanted none of it. "Mrs. Gardiner. As this is a private matter between employer and employee, it doesn't require my presence."

"Ah, my dear, but it does," Rosie said. She picked up her teacup and stalled, probably to gather herself rather than to specifically annoy Giselle, before she placed the cup in front of the French-style phone on the side table. "With the funeral tomorrow, and about to be short a nurse, I'll need your help with the children. At least until we can hire a replacement." Rosie pulled a dainty, lace handkerchief from her sleeve and dabbed under her eyes. She glared at Carol. "You're free to leave. I'll have the check for your services forwarded."

Carol stood. "Thanks." Guess further need for politeness no longer existed.

Rosie glanced at Giselle after they both watched the disgruntled nurse leave the room. "Is there anything I can get you?" she asked. An emotion other than the pain of losing a child beckoned from Rosie's eyes before Rosie lowered her gaze to her hands resting on her lap. Would she share whatever concerns unsettled her? Giselle lowered her voice to express her concern. "Rosie?" No need for formality from her either, right? "What troubles you?"

Rosie's twisted the handkerchief so forcefully it resembled a lace corkscrew. "I visited Charles at the mortuary." She looked up; fresh tears clouded her eyes. "It was so cold there. I hope he'll be all right with the suit I brought."

Giselle knew he wouldn't care, but grief was powerful. The inanity of the comment made her wonder if she had similar thoughts that she'd been unaware of with

Uncle Preston, then with Reginald. "I'm sure he'll be fine."

"I hated leaving him there. He's still so young." Rosie heaved a burdened sigh. "Do you know that Edwin won't be at the service tomorrow night?"

She hoped her surprise wasn't too noticeable. Calmly, Giselle said, "No, I had no notion at all. Is there a proper reason?" What could constitute a proper reason? They spoke of Edwin, after all, so the prospects were endless for anything which didn't include family.

"Something about being named the president-elect of the local medical society. I can't remember the full name. I wish he'd reconsider. No one would fault him for being with family during our mourning." Not that the formal name was relevant, Giselle thought, but the little things took attention from death. Another labored sigh. "I guess I need—" Rosie pinned Giselle with a pleading gaze. "We both know neither Nurse Keillor nor Edwin got on very well, but she did her job well." And in relative quiet, while keeping Uncle Reginald out of your hair, Giselle reasoned, suspecting where the conversation led.

Giselle decided to jump straight to it. "You want me to ask Nurse Keillor to return? To replace Nurse Newman?"

"It would be understandable if she's already accepted employment elsewhere. If not, then who better than someone familiar with the house and our expectations?"

"I don't know," Giselle said. Would Elspeth even consider returning, whether available or not? She, for one, saw benefits from her reappearance. Elspeth's presence would help with the children since she stood a better chance of knowing what Edwin's attentions were facilitating in their care. Just because Giselle believed his motives were opposite from his medical code of ethics didn't mean he did anything wrong; and presenting a fair imitation of a dolt didn't mean much to some. It hadn't forced Trent to demand Edwin stop tending to family members.

"Could you try?" Rosie said, clearly irritated. "It would be easier than asking Doctor Trent to locate another available nurse." The request accomplished two missions for Giselle. A reason to visit Elspeth without being questioned about it later. And a chance to have Elspeth close, to question Edwin's motives with her, as well as help Giselle regain her lost feeling of safety.

But she also didn't want to appear too eager to see Elspeth. Rosie was a gossiper. Surely Edwin would get wind of the matter and interrogate Giselle later. "I'll take care of it first thing tomorrow. It's getting dark and too late to be out and about unescorted." Although, maybe they already suspected she and Elspeth to be in communication. Rosie seemed under the impression Giselle had no problem contacting Elspeth.

"I'll have a hired carriage brought round with instructions to wait once you arrive. Should the nurse not accompany your return, I'll have Edwin retrieve you later in his horseless carriage." Oh, goodie, Giselle bemoaned silently. Regardless of Elspeth's response, she'd find her way home. No way did she intend to find herself trapped alone with Edwin. Rosie reached for the handset.

While she made the call, Giselle walked outside to wait. She resisted the impulse to change, put on a prettier dress than the one she wore around the house all day, but that would raise too many eyebrows. Of course, she reasoned silently, Elspeth appeared to accept her no matter such trivialities.

****

The suite door was open when Giselle arrived. Elspeth

sat behind the desk in the parlor area; her attention focused on the scattered papers on top. Elspeth wore trousers and a masculine buttoned shirt, clothes comparable to those she wore when Giselle visited days ago, and her dark brown hair pulled back by a wide silver barrette. Without the tight bun, the looseness of the thick strands made Elspeth's features soften, appear less narrow and severe. Giselle appreciated the woman and the scene, probably more so if Giselle's mission weren't so grim.

The simple sight of Elspeth warmed her heart regardless, and Giselle gazed for as long as she could without attracting Elspeth's attention and startling her. Feeling she bordered toward creepy after so long, Giselle crossed the threshold into Elspeth's suite. She closed the door behind her, not wanting anyone to walk in or hear their conversation.

Elspeth raised her head, her gaze drilled into Giselle's, first with surprise and followed with worry. "Giselle, what's wrong?" she asked, rushing to her side. She hadn't intended to, but Giselle clutched Elspeth into an embrace and released the tears she'd managed to contain to the privacy of her bedroom. When her crying slowed, Giselle stepped back. "Tell me what's happened, Ellie."

For a moment, Giselle paused in surprise. Only the Colonels' used the nickname. Had Elspeth used it before this? If she had, did Giselle not realize because Elspeth slipped into her small circle of loved ones? Elspeth must have understood the name usage as she apologized immediately. But Giselle realized she liked the way the name sounded on Elspeth's lips, soft and tender. "No, don't apologize. I like the way you make it sound." Then she flushed in embarrassment at her admission. Elspeth didn't make the nickname sound childish. She'd never asked the Colonels to cease the use when she got older because it brought them such joy to have something no one else in the family had with her.

Giselle allowed Elspeth to tug her toward the couch, their hands clasped. She'd let the cab driver go, not wanting to rush this visit, wanting every minute she could get. Giselle needed this time with her friend. "You're not sleeping. You have some bruising under your eyes. Nightmares? Or is something else going on?" Elspeth reached up and brushed stray strands of hair behind an ear. Was it a conscious action? Giselle wondered. But she wouldn't complain.

"Are you saying I look awful?" She grinned and raised an eyebrow to acknowledge the teasing.

Elspeth lowered her gaze, clearly bothered by her own words, anyway. Giselle couldn't acknowledge the tender touch without further distancing them. Getting closer to Elspeth was her goal, not the other way around. Better she deals with her reason for being here. "The Gardiner's need your help. Rosie specifically asked for you."

"I'd rather n—"

"Please, Elspeth, hear me out?" she asked. Elspeth nodded. "Charles is dead. The girls are all ill. One of the three nurses hired to help quit a little over an hour ago. And I still think Edwin is attempting to kill them all."

"Update me on everything you can," Elspeth said with a frown.

Giselle did. She related the events from when Elspeth's services were terminated to the conversation with Rosie to enlist Elspeth's return. "I don't know how much longer the other nurses can or will hold out. Nora is still upset with what Edwin had her do to Charles." In truth, Nora was so inconsolable she appeared near-catatonic most times. Giselle felt the tears build in her eyes as she remembered how deflated the woman has been since Charles died. The spirit Giselle once witnessed a hint of, was now evaporated.

"Whoa, relax," Elspeth said, pulling her closer. Giselle didn't fight the contact, and she melted into it. She wrapped arms around Giselle's waist, where her chin rested on top of her head. Giselle felt cocooned in adoration. "You need to take care of yourself. I couldn't bear it if something happened to you." The intensity in Elspeth's tone surprised and soothed her.

Despite knowing Rosie waited for her return, Giselle needed answers. Did Elspeth feel friendship or something more for her? The days would be long and made uncomfortable if she longed for a woman who didn't return her affections. Giselle rested her hands atop the long-fingered ones at her waist. "Elspeth? Can I ask a question and get an honest answer?"

The chin on top of her head quickly shifted away. "I've never lied to you," Elspeth said. Giselle tightened her grip when she felt Elspeth pull away.

"I believe that," she said, scooting back a little. Giselle realized Elspeth would never be the first to broach the topic of what was happening between them. Many nights of little to no sleep gave her plenty of time to think. Time to realize Elspeth would be afraid of Giselle's reactions if she announced the growing attraction between them. She knew that was what had to be happening to her. Giselle never missed the company of her sometime suitor's or her other female friends. "But you need to know something. I get the queerest feelings when I'm with you. In a good way, I think."

Giselle felt the vibration of the fingers against her back from Elspeth's deep chuckle. "You think?" Elspeth asked. Before she could respond, Elspeth squeezed herself away from her, jumped up and away from the couch, and paced agitatedly. "Have you any idea of the implications? What this would mean should anyone find out? And over feelings that you think you have?"

"So, you don't feel the same?" Giselle felt foolish. "I'm so—" She needed to get away from here, from the embarrassment she'd brought on herself. Before she humiliated herself further by crying. It was bad enough the resulting situation would upset Rosie not getting Elspeth back. She'd have to call Dr. Trent, ask he find another nurse. Giselle only managed to stand and turn before she felt Elspeth at her back, arms holding her in place.

"Stop, please," Elspeth whispered in her ear, her tone pleading. "This is hard for me, Ellie."

"Caring for me, or for admitting it?" Another deep rumble of amusement gave Giselle a pleasurable shiver, even if she was hurt. Elspeth's hands clutched at Giselle's upper arms. "Are you laughing at me?"

"No, sweetheart. Laugh with you? Anytime. Laugh at you? Never." Elspeth pulled back, and Giselle missed the contact. Elspeth's hands stayed on her arms, but Giselle didn't turn around. "I care for you more than friendship dictates. But other than the abhorrence others believe in our kind of caring, I'm so much older than you. You are still so young."

"Too young to know my own heart? You believe me to be a child?"

Elspeth's fingers squeezed gently. "Not a child by any means. However, how can you know your own heart? What have you to base it on? The world is open to you for all its wonders. There is a lot for the world to show you, teach you."

Giselle did turn to face her then. "The world has no interest if you're not sharing it with me. I have no great or noble aspirations. I only wish to love and be loved. You make me want those things."

"Oh, Ellie." Elspeth raised a hand and cupped her cheek. "Have you any idea what you're asking of me?"

She stepped closer, putting her hands at Elspeth's

hips, and bit and released her bottom lip. "Not entirely. So, I guess that does make me a child. I only know I feel safe with you. Comfortable enough periods of silence aren't unpleasant." Closer still. "I'm a willing student. Teach me, please?"

Elspeth's eyes darkened with desire. Giselle felt an unexpected ache between her legs, which became moist when Elspeth gently pressed her lips to Giselle's, then broke the kiss all too soon. "Much as I'd like to continue this charming activity, I believe they expect you back."

Giselle sighed heavily. "Must we stop?"

"Yes, Ellie, we must." Giselle couldn't move, her limbs weighted with want, so accepted it as positive when Elspeth put distance between them. "I'll call James for a ride, and then I'll pack my valise while we wait."

"What are you going to tell him?" she asked. Her heart pounded a near painful beat in panic.

"Relax, sweetheart. We get a safe ride, and we can update him. He'll know about Charles, but not the rest." Elspeth placed the call to James, somewhat surprised he was available but didn't question their luck.

Giselle followed Elspeth as she strode to her bedroom and packed. "Thank you for doing this."

"I can imagine how difficult this is for you." Elspeth gazed at her with a sad expression. "You've lost so much, and I can't guarantee it will get better, Ellie."

"This entire situation is predicated on the fact men have the last word, and our women's voices mean nothing." Giselle sat on the corner of the bed, watching Elspeth work. "At least we have a better chance if we're together. Heck, your presence alone, and the fact Rosie asked for you has to mean the circumstances can improve." She shrugged. "If not, then at least I'm not alone. I feel better knowing you'll be near."

Elspeth finished packing and moved closer. "Ellie, are

you sure you want more than friendship?"

"Who said we can't still be friends?" she asked, teasing.

"At any time, you realize it's too much, more than you expected, tell me. I won't hold it against you. Ever." Elspeth kissed her again, her lips warm and pliant against Giselle's.

"You keep kissing me like that," Giselle said, "and I'm pretty certain you won't ever get rid of me."

"Hello?" James's voice came from within the suite.

"Just a minute," Elspeth said, picking up her carpetbag. "Let's nurse some children to health and move you in here permanently."

"Sweet talker, you," Giselle said. She smiled, then sobered. "I look forward to that end, very much." Elspeth took a hand in hers, and Giselle let her lead them to the outer suite and James. Silently, she prayed the kids got well soon. Giselle was looking forward to a future with Elspeth away from any Gardiners.

Chapter Fifteen

"Thank you, my dear, for looking after the children tonight," Rosie said. Giselle stood in the foyer as Rosie prepared to leave for Charles's funeral. Transportation hadn't arrived yet, and Astoria was still with Edwin as he dressed for his excursion.

"Take all the time you need," Giselle said. "The nurses and I have everything under control."

"Be sure that you do," Edwin said as he and Astoria walked into the foyer. "Call Dr. Trent for any trouble. Tonight is too important to have you bother me."

"Of course," Giselle said, barely able to control an eye-roll. She'd call James before Trent. A knock on the front door saved her from needing to spend any more time in their company.

Edwin pulled the door open. "Your ride, ladies." He extended a bent elbow to each as they left. Giselle gladly closed the door behind them.

"Feel the need to bathe?" Giselle startled, not expecting Elspeth's voice, or the brush of her warm breath to her neck, behind her. "I'm sorry."

She turned toward her. "Don't be. You're right. He does make me feel dirty." Giselle shifted closer and lowered her voice. "Is everything okay?"

Elspeth nodded. "Rosalind was almost asleep, Blanche and Susan are asleep, so I told Helen to look after them for a while. I sent Nora to bed since she needs the quiet most." She nodded her head toward the kitchen. "Thought we'd have some tea before I take over for Helen."

"Sounds wonderful." She followed Elspeth into the kitchen. Giselle was surprised to see Lottie hadn't left for the evening. "Lottie, why are you still here?"

Lottie shook her head. "Last minute demands from his royal highn-ass."

"Lottie," Giselle said in surprise, barely able to suppress her laughter.

Elspeth didn't bother smothering her reaction, breaking into a huge smile. "I've missed you, Mrs. Kaplan."

"And I missed you," Lottie said. She glanced from Giselle to Elspeth. "It's nice to see you relax some, both of you. I wish there were more opportunities for genuine laughter in this house."

Giselle pat Lottie's hand where it lay on the small butcher island. "We'll get the children healthy, and maybe it will keep Edwin away from the house for a while."

"Wish something would," Lottie said. "Might as well move in permanently, with as often as he's been here these last few months. If I didn't need this job, I'd've hightailed it outta here with the nanny."

"You can always come work for me," Elspeth said. Her look of surprise alerted them she hadn't realized she'd spoken aloud.

"That's not a bad idea," Giselle said. She studied Elspeth for a moment. "You'd probably have to offer rather nice incentives to pull her away for this job, which she's maintained for quite some time."

"What are you two going on about?" Lottie asked.

"Nurse Keillor is soon to open a nursing home. The residents will need to eat." Giselle raised her eyebrows, then stage whispered, "I can put in a good word for you with the boss."

"That's wonderful, Elspeth."

"Thank you. I still have some renovation to complete. And I must finish here, first." Elspeth gazed at her with such warmth that Giselle felt flushed. "Then, I plan on whisking Giselle away to be my financial manager."

"Bless you for that, nurse," Lottie said, her tone serious. "Without you and the colonels, this is not a good place for our Giselle." Lottie heaved a sigh. "I should be off. My family has been understanding, but not happy about these extra hours so close to the holidays."

"Yes," Giselle said, hugging Lottie. "Go home to your family."

Lottie went to the small cleaning supply cupboard that held her coat and purse. As she put her jacket on, Elspeth said, "Mrs. Kaplan, give some serious thought to what Giselle proposed. If you can't accept on your behalf, maybe you can recommend a substitute. No one will be as good as you, of course, but the second-best will need to suffice."

"I'll do that, Elspeth," Lottie said, her tone serious. "Thank you."

"No need for that among friends." Elspeth smiled. Giselle wanted to hug her right then. Not that she needed inducement other than proximity. How could people not see the tenderness of Elspeth, focusing only on the negative?

Hand on the doorknob, Lottie stopped and stiffened. She twisted to stare at them. "Oh, I nearly forgot."

Giselle took a step closer to her. "Something wrong?"

"I wouldn't know but wanted to tell you of something that happened today." She frowned. "Little Susan offered me a piece of chocolate, which I accepted without thinking. After eating it, I thought about your food concerns. I asked where she got it, and she told me Edwin brought them a box of sweets."

"Did you take the sweets from them?" Elspeth asked.

"I'm sorry. By that time, Susan's offering was all that remained."

"We appreciate you for sharing this, Lottie," Giselle

said. "Not much you can do."

Elspeth smirked. "Can't know whether Edwin tainted anything. I want us cautious, but not fearful."

"Ha," Giselle said. "It seems a good possibility. Anyone in this house with contact with him has fallen ill. Or died." A warmth to her lower back let her know Elspeth offered support from the contact.

"So far, the youngest girls are all right," Elspeth said softly. "All we can do at this point is to keep an eye out for changes."

Lottie opened the door to the cold night air. "You may also need to note that Blanche's friend, Jayne Price, spent a good part of the day visiting. Can't imagine she turned down sweets." She shook her head. "Good night, girls."

Giselle and Elspeth echoed her salutation before the kitchen door to outside closed. "Suppose I need to make a note of the visit and the sweets."

"Do you think he poisoned the candy?" She leaned into Elspeth. Could Edwin be that vile? "They're just children," Giselle said.

Elspeth put an arm across her shoulder. "No, Ellie, they are obstacles." Giselle shuddered. "Come on. Let's relieve Helen. Then we can enjoy a little peace before the adult Gardiner's return."

She hoped they were overreacting. Hoped the children wouldn't meet the fate of the Colonels and that of Charles. Much as Giselle tried to imbue a positive light upon the situation, her heart told her events instituted by Edwin weren't over yet.

****

James knew about the events at the Gardiner house

from Elspeth. He and anyone in Maple Woods with a newspaper also knew Charles Gardiner was dead. Three dead in a little over a month, in the same house, was unprecedented. The only reason he could figure that the oddity went unquestioned would be due to the age of two family members.

Tonight, the service for Charles took place a few miles away. A reasonable expectation was for the family to attend the funerals of relatives. Normal, however, didn't appear to concern Edwin Merrick, who currently held court in the corner of the room.

He hadn't wanted to attend tonight. Probably could have used an excuse to explain his absence, but courtesy to a fellow physician had an advantage. James wanted to watch Edwin, wanted to stay in his good graces until the tragedies afflicting the Gardiner house ceased to exist. Especially now that Elspeth returned to offer aid. James recognized the real reason behind Mairi's offer. It would be impossible for her to leave the charming Giselle alone in the face of possible danger.

The more information Elspeth provided, though circumstantial at best, had him worried. The illnesses were too coincidental, in a short time, to be anything other than contrived. He grinned. Leave it to Elspeth to play the knight to Giselle's damsel in distress. James was delighted for her happiness.

"What's so amusing?" a voice asked beside him. James was so preoccupied with internal speculation he hadn't realized Edwin left his spot to schmooze.

"Remembering a conversation from earlier in the day with a beautiful woman."

"From that grin, it must have been a doozy," Edwin said, before taking a deep pull on the drink in his hand.

James didn't want to converse with Edwin; the man made his skin crawl. If Edwin affected him this way, no wonder Mauri worried about Giselle. Best to keep the conversation light. No need to raise any eyebrows. "How was Thanksgiving?" James asked.

"Didn't go," Edwin said simply. "Wife and I had other plans. I asked the family to postpone it, but Mother had a trip to Chicago with friends." He grinned, all teeth, and pushed up his spectacles. "Probably best, from what I hear. Thinking the family's succumbed to some awful bit of bad medical luck. Maybe even typhoid."

James frowned. He learned from Elspeth via Giselle, Astoria and Edwin were present for the holiday meal. At the time, it hadn't seemed a critical bit of news. He wasn't about to verbally call Edwin on the matter as it may prove vital to Giselle's and Mairi's safety. Why did Edwin feel the need to lie about the event? Was he setting up an alibi? Why would one be necessary unless you were guilty of wrongdoing? Since when had the surviving family been diagnosed with typhoid? "Ah, too bad, since holidays are meant for sharing with family. There's always Christmas."

"I suppose."

"How are those specimens working for you?" he asked. James didn't want to give Edwin a chance to quiz him on his personal life. Not that Edwin would miss the opportunity to keep the moment about him. He was the man of the evening, after all.

"Oh, fine, fine." He drained his glass and rocked back on his heels. "Good to keep the brain busy. Plan to achieve great things, Jimmy, my boy."

It took a concerted effort not to flinch at the flippant use of the name. Many people could plan to achieve greatness, but it didn't guarantee it would happen. Edwin didn't strike James as the achiever of anything more than gross annoyance upon others. "Good luck with that," James said, straining to hide the sarcasm.

"Don't need luck," Edwin said, tapping a finger to his

temple.

Right. Whatever floats your boat, Eddie, my boy. "So, congratulations, by the way."

"Ah, thank you." Edwin smiled. The expression made him appear creepy rather than pleased. "Must keep impressing the wife, you know."

"No, I don't know," James said.

Edwin gazed in his direction. He dropped his empty drink glass on the tray of a passing waiter. "Maybe you will understand if things work out with the woman who made you smile like the cat with a canary." Edwin laughed at his own joke. "Need another drink. Enjoy your evening."

James watched him walk away. He'd done all he could do this evening, overdosing on disagreeable sensations from Edwin. He needed a hot shower. Had the possible negative situation in the Gardiner house not existed, James would berate his sister for suggesting even a second in that horrid man's presence.

How had Mairi and Giselle managed?

Chapter Sixteen

Elspeth was glad to see Nora and Helen looking a little better this morning. Sleep did wonders for them. They exited their respective rooms just as she knocked on Giselle's door. "Good morning, ladies. Shall I meet you downstairs for an update after you've checked on the children?" It was agreed, when she'd introduced herself on arrival, Elspeth would take charge as the senior nurse. She wouldn't usually agree to the need but believed it best to be the go-between with Edwin and the Gardiners. She caught the small smile from Helen right before being yanked into Giselle's room.

Warm lips pressed firmly against hers as her body pressed against the closed door. No sooner had she melted into the kiss, Elspeth removed the contact. "I enjoy doing that. Please, say we'll kiss often," Giselle said.

"Kissing me like that will assure a lifetime of no complaints." Elspeth grazed a finger along her cheek. "Sleep well?"

Giselle tilted her head into the caress. "Mmhmm." She raised her head and gazed into her eyes with such tenderness Elspeth knew her heart was entirely in the young woman's hands. "It's helped considerably, knowing you were near."

Elspeth smiled at the statement. "Knowing I was near should you require me keeps my nerves in check." She leaned in and placed a kiss to Giselle's forehead. "Now, I shall hurry and get the Gardiner girls better so we can get back home."

Tears clouded Giselle's eyes. "Home. Sounds wonderful."

"It will always be yours, for as long as you want it. You understand that, right?" Elspeth hoped Giselle would consider her place was with Elspeth. She suspected the younger woman might not feel the same after a few years, but Elspeth would gladly accept any time they could share, no matter how minimal.

"Quit that," Giselle said. She drew her closer, wrapped hands at her waist, and Elspeth sighed at the comfort the embrace brought her.

"Quit what?" Elspeth asked. "Didn't do anything but enjoy this moment."

Giselle sniffed. "You're thinking negative thoughts."

Elspeth frowned. "How could you suppose that?"

"Your face got all scrunched up." Giselle gave an exaggerated frown, complete with pouty lips.

"I did not," Elspeth said.

"Maybe not as bad as I implied just now, but your expression did get rather serious." Giselle's features sobered. "Please, Elspeth, don't look at me as if I'm still a child. See me for someone who cares for you, without an age barrier."

"I'm trying, Ellie, I assure you."

Giselle playfully swatted her shoulder. "Try harder."

"I promise—"

A sturdy knock sounded on the door, and they moved away from the other. "Nurse Keillor?" Elspeth opened the door to Helen, who glanced regretfully toward Giselle. "My apologies, Miss, for the interruption, but," her gaze returned to Elspeth, "you need to see Nora in Rosalind's room. There's been a development."

"Of course." A glance to Giselle, a nod of understanding, and Elspeth left the room and followed Helen downstairs. While Helen moved toward the youngest girl's shared bedroom, Elspeth strode to Rosalind's.

"What can you tell me?" Elspeth asked as she entered the room. Rosalind appeared to be in pain, though sleeping, her sleep was fitful. She determined after she listened to Nora, to call her brother in on this matter, to see firsthand some of her concerns addressed. Trent and Merrick be damned.

Nora glanced toward her, then returned her gaze to Rosalind. Nora conveyed the information in a mere whisper. "As you may be aware, Rosalind is deathly afraid of needles, so Doctor Trent ordered them terminated in her case." Elspeth nodded, even as Nora pulled her into a corner for more privacy. "She just passed out but shared something disturbing." Nora hesitated before adding, "About Doctor Merrick."

"Which is?"

"As Rosalind explained to me a moment ago, Doctor Merrick came into her room late last night. He had a needle. She claims, even as she dodged away from him, he grabbed her arm and shoved the needle into her. Because she fought him, he drove the needle into her upper arm, just above the elbow."

"Did he explain what he was doing?" she asked, suspected he wouldn't feel the need, especially to a female child. "Did you check the area?"

Nora gave a swift nod. "The arm is an irritated red, confirming her story. But he didn't say anything, didn't even turn on the light, Rosalind claims." They both went to Rosalind; Nora carefully produced the injury for her inspection.

"Stay with her," Elspeth said. "Don't leave her side until I tell you otherwise, particularly if Merrick returns. I'm calling in another doctor, one I trust. Enough is enough. These children need proper attention."

"Yes, ma'am," Nora said. As Elspeth left, she thought she heard a relieved sigh from the other nurse.

Elspeth went to the nearest phone, on a table at the far end of the second-floor hallway, where she promptly called James. She gave him a very brief account of what happened to Rosalind, only disconnecting when assured he was on the way. She made her way down to the kitchen, where she found Giselle speaking with Lottie, who promptly asked if she'd like tea.

"With the cistern water," Lottie said.

She only hesitated a moment before conceding. The need for tea outweighed her concern for contamination. "Thank you, Lottie," she said as the cup passed to her. "I wanted to let you know to expect a visitor at the back door. I've asked another doctor to stop by. His name is Doctor Campbell." Elspeth smiled at Giselle's raised eyebrow. "I believe we need a fresh pair of eyes on this peculiar situation."

"Should I bring him up the servant's stairwell?" Lottie asked.

"I can take him up for you," Giselle offered. "Has something else happened?"

Lottie brought a hand to her chest. "None of the other children has passed, have they?"

"No, but Rosalind's condition has worsened." Elspeth took a couple of sips of tea. "I hope to have her seen by Doctor Campbell before Merrick gets wind of it."

"Is there anything I can do?" Lottie asked.

Elspeth shook her head. "No. However, you probably want to deny any knowledge of his presence should either Merrick question you." She glanced at Giselle. "I'd rather not have you involved either. But I'm convinced relegating you to your room will cause more difficulties for me."

Giselle grinned mischievously. "How quick you've come to understand me."

"Send James up as soon as you can." Elspeth gave Giselle one more smile before she darted away, afraid if she hesitated any longer, she'd furnish more than Lottie would want to witness between her and Giselle. But, oh, how she wanted to hug or kiss Giselle—just because.

****

When James found her in the hall after he examined the three Gardiner girls, Elspeth barely contained her nervousness at his conclusions. "Thank you, James, for involving yourself in this. I don't want to put you in a bad spot with your colleagues, but I'm truly worried."

"No worries, Mairi," James said quietly. "Ease your fears. I called the younger Doctor Trent and explained a bit of the matter."

Elspeth winced. "What did you tell him?"

James squeezed her upper arm. "It's all right. Gerry, unlike his father, will do whatever he can to avoid Merrick and is not a fan of him in the least. He'll explain it so that it becomes his idea for sending me over. We've agreed a nurse called for the senior Trent who was unavailable, Gerry wasn't able to assist and, thus, I'm to the rescue."

"I'm sorry we have to handle things like this. It's so unprofessional." Elspeth pinched the bridge of her nose in hopes of alleviating some of the pressure building into a headache.

"Which makes it uncomfortable for you, but now I have a better understanding of what you've shared on previous occasions." He flashed a lopsided grin at her. "Need to fix matters so you can move on with a particular auburn-haired beauty."

"James."

"What? I'm happy if it's what you want. She's delightful, especially when I inquired about you on our journey upstairs, and she battled not to smile, lost to a blush."

Lowering her voice, Elspeth said, "She'll be moving into the house when this matter is finished."

"Perfect. We'll have to—"

"What's going on here?" Edwin bellowed from the top of the second-floor landing. "Doctor Campbell?"

"Showtime," James whispered near her ear before he acknowledged Merrick. "Ah, Doctor Merrick. Filling in for Trent. He's feeling a bit under the weather, and he didn't want to leave you without a replacement."

Edwin scowled at them. "Something I should be aware of?" He glared at Elspeth and moved threateningly toward her. "Why didn't someone notify me of a problem, Nurse?" His disdaining tone caused James to glower at the back of Edwin's head before he shifted as if to protect her.

Elspeth gave a barely perceptible shake of her head; one James would catch even if Merrick didn't or wouldn't waste time observing. "Time was of the essence."

"Time for what?" he demanded.

"Really, Edwin," James said. "What matters is the care of the children. The oldest girl has suffered a setback, from what I understand, of her original ailment."

"Setback?"

"Yes," James said. Elspeth caught the gleam in her brother's eye. He was angry, which meant he'd not pull verbal punches. His tone hardened when he asked, "Did you give Rosalind a shot last night?"

Edwin seemed startled. "Um, yes, I did."

James held up a finger to halt Edwin. She wondered if James enjoyed taking advantage of his seniority, which he'd never use on anyone else. "Nurse, would you get the nurse who looked after the child this morning."

"Yes, Doctor," Elspeth said, then left to retrieve Nora, who wasn't far away. "This is Nurse Hunter."

"Nurse," James acknowledged before returning his attention to Merrick. "Trent discontinued the use of needles with the child, because of her fear of them."

"Well, yes, but—"

"But what, doctor?" James asked, tone harder as he interrupted Edwin.

On the defensive now, two nurses to witness his interrogation, Elspeth watched Edwin grow annoyed at being questioned. "I checked on the children last night. My duty, James, as their doctor and their brother-in-law. I found Rosalind's pulse was erratic, so I gave her a hypodermic of camphorated oil."

Elspeth, and Nora, if her frown any indication, was skeptical. When she'd inspected the newest injury, she hadn't noted the smell of camphor. If he'd injected Rosalind with camphor oil, the scent would be on her arm or her bedclothes, where stray drops would have spilled.

"Camphorated oil? Didn't detect it, but that's beside the point. Her arm, when I examined her a moment ago, was disturbingly swollen. Whatever the reason, I've instructed Nurse Hunter not to leave Rosalind's room." James directed his gaze at Nora. "You may return to the patient. Continue to monitor her erratic pulse. I'll return in a moment with further instructions as to the care of the newest injury."

"I'm sure I can take care of it," Edwin snarled.

James quirked his head to the side. "I'm certain you can." His sarcasm appeared lost on Edwin, but Elspeth heard it. "However, Doctor Trent has asked me to handle matters in his absence. He's concerned for your health, too, Edwin. The last month has placed a lot on your plate." He glanced toward the ceiling as if deep in thought. "What has it been? Three deaths? And now three young girls are ill. It's too much for one man, no matter how proficient he is at his craft."

Elspeth wanted to roll her eyes at the compliment, even if she knew James wished to appear on Edwin's side. Edwin fell for it. "Yes. Yes, you're right. Since you're here already, maybe I should take a moment or two for myself." He extended a hand in James's direction, who returned the shake. "Think I'll see if the wife has Christmas shopping left to complete."

Surprised at how quickly he capitulated, Elspeth and James watched as he returned to the first level. "Unexpected," she said.

"Not really," James said. He took her elbow, walked her to Rosalind's door, and stopped outside. "I'd say he's already planning a workaround."

"Working around us?"

"Yeah. Trent would defer to a younger doctor, in this case, Merrick."

Elspeth groaned. "Please tell me you don't think we are imagining things."

James shook his head. "No, I don't. I've taken blood samples from the youngest girls. I'll have to assume whatever ails them is what is affecting the oldest." He paused. "You mentioned Merrick recently brought in bottled water?"

"He's bringing it in personally, for the family's health," she said.

"Then I had best take a sample with me."

"James, do you know what is wrong with the children? What he's done?"

"Not yet, but I may have a suspicion. I sure hope I'm wrong." He smiled lovingly at her. "Answers won't come quickly, Mairi. Keep you and the nurses safe as best you can. I have no fear you're already doing everything to keep Giselle far from Merrick."

"You know me too well." Elspeth couldn't stop the flush of color to her cheeks. She was able to control her emotional reactions with everyone but her brother.

He cleared his throat, a stern expression on his face. "I have an important question to ask before we turn to current matters." At her nod, he lowered his voice and shifted close to her ear. "Do you think Nurse Paige would agree to dinner with me?"

Elspeth snickered. "Probably, little brother."

"We can double date." He waggled his eyebrows at her.

She shook her head. "Fine, but please refrain from an open courtship until we've dealt with solving this present crisis."

James sighed dramatically. "If I must."

"You must." Voice low, she added, "If I must postpone my flirtations, so can you. Ow." He playfully pinched her cheek. "Heard that." Elspeth gave the only response available to her. She straightened, glared at him, and opened the door to Rosalind's room. "Shall we, Doctor?"

Chapter Seventeen

The morning following James Campbell's visit, Giselle went to the nursery to spend time with Susan and Blanche. She offered to spend time with Rosalind, but she spouted she was too mature and felt too miserable to be coddled. Giselle thought it just as well since the younger girls were better suited to her time than the spoiled teenager. What she had hoped to avoid was not to be. Both the youngsters were still in bed; and, their guest, Jayne, was putting on her coat. Giselle had been surprised the girls could have an overnight visit so soon after the death of Charles, but glad permission was given. The girls needed activities to take their minds off of the tragedies in the house, even if they still had to wear mourning black.

"Are you off for home so early?" Giselle asked.

Jayne nodded solemnly. "We aren't feeling well."

"Oh," Giselle said, glancing toward Helen. "What's wrong?"

The nurse closed Jayne's overnight bag, which she'd been packing. "So far, just a general malaise. I've shared with Nurse Keillor when she came 'round, and we'll keep an eye on things."

"And?" she asked, glancing toward Jayne. It would not go well if Jayne contracted something lethal while at the Gardiner home, worse if no one alerted the family of the possibility.

Luckily, Helen was quick to catch on to her unspoken question since she didn't want to alarm the young girls. "Dr. Campbell has been apprised."

"Wonderful." Giselle picked up Jayne's bag and addressed the young girl. "How 'bout I walk you downstairs and stay with you until your ride arrives?" Jayne nodded. "Perfect." She addressed Blanche and Susan. "Once Jayne is safely on her way, I can come back and read to you, if you'd like."

Blanche brightened. "Can you read more from *The Wind in the Willows*?"

Susan giggled. The diversion was working for the seven-year-old. "Ooh, Mr. Toad is getting a motor car."

"We most certainly can, and you're right, Susan. The caravan crashed," Giselle said. "Be back in a moment to read the next adventure."

Giselle walked Jayne downstairs, staying with her until the arrival of her father, then returned to the younger Gardiner girls. Helen sat quietly in a chair behind her while Giselle raised her skirt slightly and sat on the side of Susan's bed and read another two chapters before she realized her captive audience was losing focus. "Are you two all right?" she asked. "Have you had enough for now?"

Helen popped up from her chair and moved closer to Blanche's bed. "Are you feeling ill?" she asked with her hand to Blanche's forehead. Giselle suspected the reaction was automatic. Helen must have realized what she'd done since she gave Giselle a wry grin. "Of course, you aren't well. Sorry."

"I doubt they noticed your little faux-pas," Giselle said quietly. "They cue on your concern."

"Should we get Nurse Keillor? Their temperatures have elevated." Helen's concern was genuine, maybe more than duty required. Giselle would label it more maternal than business-like.

Giselle shook her head. "That's not necessary right now." Elspeth had explained to her, last night, that James took blood samples and ordered rest with plenty of fluids for them. He also replaced the bottled water in the kitchen with a duplicate, removing the one provided by Edwin. Elspeth had further explained, though he didn't know the prognosis, James intended to eliminate all possible causes, even taking what remained of the candy Edwin gave the girls. "Why don't you go get a cup of tea," Giselle said. "Take the breaks while you can, before Edwin makes a pest of himself. Don't neglect the opportunity when presented."

Helen seemed poised to argue, then shook her head. "I can't argue with your logic. I'll be but a moment."

"Take your time," Giselle said, tucking blankets around the now sleeping girls. She then sat in the chair Helen recently vacated. Her thoughts shifted to Elspeth, as was becoming a common theme lately, not that she'd complain. Immediately, images of Elspeth when they'd kissed populated her brain. Her body warmed, not so much from the flush, but her body's responses to the remembrances. Despite all the sad changes in her life lately, Elspeth was the singular bright spot, the one thing she could focus on and look forward to a future with.

Her thoughts were interrupted by soft whimpering. Giselle stood and glanced toward the girls as she moved to stand between their beds. Susan's brows furrowed in her sleep, and her bottom lip quivered. She realized the youngest Gardiner child was having a nightmare. Giselle sat on the side of Susan's bed and grazed her fingers across the girl's sweat-dampened forehead. "Shh," she repeated. Giselle wanted to relax her, not waken her, and hoped the slight physical contact achieved her goal of halting the nightmare. It didn't.

Susan's eyes popped open and pinned Giselle in their startled gaze, blinked once, twice, and focused. Scrambling on her knees, Susan crawled to Giselle, wrapped her tiny arms in a vice-like grip around Giselle's neck, and cried. A moment later, the little girl said, "I don't want to die, Giselle."

Giselle hugged her tighter. "Oh, honey." Instinct automatically prompted her to respond that wouldn't happen, but she didn't want to lie to the girl. With James's intervention, Giselle hoped that horrid results would be averted. She lightly stroked her palm down Susan's hair, rocking them side to side. "We have nurses who care very much for you. Nurse Keillor is making sure of it. She even has a special doctor helping to figure this out." Giselle leaned back, tapped a finger under Susan's chin, and gazed directly at her. "I'll be here whenever you need me."

"Promise?" Susan asked.

"Until Mother sends her away," Blanche said brusquely. Giselle hadn't realized she's wakened.

Fresh tears fell from Susan's eyes. "But why? You spend time with us."

"Because we're growing up. We're not supposed to be getting attached." Blanche crawled from her bed onto Susan's, putting an arm around her shoulder.

Susan stared at Blanche with an earnest expression. "But I want her to stay here with us. I love her." Did she forget I'm sitting right here? Giselle wondered.

Blanche rolled her eyes. "We're children. We don't get a say." Giselle had to bite back the grin demanding release. Blanche was on the cusp of adulthood, but hanging as best she could to the last remnants of childhood. She was bright but tended to downplay her intelligence except for moments like this, and rarely in front of her other, older family members.

Giselle's heart broke, realizing a small extension of the Gardiner family seemed to care about her, what happened to her. She couldn't guarantee the future's outcome but felt she needed to offer some assurances. "Well, I say we can stay in touch if you wish. We can work it all out when you both get healthier." She smiled and tapped a finger to Susan's nose. "Because I love you, too."

The door opened, and Helen slipped in. Helen raised a questioning eyebrow in her direction. Giselle gave a slight shake of her head, turned a wry face to the girls. "Uh-oh, I've been caught interrupting your rest. Lie down and close those eyes."

Both complied, but Blanche opened one eye slowly. "Another chapter might help us, Giselle."

Giselle gasped in feigned surprise. "Are you saying the story puts you to sleep?" Susan giggled. "Or my narration does?"

"Read," both girls said simultaneously before giggling.

The response filled Giselle with hope. If a positive attitude had any healing qualities, Blanche and Susan would make it through this.

****

Giselle entered Rosie's sitting room, intent on updating her on the changes to Susan and Blanche. However, she found the Merricks were present.

"There must be something wrong, I tell you, no matter what you believe." Beside Rosie was the paper packet of a headache powder Edwin produced a couple of days earlier and a glass of water. Rosie's headaches were frequent, so no one questioned her complaints. "Astoria, have that abysmal water thrown out."

"Mother?"

"The water. The water from the huge bottle that you've brought in, have it emptied. It's the foulest stuff ever put in my mouth." Rosie gave a shudder, which brought her gaze to Giselle in the doorway. "Yes, my dear."

"I wanted to let you know all the children are resting. And to see if there was anything that I could do for you, but I see you have your daughter to assist. I'll take my leave." Rosie waved a hand dismissively. Giselle hastily exited before anyone could comment or ask something of her. Specifically Edwin, but he seemed a tad preoccupied. Giselle could still hear Rosie's complaints from the library, where she stopped to get a new book for herself.

"Edwin, I feel worse than before I drank that vile concoction. I need an emetic." A pause. "Are you listening, Edwin?"

Merrick stepped into the hall, followed by Rosie and Astoria. Giselle, from her position in the library, noticed Edwin appeared to be taking his time filling the order. Rosie strode angrily around him and headed for the guest bathroom.

Curious, Giselle moved closer to the library entrance where she could observe yet remove herself from view should anyone look in her direction. Rosie decided to—literally—take matters into her hands. She rammed a finger down her throat as she entered the bathroom. From the sounds, Rosie no longer required the emetic.

Some moments passed before Rosie was composed enough to leave the bathroom. She glared at Edwin. "Is this an example of the attention you're providing my children?"

Astoria came to her husband's defense. "Mother, it's because of the superb care to the girls that he's tired now. How could he possibly have known your need to be so immediate?"

Superb care? Giselle wanted to laugh. Was Astoria that blind to her husband's incompetence? Or was she a willing accomplice in his plot?

****

Elspeth relieved Nora of her overnight vigil for Rosalind at dawn. She sat in the chair beside the small table and reviewed the logbook used to track the patient's progress. Nora's log entry recorded a normal temperature and pulse, for which Elspeth was happy. Her relief was short-lived. Merrick entered the room without so much as a knock to announce himself. From the surprised expression, which he quickly hid, he probably suspected Nora to be in attendance. Elspeth was glad to provide disappointment to him.

"Morning, Keillor," Edwin said, his lip curled in a sneer.

"Uh-huh," she said. Elspeth gave tit-for-tat since he intended to be discourteous.

She kept her gaze on him as Edwin moved closer to her, picked up the log she'd just put down, and picked up the box of capsules on the table. "Is Rosalind still taking these?"

"Yes," Elspeth confirmed. The doctors neglected to share with Elspeth the boxes content, a prescription the sixteen-year-old took several times a day under Doctor Trent's orders. As the pills created no ill effects to date, Elspeth never openly questioned their use.

"When is the next capsule due?"

Read the log, Merrick, instead of glancing at it, she wanted to tell him. Instead, she replied, "In an hour."

Just then, the door flung open, and Astoria appeared. "Nurse—" She gaped at Elspeth, who waited for the woman to state her reason for bursting in on them. "Oh, ah, I think there's a problem with Blanche."

Despite the warning bells telling her not to leave the

room, Elspeth rushed out to check on Blanche. When she entered the nursery, Helen glanced at her in confusion from where she read in the chair. "What's wrong?" Elspeth asked, noting Susan and Blanche both asleep.

"Nothing," Helen replied. "Why?"

"Astoria said—" Elspeth took another look at the children. "Under no circumstance are you to leave this room. Okay? Not for anyone but me."

In the hallway, Elspeth caught a glimpse of Edwin and Astoria at the stairwell landing. Astoria shot her an expression that dared Elspeth to confront her. She didn't; instead, she rushed back to Rosalind. Everything seemed as it had when she left it minutes before, down to the still sleeping Rosalind.

Two hours later, Nora returned with a tray for Rosalind. "I can take over now." She put it on the table since Rosalind slept, if a little fitfully.

"Did you get enough rest?"

Nora shrugged. "I couldn't sleep. This house gives me the creeps, like one of those gothic novels."

"Yes, I know what you mean," Elspeth said, glancing at the bed to make sure they hadn't disturbed Rosalind. "A bit surprised that you're a gothic novel devotee, though."

"We all need our guilty pleasures. And, you know, now the saying is right. Truth is stranger than fiction." Nora tapped the logbook. "Anything I should be aware of happening in my short absence?"

Elspeth wasn't the gossipy kind, and that's what talking about Merrick felt like, but the three nurses needed to have all information to protect the children. In this case, it was necessary to share. "Another visit from Merrick. I tried to stay in the room, but Astoria came in and said something was wrong with Blanche. By the time I realized she was okay, only a minute or so passed, and the Merrick's were walking downstairs."

"Do you think he did something to Rosalind?"

"I honestly don't know. Rosalind appears fine." Elspeth shook her head. "But we're speaking about Merrick. His presence could mean something, could mean nothing." She rubbed her eyes with the heel of her palms. "We need to be smarter about how we handle this."

"What are you thinking?" Nora asked.

Elspeth bit her bottom lip. She didn't want to stretch their exhaustion any further than Edwin did already. Moreover, she didn't want to involve Giselle, but Elspeth was at her wit's end to find a course of action to protect the children best. "I need you to ask Giselle to come to Rosalind's room. Then, stay with Helen. No matter what happens, we always need at least one of us to be in the patient rooms at all times constantly."

Nora tilted her head toward the bed and smirked. Her voice a low whisper when she said, "Are you sure you don't want me to handle the little princess?"

"Thank you, Nora, but I can handle her." Elspeth shook her head, not even trying to hide the automatic grin.

****

Rosalind was awake and eating when Nora dropped by with Giselle, then left to join Helen.

Ever polite, Giselle glanced at Rosalind and smiled. "Good morning, Rosalind." The girl mumbled her reply. Obviously, courtesy didn't matter when in a sickbed or responding to the family's unwelcome orphan.

Elspeth smiled grimly at Giselle. "Let's talk outside," she said, following her out. In the hall, Elspeth explained the early morning visit by the Merricks. "Am I being paranoid? Because I don't know. Edwin's hands aren't clean, but I can't find everything he does as being suspect, can I?"

"Sure, you can," Giselle said, then snickered. She squeezed Elspeth's upper left arm. How very much Elspeth wanted to pull her into a hug. She craved contact with Giselle. Part of her tried to suppress the feelings for all time, but her heart couldn't help itself. Elspeth wanted this situation to speedily resolve so they could return to her home and put all this misery and stress behind them—as far as possible, given the losses suffered as a result. "How about I bring us up some tea. I can remove Rosalind's tray," Giselle suggested.

"That would be lovely," Elspeth said. "Take your time. Rosalind needs her bath." When Giselle left the room on her task, Elspeth noted it was time for Rosalind's morning medication, and selected one from the pillbox, then proceeded to complete the young girl's morning bathing routine. With the task done, Elspeth wandered to the window while Rosalind lay back on her pillow. The window coverings were open, and Elspeth glanced outside at the snowy lawn below. She saw the buggy parked in front, and Doctor Trent as he made his way up the short hill toward the front door. "The doctor has arrived," she said, determined to enjoy the view for as long as duty allowed her.

Rosalind's voice brightened. "He'll come here directly," she said. "Doctor Trent always starts his rounds with me."

Elspeth turned and stepped to Rosalind's bed, just as the door opened to admit Trent, followed by Giselle with tea service tray in hand. Giselle placed the tray on the table and quietly slipped out of the room. Elspeth hoped she hadn't gone too far.

"How is my patient today?" Trent asked, placing his medical bag on the nightstand and reaching for Rosalind's wrist to take her pulse.

"About the same, sir," Rosalind said, never one to deviate from her internal script. Her face, with half-lidded eyes, held the same forlorn expression as always. Elspeth shifted to the bedside opposite Trent, focusing on Rosalind. Either the girl was becoming a better actress, or—

Rosalind suddenly started to shudder. Her body arced in a trembling motion, and Trent dropped his grip on her wrist. The girl's neck went rigid; head slammed back into the pillows, then her opened eyes blankly stared at the ceiling. Soft sounds tumbled from her lips, but they were nonsense words trickling in senseless mutterings.

Elspeth grabbed Rosalind's wrist. She found no pulse. With a glower to Trent, she demanded, "Do something, Doctor. I've lost her pulse."

He gave a shaky breath, stuffed his hands into his bag, and pulled out a small vial and syringe. "Morphine-nitroglycerine injection," Trent said. Mere seconds later, Rosalind gasped, her eyelids falling closed. The injection worked. "She'll sleep for a little while, but should be alright."

Baffled by the situation, Elspeth asked, "What happened?"

Trent shook his head, his gaze on Rosalind, his brow furrowed. "I can't say." Elspeth doubted that the older man was aware of how openly he spoke to her. "What has she done in the last hour?"

"She's taken her morning medication, bathed, and had breakfast. All part of her usual routine," Elspeth said. "Rosalind showed no indication of distress, not until you where here to witness the results."

Still frowning, Trent picked up the pillbox and stared at the contents. He emptied the pills into his palm, then stuffed them in a pocket. Trent then retrieved a bottle of pills from his bag, counted out a few, and placed them in the pillbox. Neither spoke. Elspeth suspected recent events were making Trent as paranoid—probably deservedly so—as the nurses and Giselle.

"This is more than an old physician can handle," he said, then stared directly at Elspeth. His hands trembled, and she knew the incident had shaken the elder doctor, probably more than he expected. "My son has explained you're familiar with Doctor Campbell."

"Yes," she said with a nod. Might as well be honest with the man. "He's my half-brother."

"Good, good." Trent pulled a handkerchief from his pocket and dabbed at the beads of sweat dotting his upper lip. "I plan to give him a call, ask him to take over the duties to the Gardiner family until this peculiar matter is resolved." He closed his medical bag with a decisive snap and turned back to her. "I'll let Mrs. Gardiner know. She'll agree, of course, trusting my judgment. I can't guarantee she won't alert Doctor Merrick of the change."

"Understood, Doctor." They didn't need to voice that Merrick could prove troublesome. Elspeth followed him to the door, sighting Giselle in the hall. When Trent started down the stairs, Elspeth waved Giselle toward her.

In the room, Elspeth whispered what had transpired as Giselle poured them tea. She also handed over a small plate with a generous slice of pound cake, sprinkled with confectionary sugar. Giselle arched her eyebrows playfully. "Lottie said you're too thin."

Elspeth grinned. "She's figured out I have a sweet tooth I seldom indulge."

"Go to know," Giselle said.

They consumed the treat, and the tea in silence, content to enjoy the quiet companionship few seldom found, let alone shared. Elspeth had only been this comfortable with James, certainly never with Maddie. Well, she thought, these feelings may not last long but would always be cherished in her heart and memory.

Chapter Eighteen

"We can't let her travel alone. I don't know what to do. Lilly should be here, but I can't leave my little girls," Rosie said. Her tone held just enough whining Edwin decided to use this bump in the road, another level of the plan he hadn't expected to occur, to his advantage.

And, just maybe, he'd get a little payback for interference by the orphan. Imagine, bringing that hideous nurse back. "Mother Gardiner," Edwin said, as he kneeled in front of her and clasped her left hand in his. "We have three nurses and Doctor Trent. The little ones will be fine. Let me collect Lilly for you."

"Oh, Edwin, you're such a godsend to me."

"May I ask a boon?"

"Yes, anything," Rosie said, though she frowned at him.

He stood. "I'll leave as soon as I make arrangements. In the interim, I ask to get the library converted into a bedroom for us. No need to continue to inconvenience Astoria with a smaller space while she remains to assist you during this tragic time."

"Of course," Rosie agreed. "You only needed to ask." Hah, take that, Giselle. You've lost your hideaway. If he could think of a reason to rid himself of the annoying nurse, he would do so. That wouldn't be an easy task. The other nurses, even Trent, deferred to her for most matters. "Are you certain you wouldn't rather have an actual bedroom upstairs?"

"No, no, until we know what is infecting the children, I'd rather not expose Astoria."

Rosie nodded, then heaved a sigh. "I understand. Well,

let me get you the information for Lilly so you can get those arrangements made." She stood, brushed the wrinkles from her dress, and left the room.

Astoria smirked. "Guess I should go pack a few things before Mother has the movers arrive." She left him standing by Rosie's chair.

"I'll need to go to my office, Tori," he said to her departing figure. He didn't wait for a response. Whether she heard or not, Astoria would only respond if she needed him to do something for her. Rosie met him in the hallway with a slip of paper, the travel information. Edwin bussed her cheek before striding out the door.

At his office, Edwin gave a polite acknowledgment to his secretary, Miss Strauss, before entering his office. Time for another order. He contacted the pharmacy, placed another order for cyanide. "The order needs to increase to a dozen capsules." The manager answered so the request received no questioning, as had happened on one previous occasion.

Edwin pulled the paper Rosie gave him from his pocket. Time for travel arrangements. This new project could work to his advantage. He hadn't expected Lilly to return to Maple Woods, not after the family fallout concerning her. One less Gardiner to claim an inheritance, and a deviant one at that.

****

Elspeth sipped her tea but couldn't tell the flavor or the temperature as she tried not to appear obvious that she mentally devoured Giselle. Who could blame her? Even in the stark black of mourning clothes, Giselle made the dress a work of art. Of course, Giselle could be naked— The image flashed in her head. She inhaled sharply, only to begin a series of coughing that made her eyes water. Giselle looked at her with concern, Lottie clearly bit back a smile, not that she put much effort into the action.

"Are you okay?" Giselle asked.

She nodded. "Went down wrong." The three of them stood around the butcher-block table in the kitchen's center.

Lottie snickered. "Lose your focus, did you?" Elspeth shot her glare.

Any response, planned or otherwise, froze on her lips when the kitchen door opened, and James entered. "Hello, am I interrupting?" he asked while glancing at each.

"No, Doctor," Lottie said. "Can I get you something to drink?"

James shrugged out of his coat and flashed her a bright smile. "Coffee would be lovely if you have it."

"Right away." Lottie nearly floated as she went about the task.

"So, how are my three favorite ladies today?"

Elspeth rolled her eyes. "You already have us all in your camp, James. Quit your flirting." She took a cautious sip of her tea. "Any news?" She hadn't needed to update him on Rosalind since Doctor Trent had as soon as he left the house.

James lowered his head. "Still have a few test results to sort through. I've also brought in another pair of eyes, sort of a second opinion. Don't want to take chances."

"And..." Elspeth swatted her brother's shoulder.

"Let me start by stating..." He cleared his throat. Lottie handed him his coffee. James took a drink, winked at Lottie, and glanced toward the door leading further into the house. Voice low, he said, "This epidemic, and I use the word loosely, is confined to this house. There are no other cases recorded in Maple Woods for this entire year.

Not one."

"Damn it, James, get to the point," Elspeth snapped.

"Typhoid fever."

The kitchen suddenly became silent. There wasn't much to say after the revelation, too much to work through. One question stood out, but she wouldn't bring it up with Giselle and Lottie. She didn't need to worry. James brought the matter to light. "Inadvertently, I may have assisted in this dilemma. As Elspeth knows, doctors sometimes share samples of cultures for research."

"And you shared with Edwin?" Giselle asked.

"Unfortunately, yes."

"It's not like you could have known," Lottie said, saving Elspeth the need to defend her brother. "You aren't the one to bring this sickness down on this house, are you?"

"No, of course not." James worked his lower lip with his teeth.

"Is there more?" Giselle asked. Smart as she was, at least in Elspeth's estimation, Giselle caught one of her brother's tells.

James leaned on the table. "I went to Merrick's office, spoke with his receptionist, who informed me Merrick was on a trip to New York. I explained about the culture, and how my culture died, asking if she'd kindly permit me to scrape off a bit of Merrick's for replanting." He focused on Elspeth, probably knowing she'd be the one to understand the meaning. "The lower half of the medium hadn't been touched, and the upper half swept clean."

"What does that mean to us laymen?" Giselle asked, with Lottie nodding furiously at her side.

"Simply put, enough typhoid germs were missing to inoculate all of Maple Woods."

"Oh, James," Elspeth said, worried what Merrick would do next. "We have to tell someone, do something."

Quietly, James said, "Relax, Mairi," he said with a gentle pat to her hand. Giselle's raised eyebrow at the name hadn't gone unnoticed either. "I took precautions when I suspected what I'd find. I brought a new tube with an identical culture, which I already added potassium permanganate and formaldehyde." He smiled at Giselle and Lottie's questioning expressions. "It will destroy the typhoid germs."

"Well, that's good to know." Lottie puttered around the kitchen and returned with a freshly cooled apple pie, which she sliced and presented to them. "This is wasted on the others."

"Lottie," Giselle said in feigned outrage.

"Oh, pooh," Lottie said, waving a hand in the air. "I've another one for them."

"What steps do we take next?" Elspeth asked. The present company was of the people in her acquaintance, and only recently, she willingly relaxed her stern persona around. She smiled at Lottie. "This is wonderful, Lottie. I certainly hope you are considering my earlier offer."

"I haven't pushed it from my mind completely, just for now."

James should have inquired of the topic's relevance at this point, but he remained quiet. Elspeth noted his preoccupation didn't affect his appetite since he loaded his plate with another slice. Not that Elspeth wanted to hear the possible reply, but she asked, "Is there more?"

"While I was in Merrick's lab, I noted another tube with disturbed growth. It was Diphtheria."

Giselle sighed. "I assume that finding is not good news."

"Depends on if Merrick's used it already, or what he plans on doing with it," Elspeth said. She gave Giselle a wry grin. "Really, James, how can we stop him?"

"We have some evidence, but nothing that couldn't be

explained away by Merrick. I've compiled some information and a timeline and presented it to some of my colleagues. We've already made steps here, removing the contaminated water and not leaving the children alone, especially with Merrick." James pushed his plate away. "At least I know I have a direction for their care, which I will begin now." He patted his stomach. "Thank you, Lottie, that hit the spot."

"Edwin's travel to New York will hopefully give the children a chance to recover," Giselle said. "The last thing we need now is more death."

Elspeth wrapped an arm around Giselle's shoulder. "This will all soon be over." She caught James's smile, returned a scowl.

"If you ladies will excuse me, I'll check on the girls." James leaned close to her ear as if to whisper, but he didn't. "Check out a certain nurse while I'm at it."

Giselle and Lottie laughed as James took the back stairs to the second floor. Elspeth frowned at his departure. As Lottie cleared up the remnants of their impromptu snack, Giselle leaned into Elspeth, which made her aware of the arm still draped across Giselle. She started to pull away, but Giselle wrapped an arm at Elspeth's waist and asked, "Nurse Paige, I assume?" At Elspeth's soft groan of confirmation, Giselle squeezed the arm holding her, and nodded. "Cute choice." Giselle paused. "For your sister-in-law. Am I invited to the wedding?"

"What—" Elspeth glanced over to find a mischievous grin spread across Giselle's lips. If they were back at her home, she'd cover that grin with her lips. Then her cheek, her neck— Elspeth squeezed her eyes closed when she felt the telltale heat of embarrassment fuse her face. Damn, how did this mere slip of a woman manage to get all Elspeth's control to evaporate?

****

Lilly Ann Gardiner was shocked to receive the summons home from her mother. But not nearly as flabbergasted as finding her brother-in-law waiting at the train station, where she would transfer for the journey to Colorado. She dropped her traveling bag beside her on the platform when a few feet from him. "Dear Lord, Edwin," she said. Lilly snugged her gloves on her fingers as a plausible excuse to avoid accepting his extended hand. She loathed Edwin and had no intention of touching him. "How bad is it?" She'd learned, from Rosie's telegram, of the death of both Colonels and her only brother, Charles. Edwin's presence could only suggest the worse.

"Calm down, my dear," Edwin said, his expression devoid of emotion. "I understood Mother Gardiner explained things."

"I know of Charles, Reginald, and Preston. Are there more?"

"No. Whatever makes you think that?"

"Why are you here?" she asked.

Edwin absently brushed at his sleeve. "I'm here to assure you get home safely, of course." He flashed a smile that never reached his eyes. "Wouldn't want someone to accost you on the trip home." His tone belied any genuine belief in the possibility. Lilly knew his feelings toward her. He detested her as much as she loathed him—excessively.

"All aboard."

They turned in the direction of the voice. Saved by the conductor, Lilly thought. Inside, Lilly sat beside the window of their compartment, placing her bag on the seat next to her. Edwin sat opposite. Just when she thought the train would never push on, the whistle blew, and the journey commenced.

Lilly blocked out most of Edwin's inane conversation, annoyed with his repetitive habit of pushing up his glasses with a finger when their position hadn't changed. She didn't know if it was exhaustion from the trip, or Edwin's proximity, that made her irritable, but she needed a moment away from him. It had barely been an hour. Lilly stood.

"Where are you going?" Edwin asked, too sharply for her liking.

"I'm thirsty. There's a cooler at the end of the aisle."

"Let me get if for you," Edwin offered.

"Do you intend to drink it for me, too?" she asked, exaggerating her eye roll for his benefit.

He snickered, reaching into his coat pocket. "A gift from my wonderful wife." Edwin pulled out a round, silver disc about three inches in diameter and an inch in height. He unscrewed the top, flicked his wrist, and produced a cup. "A collapsible folding cup. I'll bring the water to you." Then he was off on his task.

The next destination in their journey brought them an extended four hour stop. Lilly and Edwin dined together in the station's restaurant, a meal strained by silence. When they finished, waiting for the train to leave the station again, Lilly picked up a paper, summarily dismissing Edwin.

"I need to make some calls," Edwin said, shifting from foot to foot anxiously.

"Yes, yes," Lilly said. She didn't care what he did, so long as it was away from her. Getting no further response from her, Edwin stormed off.

Lilly was glad to see him go, relieved even, though it would be for only a short time. Edwin had given quick responses about what to expect when they returned to

Maple Woods, and she worried he downplayed the situation. A few years had passed since she left Colorado for a look at the world outside the confinements of the family expectations.

She hadn't missed home too much, her brother and three of her sisters too young for communication. Astoria, subsequently Edwin, too strict in their social significance to appeal to her. Lilly was glad to get away. The only one Lilly enjoyed spending time with was Giselle. Even their letters were entertaining and brought her joy. At least until that, too, was ended by her family. Lilly wondered how Giselle faired without the Colonels.

Giselle was a delight, inquisitive, and openminded. It was an odd combination to witness, the older men hanging on Giselle's every word and deed. She brought out a side of them that no one else in the family managed. Not that they tried. Lilly wasn't close to them, either. But she never disrespected or disregarded Reginald or Preston as the rest of the Gardiners had done.

Lilly considered asking Edwin about her but hadn't missed that he hadn't mentioned Giselle in any of his updates. Was Giselle okay? Or had the young woman ruffled the Merrick sensibilities? As if called by her thoughts, Edwin returned to his place across from her seat. "Did you get everything taken care of?"

Edwin nodded. "Duty is never done for a doctor. What with my practice, research, and having just taken the position as president-elect of the Jackson County Medical Society."

Yes, she thought dismally, let's toot that horn of yours yourself. No one else will do it for you.

"You're probably right." She focused out the window. "I'm surprised you aren't using this opportunity to enjoy the time away from work, focus on doing something enjoyable."

His quick grin was predatory, and Lilly suppressed a shudder. "Oh, I'm doing something enjoyable, and in the realm of work." How cryptic and ominous can Edwin get?

Lilly rubbed her forehead. As the train left the station for the final leg of the trip, Lilly felt the onslaught of a headache.

Chapter Nineteen

Giselle stopped her downward trek in the middle of the staircase when the front door opened. Lilly, Edwin behind her, walked through, stomping feet and brushing snow off. Lilly removed and hung her coat and hat on the coat bench seat, added to the foyer when winter started in earnest, and dropped her travel bag to the floor. She suspected she'd be reprimanded for her actions later but rushed down and pulled Lilly into a tight embrace. "I've missed you."

Lilly returned the hug and whispered in her ear, "Missed you, too. Promise to make time for me and a chat later."

She pulled back and nodded. "Gladly."

"I should think you'd want to see your mother after your trip," Edwin said, his displeasure evident. "Mother Gardiner is the one in need of your presence, after all."

"Yes, of course." Lilly grasped Giselle's hand. "Do come with," Lilly said. Giselle heard the hint of a plea in her tone. After a long train ride with Edwin as an escort, Lilly probably hoped for a familiar and comforting person by her side. A charge she'd willingly provide her. There were dark smudges under Lilly's eyes, and her features looked pained. Plus, she had a slump to her shoulders that Lilly wouldn't usually allow anyone to see. Much like Elspeth, Lilly seldom, if ever, let her public persona slip.

Leaning close, Giselle asked, "Are you alright?"

"A bit of a headache," Lilly said. "I'll be fine when I settle."

"Let me get you some tea." Giselle started to move away, but Lilly's hand squeezed hers, holding her fast.

"Mother will have some, I'm sure." Again, the tone

hinted at a silent plea not to leave her. Giselle kept her place at Lilly's side as they entered Rosie's parlor.

"Oh, Lilly, thank you for coming home," Rosie said, rising and holding her arms open for Lilly to return the embrace. Lilly released her hand and stepped toward her mother. Unlike the greeting she and Lilly shared, Rosie placed her hands on her daughter's shoulders, and the two shared air kisses. "Now, what's left of my family is complete."

Edwin, never one to appreciate being ignored, moved between them. "There, there, Mother Gardiner, let's not stress ourselves." His insincerity was so obvious. How could Rosie stand it?

Lilly stepped back and drew Giselle to the couch and sat. "Leave her be, Edwin. She's fine." Rosie sat in her chair. "Would you be so kind, Mother, as to pour me a cup of tea?"

"Yes, of course, dear." Once she passed the tea over to her, Rosie said to Edwin, "Astoria is in the library. We've had it set up as you requested. Go say hello to your wife."

"As you wish." Edwin dropped a kiss on the top of her head and walked out of the parlor.

"I've had your room aired in preparation for your return."

"Thank you," Lilly said, then rubbed roughly at her forehead.

Giselle worried something other than fatigue bothered Lilly. "Are you certain you're okay? I'm sure I can find someone to check on you."

Rosie sniffed sharply. "We have three nurses on staff. Might as well make use of them." Giselle stiffened. It wasn't as though Elspeth...any of the nurses invaded the house willingly for anything other than work: but here to serve a purpose.

"It's probably just exhaustion from all the travel."

Lilly smiled wanly. "Isn't like I've been living with all the illness you both have in the last months. Edwin filled me in somewhat, but his responses were rather clinical."

"The girls are improving." Giselle didn't want to be more specific with Rosie in the room, not that Lilly didn't know the varied personalities of her sisters, no matter how long she'd been away. Some things rarely changed in people. "I could take you up to see them."

"No, Lilly, I'd rather you didn't," Rosie said. "Not that you couldn't remember the way on your own." Rosie flashed an irritated glance at Giselle. "After the long journey, I wouldn't want you to arrive, only to become ill finally. In fact, it would be best if you stayed at a hotel for a while."

"Yet you aired and offered my old room moments ago, knowing I'd stop in on the children, even if nothing more than sibling duty." Lilly's voice grew sterner with every word. "Why the sudden change of heart?" Giselle suspected Rosie wished to avoid her and Lilly talking, maybe sharing information Rosie believed better unsaid. Not that she would voice those thoughts aloud in this house now Edwin and Astoria were in residence.

"I couldn't bear anything happening to harm your health when you've just arrived," Rosie said.

"But the girls are getting better, right? Surely Edwin would—"

"Edwin isn't the principal doctor in this matter."

"Oh?" Lilly glanced at her, and Giselle gave a barely perceptible nod. At least she hoped Rosie didn't notice her confirmation.

"Yes, well, he is rather close to the matter. It's too much to ask of him with the family involved." Again, Lilly glanced at her for confirmation. Giselle raised an eyebrow, hopefully conveying there was more to the story.

Lilly rose from the couch, and Giselle joined her.

"Then I should check into a hotel and settle in. I could use the rest."

Rosie stood too. "I'll call over and have a room reserved for you. Hopefully, despite this necessity, you'll visit soon."

"Of course, Mother."

"I'll walk you out, Lilly Ann," Giselle said. "Better yet, Lottie asked after you when she learned you were coming. It would be nice if you could say hello. I could take the opportunity to call you a cab."

"I'll handle that when I reserve her room," Rosie said.

"Thank you, Mother. I'd love to see Lottie again. Has she changed at all?" Lilly gave Rosie a quick hug and followed Giselle to the kitchen. On the way, she playfully slapped Giselle's shoulder. "Quit with the Lilly Ann. You know I go by Lilly only."

Giselle laughed. "Is Lilly highfaluting enough for your cronies?"

Pausing with a wicked grin gracing her lips, Lilly said, "Easier for the ladies to shout out."

Although she blushed at the image that popped in her head, Giselle shook it away. "Oh, we have so much to catch up on. Besides, I didn't want Rosie to think we renewed contact."

Lottie honestly had asked after Lilly, and their reunion was warmer than the one shared by mother and daughter. Wasn't surprising given the differences in Rosie's and Lottie's personalities, even if Rosie would accredit it to expectations of social status.

After a few moments of small talk, Lilly asked, "Be truthful, are the girls going to be all right? I'd rather not lose another sibling, whether we're emotionally close or not."

With a snort, Lottie glanced from Lilly to Giselle and said, "Better now that Doc Edwin isn't involved. Elspeth did the family right by bringing Doc James in on this."

"Elspeth?" Lilly asked, both eyebrows raised in curiosity and question.

"Nurse Keillor is the head nurse." Lottie lowered her voice conspiratorially, shifting closer to Lilly. "She's sweet on Giselle."

"Lottie," Giselle exclaimed, her face flaming in mortification.

Lilly gave a gleeful squeal. "Oh, do tell."

From outside, the honk of a car horn sounded. Giselle knew he'd also walk to the front door to retrieve any luggage for his passenger. She plucked paper and pen Lottie kept in a drawer for grocery lists and wrote Elspeth's address before handing to Lilly. "Rosie expects me to leave as soon as the children are well enough. This is where I'll be when I'm no longer here." They heard the doorknocker sound.

"Let me settle in, Giselle, and then we will definitely make time to talk." Lilly kissed Lottie's cheek, then Giselle's. "I can't wait for you to explain Elspeth." With a light slap to the cheek she'd kissed, Lilly glided out of the room.

Giselle glared at Lottie. "I can't believe—"

"Am I wrong?" Lottie asked seriously. "We both know Lilly is the only one around here who cares and will be happy for you."

"You shouldn't even know," Giselle said. She lowered her head, not sure she wanted to see Lottie's expression to her next question. "Do you think me wicked and aberrant?"

Lottie closed the distance and pulled her into an embrace. "Never. The way you both look at one another could only be a blessed thing." Lottie pulled back and stared into Giselle's eyes. "I only spoke because I knew Miss Lilly would understand and keep the secret." Tears filled Giselle's eyes. "Besides," Lottie said, moving a few steps away. "Teasing you brings joy to my heart." Lottie inhaled deeply, then stabbed a finger toward the stairs. "Off with you. I've work to do."

Dismissed, Giselle did as she was told.

****

James followed Elspeth from Blanche and Susan's room. She turned toward him in time to see him wink at Helen before the door closed. Elspeth shook her head and placed her hands on her hips. "Helen is a brilliant and charming young lady, James." He nodded agreement. "However, she's not experienced enough not to get caught up in the games of men. That said, if you are toying with her affections, you'd best break it off now. I'll not stand by and watch you hurt her, brother or not." Their conversation wasn't loud, but Elspeth glanced around for prying ears.

"You know me better than anyone, Mairi, and accept I haven't the best dating record." James closed the distance so no one would overhear his reply. "Helen is younger than my usual conquests, I admit." He grinned broadly. "And she's such an adorable if small little package." James's expression grew serious. "If no other good has come from this house, believe me when I tell you that I'm not trifling with Helen's affections. My intentions are honorable toward her."

He was right about the house. Elspeth would never have believed someone as pure and unique as Giselle would look twice at her, let alone kiss her with as much passion as Giselle managed. How could she be surprised that Helen Paige couldn't mean the same to James? Maybe the Gardiner tragedy had produced adoration both could build on, grow for their future. She gave him a wan smile. "I hope so. Mother has waited long enough for us to concentrate on more than our careers."

James tugged on her arm, walking them to the third-floor staircase for a little privacy. They sat together on the stairs. "At least you haven't suffered the parade of prospective mates in the meanwhile."

Elspeth felt the color drain from her face. "No, guess I haven't."

"Oh, Mairi, I'm sorry. I—"

"It's okay. Our mother may recognize my position with the heart but will hardly be accepting. I'm the family embarrassment."

"Not to me." James leaned into her shoulder. "And we both know she's only interested in grandchildren, not my future wife."

"Please," Elspeth said. "Of course, she's interested in your wife. She needs someone to be all girly with her."

"Hadn't thought of that part." Elspeth chuckled when he put an elbow to his knee and dropped his chin to his palm. "Better hide my entertainment funds before our mother takes the wife shopping."

Elspeth shook her head, then slung an arm across his shoulders. "Dear me. You are serious about her. You've jumped straight to mother-daughter-in-law jaunts for shopping."

"Yeah, pitiful, right?"

"No, James, I'm happy for you." She removed her arm from him. "So, back to duty. What's the prognosis? Are the girls ready to be released from our care?"

"Much as I despise Merrick's constant presence downstairs, I don't think he'd try anything like this again. If anyone in the house were to get sick too soon, he would be the obvious suspect."

"Yes, I agree. Especially if he is currently residing in the home. Guess he'll need another way to get to the family coffers," Elspeth said.

"I'm still composing documentation to keep Edwin from concocting and performing another plot against these poor kids. And I haven't kept everything to myself."

"Do you think Edwin would come after you?" Elspeth wouldn't put it passed him.

James dropped his arm and shook his head. "Honestly, Mairi, I want to see all of you, especially you and Giselle, out of this house as of yesterday." He focused directly on her. "I'm more afraid for the safety of you and Giselle. A man who can kill his wife's siblings will have no qualms about two women."

Elspeth gave a squeeze to his knee. "The sooner you give Mrs. Gardiner the all-clear, the sooner all of us can leave here." She stood, and James followed suit. "One last thing."

"What's that?"

"It's cute when you worry."

****

"That's great news, Rosie," Giselle said, hoping her enthusiasm wasn't evident. Once again, Rosie called her to the parlor. She'd spent more time in this room over the last couple of months than she had over the decade she'd lived here.

"I've informed Nurse Keillor. She's to arrange things for her departure, and that of the little nurse."

"Nurse Paige," Giselle said.

"Whatever." Rosie waved a hand dismissively. "I will keep Nurse Hunter for a while longer to tend to Rosalind.

She's always had a delicate constitution, you know."

Right, delicate. "I'll also pack my things, to comply with your original wishes to be gone after the school semester finished." Giselle stood.

"Actually, I'd like you to stay on another week, to make sure there aren't any recurrences during Christmas Day activities. The children will be expending a great deal of energy. Anything could happen."

Giselle swallowed, reigning in her flash of anger. The last stab in the back was to ruin her Christmas. Rosie knew, with Blanche and Susan to think of, Giselle wouldn't deny the request. Well, two could play this game. "Of course. But I'll need to include personal time to procure new accommodations and move most of my things."

"Take what you need." Giselle intended to take a lot of time. "After what the children have been through, we must keep the holiday as normal as possible." When Rosie didn't add anything else, Giselle assumed she'd been released, and went directly to her room. Her door had no sooner closed when there was a knock.

Giselle opened it to Elspeth, the very woman she wanted and needed to see, and wrapped Elspeth in a tight hug. "Hey, what's wrong?"

"Rosie wants me to stay until after Christmas day. Told me the girls need normalcy."

"Of course, she did." Elspeth chuckled into her hair. Then Giselle felt the soft touch of lips brush her temple. "What else did she ask from you?" Elspeth pulled away, and Giselle let herself get tugged foward and pressed into a chair. She squatted in front of Giselle, her hands resting just above Giselle's knees. The concern in Elspeth's gaze was like a balm to her heart.

"That's about it." Giselle covered Elspeth's hands with hers. She could feel the warmth from Elspeth's touch, part of her wanting to beg for more. Giselle blinked rapidly, hoping to dispel the picture created, concentrate on answering. "I was assured to be here for Christmas day, but there were a lot of things I needed to do to procure a place of my own."

"Much as I want you with me full-time," Elspeth said, rubbing her thumbs against Giselle's dress-clad legs. "Until that happens, I'll welcome any chunks of time we can share." Elspeth shrugged. "Lord willing, we'll have too many shared Christmas's to remember to count them."

Giselle cupped Elspeth's cheeks. "I'd like to spend as much time with you as I can get away with if you don't mind."

Elspeth removed Giselle's hands one at a time, placing a kiss to each palm as she did. "Ah, my dearest Giselle. Every minute with you will be an eternity in my heart."

She couldn't contain her laughter. Giselle asked, "How are you single when you're so sweet?"

"My heart recognized that it waited for you," she replied, her tone and expression serious.

Giselle stood, drawing Elspeth up with her. "You should go, get out while you can. I plan to finish packing all but the essentials for a few days. If you haven't a problem, I'd like to stop by tomorrow and drop a few things off."

"I'll be counting down the hours." Elspeth lightly wrapped her arms at Giselle's waist, causing her to shiver in delight from the comfort the contact brought to her.

"So shall I." Giselle leaned in, intent on giving Elspeth a goodbye—for now—kiss that neither would forget.

Chapter Twenty

The next afternoon had Elspeth filled with joy. Giselle was here, in her room, unpacking a good majority of clothing and personal items. They'd worked out a time for a deliveryman, directed by Lottie, to pick up most of Giselle's belongings. Neither Elspeth nor Giselle wanted to chance further changes placed by the Gardiner's.

Elspeth, preoccupied with touching up the paint to a few spots on the wall in their private sitting room, was startled when the suites outer door opened and an impeccably dressed woman of about thirty years breezed in as if owning the place. The stranger extended her hand in greeting. Elspeth shifted closer and clasped her own with the hand offered.

"Lilly Ann Gardiner, and please drop the Ann." Her voice was as direct as her visual appraisement that left Elspeth with a feeling of the need for more clothing. "My, my, oh my. Not a beauty, but handsome enough in your own right."

"Elspeth." She raised an eyebrow. "Not certain if that was an insult or compliment, but thank you. Is there something I can—"

"Lilly," Giselle said as she exited the left bedroom. "When did you come in?"

"Just walked through the door. Getting an eyeful of your girlfriend." Lilly removed her outerwear and tossed it on a chair, then moved to warm her hands at the fireplace. Elspeth looked on as Giselle pulled her in for a hug. She knew from conversations with the children, and an odd word here and there from the adults, that this was the Gardiner daughter who lived in New York. "Is my whole family—present company aside—filled with blind fools?"

Giselle chuckled. "As you've excluded me, let's go with positively foolish. You should probably clarify the statement, in case you intend to test me later."

As if she weren't present, Lilly stared at Elspeth, and Giselle followed in the path of focusing on her. "Your Nurse Elspeth is supposed to be sour and wicked-looking, unable to smile due to being unbending."

"Stoic." Giselle nodded. "And let me guess. Edwin mentioned a metal rod stuck in an unmentionable place?"

"Yes, the polite explanation, thank you." Lilly glanced from her to Giselle. Elspeth hoped this teasing episode, of which she was the target, was about over. "What am I missing?"

"Nothing. You see Elspeth as I do." Giselle left her side and came to Elspeth, giving her a side hug and not letting go. Elspeth glanced down at her, still in awe of the unconcealed emotions of caring in her expression. "As I've always seen her. Even in her stiff and formal identity, Elspeth is pleasing to look upon." She smiled mischievously, her dark green eyes twinkling. "And breathtaking in her man-clothes."

Elspeth tapped a finger under Giselle's chin. "Man-clothes, huh?" Odd that it should be so, but she felt a bit excited that dressing in buttoned shirt and trousers could please the beautiful Giselle.

"Don't forget the breathtaking part."

"I won't forget." She was about to lean in for a kiss until she remembered they weren't alone. Elspeth needed to remember to lock the suite door. Too many people have made a habit of letting themselves in. "Can I get you coffee, Lilly?"

"I'll take some," James announced from the doorway, Helen at his side. She'd have rolled her eyes but doubted the action would have any effect on her uninvited company. So much for finishing the painting and relaxing with Giselle. Preferably fine tuning their kissing—and caressing. Those thoughts shattered when her brother introduced himself and Helen to Lilly.

"Please, make yourselves comfortable. I'll be right back," Elspeth said. She declined Giselle's offer of assistance. "Enjoy your visit with Lilly. Ignore James and whatever nonsense he comes up with."

By the time Elspeth returned with the tea trolley, and cookies Lottie sent with Giselle today, James and Helen were on the couch, with Giselle and Lilly seated in the chairs. Elspeth stopped the trolley beside Giselle and provided coffee for anyone interested, which turned out to be everyone. Giselle passed the plate of sweets.

Once everyone was fed and watered, Elspeth turned to her brother. "What brings you here? If you came to help with the painting, you're too late."

James shook his head. "I may be your brother, but we both know I'm not the house-handy one." He gave a hesitant glance toward Lilly. "And, well, I—"

"Go ahead, James," Giselle said. "Lilly is trustworthy."

"Better yet," Lilly added. "I'm not an Edwin fan. Does that cast a vote in my favor?"

He looked at her, and Elspeth shrugged. "What do you have?"

"I don't want to upset you ladies with grisly details," James said. He shifted uncomfortably.

"It's okay, James. We're not wilting flowers." Elspeth sat on the arm of Giselle's chair. "As long as the details aren't too gruesome, I believe we can handle whatever you have to say."

"If you're sure." James cleared his throat. "I, and my colleagues, have tested the samples of blood and water that I managed to get from the Gardiner home. We tested those against the culture I removed from Edwin's office. They are a direct match."

"Are the results what we suspected?" Elspeth asked.

"Yes, it's—was—typhoid." James cleared his throat, flicking a nervous glance toward Giselle.

"Go ahead," Giselle said. "I presume he murdered the Colonels. I also know it was by lethal means, which painfully took them."

"As do we, Giselle. We are preparing to have the Colonels and Charles autopsied." James appeared hesitant to meet Giselle or Lilly's gaze. "The stomach contents need testing, but there is a glitch."

"A glitch?" Lilly asked.

Giselle asked, "What glitch?"

Elspeth rested her hand on Giselle's shoulder and gave a gentle squeeze. "Please, James. I'm about to disown you. Say it fast, like you did as a kid." The corner of James's lip quirked in an attempted smile.

"It's too soon to frighten our girls with childhood stories," James grumbled.

"Tell them," Helen said, tapping a hand to James's clenched fists.

"It's winter after all," James finally stated. "We have to let the bodies thaw before we can do any testing, to preserve the evidence and the integrity of the bodies. Unfortunately, that will be a time-consuming effort."

"Yet, you do intend to stick with it?" Lilly asked.

"Yes, of course. I don't want any of you to think I've given up on finding the proof to hold the responsible party accountable."

Lilly snorted. "We know Edwin is at fault."

"Ah, but the proof is required to assure we can bring him to justice."

"You don't have enough of the germ specimens, water, and blood?" Giselle asked, frowning.

Elspeth rubbed Giselle's shoulder, hoping to bring comfort.

"Of the typhoid poisoning, yes. But we don't know the specifics of what took Reginald or Preston from us. That knowledge is important to our case."

Elspeth felt Giselle tremble. She leaned in close to Giselle's ear. "Are you tired? I could have James drive you back to the Gardiner's."

Rather than respond to the question asked, Giselle gave her a quick smile. "How about we kick these interlopers out and clean up."

She pushed herself off the chair's arm. "You heard the lady. All intruders must vacate the premises." Elspeth stuffed her hands in the trouser pockets. "Unless you're prepared to paint and renovate."

"That's our cue, Helen." James rose from the couch and extended his hand. "Gentlemen don't do manual labor. We take beautiful women to dinner."

"Wow, James," Elspeth said. "No wonder you're still single. Is that how you woo a woman, state a personal failing, then toss the lady a compliment?"

He winked at Helen. "Is it working?"

Helen blushed, flicking a glance in Elspeth's direction. "Depends on where you take me to dinner."

"Would you like to join us?" James asked Lilly.

"Oh, no, no," Lilly said. "I'm no one's deadwood." She rose and brushed out the wrinkles in her dress. "Besides, I'll be dining with—" She stared at Helen. Elspeth had the same question. How open-minded was the quiet little nurse? Lilly raised her chin. "Someone I met at the hotel."

James guffawed. Helen giggled, blushed, and asked, "Is she pretty or smart?" The room grew silent, broken when James started laughing.

After a moment, Lilly shook her head. "Both. But

more importantly, she's fun."

"Can we give you a ride to the hotel?"

"That I'll accept." Lilly smiled.

"Giselle? A ride?"

"I've still a few things to do here, thank you."

After they said their farewells and left, Elspeth hastily secured the building's doors, half tempted to barricade the suite's door. Problem with that idea, Elspeth didn't know if Giselle was staying. Before she could ask, Giselle pushed the trolley into the kitchen. Elspeth followed. They washed and dried the tea service items in silence. A comfortable feel of domesticity filled Elspeth, never expecting she'd experience a moment like this.

Then there was nothing to keep them occupied in the kitchen. "Guess I should clear up the painting supplies."

Giselle reached up and tugged at the collar of Elspeth's shirt. "You were nearly finished, weren't you?" Elspeth's vocal cords felt paralyzed, so she nodded. "Will anything be irreparably damaged if you leave it for tonight?"

"No."

"Good. I'd like to stay here tonight, get used to my bedroom. I've let Rosie know I wouldn't be home. There are a few things to do before bedtime." Giselle bit her lip. "You can say no. You aren't expecting me to—"

"Okay." Elspeth wondered what Giselle would have done had she said no, but suspected she'd have gone to Lilly at the hotel, rather than go to the Gardiner house. Maybe Giselle knew Elspeth would never turn her away.

Elspeth's pulse increased when Giselle shifted closer; their bodies were nearly flush. "Maybe we could just sit on the couch and relax for a while?"

Did Giselle think Elspeth would refuse her? Could refuse her? Elspeth took Giselle's hand, turned off the kitchen light, and walked them into the living area, dimming the lights as they went. She led Giselle to the couch. "Let me stoke the fire," she said. Once the fire burned brighter, Elspeth moved to sit beside Giselle, who immediately leaned into Elspeth, head resting on her chest.

She brushed her lips to Giselle's temple. Elspeth smiled. This is what makes life worth living.

****

The bed was comfortable, the bedding soft and cozy. Giselle couldn't ask for anything more unless it was to find solace in slumber. But sleep wouldn't come to her.

Her mind continued to focus on the evening's events. A visit by family and friends she liked. The mutual camaraderie over the wonderful meal prepared by Elspeth, the conversation light and entertaining. The teasing as they shared the duties in the clearing and cleaning of their repast. Moreover, the casual and gentle brushes of touch, as they moved near each other, passed a dish or cup between them. Then, there were the glances, the locked gazes before one or the other caught themselves and turned away. Had she really seen tenderness, possibly love in Elspeth's eyes? Could Elspeth look upon her and truly see her as something other than a friend? Did she see, recognize, the attraction Giselle held for her?

Giselle sighed heavily, turned onto her side, and grasped the pillow tightly to her. She needed to cease focusing on Elspeth, what she did or didn't feel, and find solace in sleep.

But shifting her focus from Elspeth only caused it to roam elsewhere for so little a time, always returning to Elspeth. Giselle drifted into an uncomfortable doze, filled with distorted images of Uncle Preston as he lay on the library's couch in distress and pain, then in the coffin. Her last moments with Uncle Reginald attempting to comfort her with promises all would work out well. Interspersed with all of these, the looming face of Edwin as he whispered, "You shouldn't avoid me," while chasing her down a hall that wouldn't end.

"Giselle," she heard the voice following her.

"No, leave me be," she shrieked back.

"Giselle, wake up." Startled by an unexpected touch, she pulled away and banged her head on the headboard. Her eyes flew open and landed on the worried face of Elspeth. "You were having a nightmare. I became worried." Elspeth frowned. "I'm sorry. I'd hoped you would be comfortable here."

"I am, Elspeth, honest. Which is why I think I had bad dreams. Fully relaxing for the first time in a long time made me too comfortable. The stress had to release some way."

Elspeth didn't look entirely convinced. "Do I need to take you home?"

"Please, no. Besides, I'm not welcomed there, and Rosie only puts up with me to be a caretaker for Blanche and Susan," Giselle said. The concern in her expression was nearly Giselle's undoing. She so wanted to be with this woman, hold her, be comforted by her. The realization hit Giselle when she noticed Elspeth clench and unclench her hand.

Giselle scooted closer, put a hand behind Elspeth's neck, and pulled her into a kiss. Surprise, and Giselle's limited experience, made the initial attempt awkward. Shifting slightly, Elspeth took control, her lips tutoring Giselle's in the education of their mutual enjoyment. All too soon, Elspeth leaned away from her. She appeared ready to apologize, which Giselle preempted with a finger to Elspeth's lips. "May I sleep in your room tonight?" she asked, then thought she might need to clarify. "With you?"

The only indication the request stunned Elspeth was the rapid pulsing of the vein at her temple. Rather than respond verbally, Elspeth clasped her hand, flipped the light switch, and tugged her into her room, which resembled the one she'd given Giselle. "Do you have a preference to which side?" Elspeth asked. Her voice shook. How nervous was she?

Giselle didn't intend to ask, afraid she'd misread the perceived shared attraction. "No, whichever you don't use will be fine."

"I usually sleep on the side closest to the door," she said.

As Elspeth turned off the light, Giselle climbed into Elspeth's bed. Despite this being her idea, she was nervous. Elspeth, hellbent on protecting her, would probably sleep at the bed's edge. There would be nothing Giselle could do to change that, short of voicing her intentions to the contrary. But was that what she wanted? Was she ready to be intimate with another person? Would it be as fulfilling as the feelings generated by the kiss that they shared only moments ago?

"Good night," Elspeth said, climbing in beside her.

"Night." There was no need to rush, right? They would have amply opportunity to know each other better, work up to intimacy. Yes, of course, they would, so no need to hurry a situation better left to a slower flow. Breathe, Giselle told herself.

Giselle pulled the sheet up to her waist, staring at the dark ceiling, feeling herself pulled to Elspeth's warm body. She lay still, hoping to be claimed by sleep, but that didn't happen. Giselle felt surprised when Elspeth rolled over onto her back, Elspeth's hand gently caressing her arm.

"Aren't you tired?" An innocent inquiry, but Giselle

didn't reply. She was alarmed. Her pulse had quickened, and her breath became rapid.

"Not as tired as I believed myself," she whispered. "Too much clattering around in my head. If I'm disturbing you, I can return to my room."

"Anything I can help with?"

She softly snorted. "You're part of the rattling items."

"I'm sorry," Elspeth said. She started to shift away, but Giselle clutched Elspeth's hand. "No, please. I want to be here with you. Want more than to sleep with you and feel safe." Giselle sighed heavily. "I want more. But I don't know how to let you know what I want."

Giselle could tell Elspeth smiled when she leaned up on her elbow. Giselle turned toward her, a soft moan leaving her lips as Elspeth's hand snaked under her nightgown, touching flesh for the first time.

"I believe you just did," Elspeth murmured.

Giselle gasped as Elspeth's hand brushed her breast. She waited, aching for her touch, sure she'd come undone if she didn't get it. But Elspeth hesitated.

"Tell me to stop, and I will."

"No. Don't stop," Giselle whispered.

Elspeth's mouth covered her own. The kiss was neither tentative nor shy, but warm and tender, even as it devoured her. Giselle burned from her toes to the top of her head. She had no wish to have this flame put out. It burned deep within her. She couldn't stop the moans, the primal sounds escaping her lips when Elspeth's hand cupped her breast when fingers captured her nipple, and it hardened to a stony peak.

This feeling was everything she'd imagined, yet so much more. Giselle had been clueless. Clueless that another's touch would make her tremble with want. Clueless that a touch would make her body hum, set her soul free. No idea a touch on her breast would arouse her to this point of ecstasy. Then Giselle realized she didn't know what ecstasy was at all. Not until Elspeth pushed her nightgown higher and exposed her breasts.

Their eyes met in the darkness; the only sound was their breathing. Giselle was almost certain only she heard the rapid pounding of her heart. By the time Elspeth lowered her head before her mouth and tongue even touched her nipple, Giselle was gasping for air. When Elspeth's warm mouth closed over her own, a low guttural sound escaped. Surely that was not from me, Giselle thought nervously.

But it was from her. And she arched closer, her hands finally moving, holding Elspeth fast against her, urging her to…to what? She closed her eyes, rejoiced that Elspeth was at her breast. Elspeth's tongue teased, then sucked Giselle's nipple into her warm, wet mouth. Giselle wasn't sure she could take much more.

Then Elspeth lifted her head, and her hands fumbled with Giselle's gown, tugging. Giselle sat up, let Elspeth remove it, and exposed Giselle's upper body to the cold night air, exposed to Elspeth's knowing eyes. Elspeth pulled her nightgown off, tossed it to the foot of the bed, and turned back to Giselle.

"Are you okay?" Elspeth whispered. As if to clarify her intent, Elspeth's hand found Giselle's breast again.

Giselle nodded. "Yes. And afraid," she admitted. Would Elspeth think her a child for the admission? Send her back to her room?

"What are you afraid of?"

Giselle squeezed her eyes closed, worried what her admission could cost her, them. She moaned when Elspeth brushed her nipple with a fingernail. Uh, goodness, what am I afraid of? Giselle opened her eyes again. "I'm afraid I won't…what if I'm not able to—"

"To enjoy?" Elspeth asked. Her voice gentle, understanding.

Giselle swallowed hard. "With you. I want to enjoy this night so badly."

Elspeth took her hand, guiding it to her breast. Giselle's fingers closed around soft flesh. Elspeth's nipple grew hard against her palm. She heard Elspeth's quiet moan, and then her mouth tentatively opened as Elspeth drew closer to her again, and her tongue explored inside her mouth. Elspeth pulled back slightly before her lips gently moved across Giselle's face.

"Do you trust me?"

How could she not? Giselle thought. But she realized Elspeth needed confirmation. "With my life."

"Trust me with you, with your body," Elspeth purred into her ear. Elspeth pressed close, her bare breasts touching Giselle's. The internal fire flamed again. "I'm going to make love to you." Elspeth's mouth moved along her jaw, then lower. She licked, then kissed, the hollow of Giselle's throat. "Close your eyes, Giselle. Just feel me. Feel my hands. Feel my mouth."

Giselle did feel. Felt the warm mouth at her breasts again, one, then the other. Her nipples were aching and hard. She was writhing with need. Giselle felt Elspeth's hand move lower, under the waistband of her underwear. Oh, my gosh. Off. Giselle wanted them off, wanted to be naked, wanted to feel Elspeth's likewise bare skin against her own.

"Please take them off," Giselle said. "Please hurry." Oh, dear Lord, when had she become so wanton? Her hands shoved at them, before Elspeth tugged them down her legs, freeing her. Elspeth must have sensed her need as she removed her underwear. They were now both naked.

Giselle pulled Elspeth back to her, her body aching, her legs opening as Elspeth urged her thighs apart. She could feel her wetness; she could feel Elspeth's moisture against her skin, and she couldn't get nearly close enough. Her hands moved, cupped Elspeth, almost frantic in her desire.

"Easy. Slow," Elspeth whispered. "Let me."

"Not slow, no," Giselle disputed. Her body was no longer in her control. She didn't know how she understood, but she wanted Elspeth inside her.

She didn't have to wait long. Elspeth's hand moved between them, her long fingers slow and sure as they glided through her wetness. Giselle's hips jerked; her clit felt swollen, hard, sensitive. Oh, and so alive. Her moan rolled into a groan as Elspeth filled her.

"You're so wet," Elspeth murmured. "So ready." Her mouth again found a nipple, her teeth teasing it.

Yes, so ready. The music of the lovemaking filled the room. The melody of the wet slickness of their skin. The melody of Elspeth's hand as it gently plunged inside her—out—back in again. The melody of their breathing, their moans. An organic crescendo.

Giselle didn't think she could take another minute of this delightful lovemaking, surely akin to torture. She didn't have to. Elspeth's hand worked like lightning, moved deep into her, her thumb hitting her clit with each pass. Giselle was panting, she knew, her body taking on a life of its own, as hips met each thrust of Elspeth's hand, plunging deeper and harder.

Her orgasm hit with blinding speed. There was no warning, no time to prepare. Giselle felt an explosion of light behind her eyes, an explosion of her senses. She couldn't stop the shout. The thrill touched her to the core. She felt her body clench and unclench, tightening around Elspeth's fingers.

Giselle opened her eyes when she felt Elspeth's mouth move past her breasts, her tongue moistening her skin, moving lower. The realization of what Elspeth intended sent her senses reeling. Giselle's body trembled, then she whimpered when Elspeth's fingers slipped from her. The anticipation of what was about to replace them nearly her undoing. She threaded her fingers through Elspeth's hair when she felt Elspeth's warm mouth nibble above her thigh. Elspeth lifted her head, her eyes clouded with desire. How had she not seen how much Elspeth cared for her? Giselle thought. A version of what she witnessed now had always been there.

"Is this alright?" Could Elspeth honestly question it? But it was there, warring with her desire, that small glint of doubt.

"Yes," she whispered. Giselle startled as Elspeth moved lower, her hands spreading Giselle's thighs as she knelt between them. Giselle's breath came in short gasps as Elspeth moved to her. Instinctively, Giselle raised her hips, offering herself to Elspeth. She didn't know what she expected. Their lovemaking was an act she'd never experienced, not that she'd experienced the first. The first touch of Elspeth's warm mouth and tongue sent a jolt of adrenaline through her. Giselle's hands curled into fists as she clutched the sheet. Her hips jerked uncontrolled until Elspeth gathered them to her, held her tight against her mouth. Incoherent sounds came from Giselle at the sheer pleasure at the feel of Elspeth's tongue as it circled her clit. Felt Elspeth's mouth close over it, sucking, teasing her tongue back and forth.

This time, Giselle felt her orgasm build, felt the thundering roll as her body pulsed. She took a deep breath, held it. Her hips strained against Elspeth's grip. Then from deep within her, Giselle climaxed. Sounds of satisfaction and fulfillment wrenched from her before she collapsed with Elspeth's mouth still on her.

Lids heavy, Giselle opened her eyes. She looked into Elspeth's eyes as Elspeth moved up her body and settled beside her, hoping to convey her feelings as she drifted off to sleep.

Chapter Twenty-one

Were angels singing? Elspeth heard one, and they were close. She left her eyes closed, stretched long and lazily, and smiled at the memory of Giselle in her arms. Giselle. Elspeth stretched her arm out and found the space the magnificent woman occupied last night empty—but still warm. She hadn't left too long ago. Another languorous stretch and Elspeth slid out of bed and dressed in her standard trousers and button shirt when in private.

She followed the musical trill to the kitchen and abruptly stopped at the sight she found. Giselle, long auburn hair pulled on top of her head and exposing her long neck, stood at the stove. With a gentle sway of her hips, spatula in one hand, and the handle of the iron skillet clasped in the other, Giselle flipped hotcakes while softly singing. During the time Elspeth watched, "Shine On, Harvest Moon" transitioned into "I Wonder Who Is Kissing Her Now."

Elspeth took that as her cue to make her presence known. Silently sliding behind Giselle, she leaned in and lightly kissed the long, creamy expanse of her neck while tracing her fingertips from shoulder to wrist. "I'm the one kissing you now and always." Giselle shivered. "Smells divine in here but isn't as heavenly as your singing."

Giselle hummed. "And your touch shouts safety and comfort." She spun another hotcake. "You don't mind that I made myself at home, do you?"

"This is your home, Giselle." Elspeth covered the hand grasping the skillet and pulled it free from the heat; then, plucked the spatula from her other hand, before turning Giselle to face her. "No pressure, darling." Elspeth cupped her cheek. "So much has changed to rattle your life. Think of these walls as protection from the world. You are always welcome to whatever I can provide you for; a day or a lifetime. All that I have is yours."

"Truly?"

"Sincerely."

A playful grin danced on Giselle's lips. "Even if you find out I can't cook?"

"But, you are cooking."

Giselle spun to finish her task. "Yes, but that doesn't mean I do it well."

Elspeth chuckled. "Trust me. You can't possibly do worse than me. My attempts are digestible, but not haute cuisine." Together, they finished preparations and brought the food to the small dinette table in the room.

"Your meal last night was wonderful," Giselle said. "I've no reason to complain. Sometimes I believe you are too hard on yourself." Both moved around the kitchen, at the table they pulled out chairs and filled plates with the ease of having done so for years. Seated, Giselle put her elbows on the table to rest her chin upon her clasped hands as if daring to be reprimanded. Elspeth wouldn't if only to enjoy the adorableness of her. "Elspeth, everything you do is done with caring and all your heart. Maybe not everything is perfect, but it's appreciated for the intent. No one could fault you."

The heat fusing Elspeth's face was instantaneous. For reasons she couldn't fathom, Giselle viewed her as nobody else, not even James, did. Giselle's words yanked on her emotions with decided force. She desperately needed to lighten the atmosphere of the situation. With a wink, Elspeth said, "Sweet talk won't keep me from consuming this wonderful bounty before us, darling."

As if sensing her discomfort, Giselle spread her linen napkin on her lap. "Bon appetite." They both ate in earnest. The food was tasty. Elspeth wouldn't need to provide polite compliments.

"I presume you'll be returning to the Gardiner house?" she asked.

Giselle nodded. "With the newest accumulation of snow, and more expected tonight, it might not be so easy to get away. Rosie will probably provide an ear full for not returning home last night."

"Can Lilly provide an alibi for you? Girl talk late into the night, and all that." Elspeth rose to get the kettle, refilling their coffee cups. She hated that Giselle needed to defend herself. Hated more that they had to hide their relationship, and not only because of their social standing. Making love to Giselle last night—Elspeth felt alive, more loved than she had in thirty-four years. Would there ever be a time when two women in love, and she did love Giselle, could openly acknowledge and display their shared joy?

"Thank you for worrying about me, Elspeth, but it's not necessary. No matter what I do, Rosie will find fault. If I'm to be chastised, might as well be for something I actually did."

Elspeth could not let the last words go without a bit of teasing despite the serious tone of the conversation. Sternly, she asked, "And do you intend to relate all we did last night to the esteemed Mrs. Gardiner?"

Giselle's expression was shocked, then slid into a smirk. "Nah, she'd be jealous. I have no intention of providing salacious details." Her feature's shifted to reflect tenderness. "I would never sully—allow anyone else to—what we shared."

The niggling of doubt took over. Elspeth couldn't bear to see the shame on Giselle's face, so she dropped her gaze to her empty plate. "Are you sorry or regretful?"

"Oh, Elspeth, no." Giselle shoved back in her chair as

she stood and rushed over, drawing Elspeth from where she sat. Then, Giselle was holding her close, her head on Elspeth's shoulders, warm breath caressing her neck. "Never regrets. The only disappointment is that I can't stay for now and always. When I conclude my familial, such as it is, duties, I won't be at their demanding whims." Elspeth felt the light splay of kisses on her neck. "I will want to repeat last night over and over until I get it right."

Elated, Elspeth shifted to cup Giselle's cheeks, and eagerly melded their lips. She moved her right hand, slid it behind Giselle's head, and deepened the kiss—and never wanted to stop. At Giselle's moan, Elspeth dropped her left hand to gather her closer, and ran her tongue lightly across Giselle's lips.

Giselle pulled away, and Elspeth wondered if she'd gone too far. Her concern must have registered on her face since Giselle put a finger to Elspeth's lips. "If we don't stop, I'll take you here in the kitchen."

"Not such a bad thing," Elspeth said.

"Not, not at all. But I need to go check on the girls."

"They abuse your good nature. Treat you like—" Elspeth stepped back, needing to calm herself. The Gardiner's never gave Giselle the respect she deserved. Didn't treat her like a member of the family; unless to curry favor for a task they wanted. Did it matter if Giselle never returned? "You don't owe them anything," Elspeth told her. And what of Merrick, he'd have no qualms to harm her when he knew she'd be leaving anyway. "Stay."

"I made a promise, dearest. Soon, we can be together, work together, to build this wonderful vision of yours."

She had Elspeth's compliance with the affectionate name, even if she didn't want Giselle to go. Moreover, Giselle was correct. "You're right. Your loyalty and dependability are the things I adore about you."

"Just adore?"

"My feelings go beyond simple adoration, Giselle, but I don't want to jinx what we have by speaking of my feelings too soon."

Giselle smiled, her eyes glistening with unshed tears. "I love you, too." With a saucy grin, she slid closer to Elspeth and started toying with the buttons on her shirt, tears gently gliding down Giselle's cheeks. "Don't ever worry that you can't speak to me about anything. Especially about feelings, good or bad." Elspeth gasped when Giselle cupped her breast. "Will you think of me tonight?"

"I never stop thinking about you." That brought on another lengthy kiss. "I'll call you a taxi."

Giselle pulled away, groaned, and headed for the living room. The taxi arrived a few moments later.

Elspeth helped Giselle into her coat, then Giselle put on her hat and gloves. As she opened the suite door and the front door, Elspeth stopped her. "If you need something, anything, even to leave in a hurry, please call me. Don't do anything to draw Merrick's attention to you. Stay away from him if you can."

"I won't do anything to jeopardize getting to you sooner rather than later." Giselle gave a quick peck to her cheek and walked out to her waiting taxi. Elspeth didn't know if it was the inundation of emotions from last night or forewarning, but she felt a surge of dread. She had to trust Giselle would use caution in the next days. Unfortunately, Elspeth couldn't involve herself until asked. Not that it would stop her from fretting.

****

"Where the hell have you been?" Edwin demanded.

Had he been watching for her? Why?

Giselle felt elation from her night and morning with Elspeth. The euphoria dampened the minute she entered the house. She had specifically chosen to come in through the kitchen to avoid seeing the family before she was ready. The only ones Giselle wanted to communicate with were Lottie, Nora, and the two youngest Gardiner's. Being attacked by this man the moment she arrived made her angry. "None of your business. Rosie is aware of my obligations requiring time away." Giselle glanced a question at Lottie, who shifted to stand behind Edwin. Lottie shook her head. Nothing had happened to the children.

"What if we needed you?" Edwin's face flushed with his anger.

"Too bad. The family can handle it like you will when I move out."

"This behavior—"

"Enough about this," she said sharply. Giselle would speak to Lottie later. Right now, she needed to get away from Edwin. "Talk to Rosie. I'm here for Blanche and Susan, and only until the day after Christmas." She hurried toward the back staircase, raised her skirts to allow better footing, intent on reaching her room and locking the door, her visit with the children postponed. She only managed to place a foot on the bottom step.

"Giselle." Edwin's voice boomed down the hall. "Rosie requests you join her in the parlor."

Fearing Rosie would demand more of her time at the house, Giselle continued up the stairs, stating, "Now isn't a good time. I have things to do." She feared he would follow, but Giselle made it to her room unmolested.

With only a couple of days left until Christmas, she finished packing all her remaining items, intent on removing items from her luggage when the need arose.

Giselle wasn't taking chances, wanting to be able to leave the house, with no reason to return, immediately.

When it drew close to Blanche and Susan's bedtime, and since no one came to repeat Rosie's summons, Giselle left her room, doing something she hadn't in an exceptionally long time. Giselle locked the room behind her.

Her knuckles were poised to knock on the nursery door when shouts from downstairs drew her attention. Giselle walked to the top of the landing and stopped. Edwin's raised voice was easy to discern, which surprised her. Edwin was, usually, able to maintain an aura of indifference. She couldn't quite make out the other voices. Whoever was here made Edwin furious. Bully for you, she thought.

Which left Giselle with an internal dilemma she didn't want to dwell on. Although barely ethical—okay, not ethical at all, but this was Edwin, so turnabout and all that malarkey, Giselle wanted to eavesdrop. Should she take the backstairs to the dining room, where Giselle would be able to hear better, if not see the participants? Or go directly to the parlor as if this were her first chance to respond to Rosie's request? Of course, ignoring the situation altogether and going about her business with the children was a final option.

A snooping opportunity was too good to pass up. Giselle quickly made her way to the kitchen, giving a curious Lottie the quiet gesture, and slipped into the dining room, nudging the door enough to hear and not draw attention to herself. Lottie followed in her wake. Unless voices were recognized, which Giselle doubted, they would need to settle for understanding the topic; and, she didn't mind that at all.

"I don't care how many times you tell me. This is ridiculous," Edwin yelled. Someone mumbled. "No, I will not calm down, Astoria. I'm being maligned."

"If you're innocent, you have nothing to worry about." Was that the elder Doctor Trent?

"I must consider the negative effects public exposure could place on the hospital. As a senior hospital administrator, I'm duty-bound to look into all complaints." Giselle didn't recognize the voice, but now she knew his position in the matter. "Maybe you should consider the ramifications this will have on your family."

Edwin roared. "Those damn nurses did this to me. I'll sue each one for these criminal accusations." Giselle's heart pounded loudly at the prospect. Lottie must have suffered the same alarm since she latched on to Giselle's arm too tightly. Elspeth would need a warning. More immediately, Nora would need to leave the house. Giselle would gladly pay any monies Nora had incurred if it meant her going without harm coming to her.

"Ludicrous. What would you gain?" Trent asked. "How do you even know who initiated the investigation?"

"Who else could it be? They're the only ones recently in the house."

"Dammit, Edwin, think." Trent. "Three deaths, one after the other, the three younger children sick, and you don't think anyone who can read a newspaper couldn't become suspicious? Anyone could have raised the alarm. Doctor Jenkins is doing his job. I'd think you would consider the hospital's reputation as well as your own, just as Rupert is doing." Giselle managed to hold her snort at the possibility of Edwin considering anything other than himself. Lottie didn't contain hers, causing Giselle to shush her again.

Rupert tried to be the voice of reason. "Have you any idea how this will harm Mrs. Merrick? Rumor already suggests you forced her into a marriage to gain access to her family, hoping to kill them, so your wife is the sole beneficiary. I've heard a bet is going with how long Astoria will live after you've reached your goal."

There sounded a tremendous crash, and Giselle wondered what Edwin damaged, and how livid Rosie would be about the loss. Lottie startled beside her.

"Oh, dear me, no," Rosie exclaimed, while Astoria snapped, "Preposterous."

"Be that as it may, young lady, we have a situation," Trent said. "We're addressing it while aiming to contain any damage. Rupert and I shall take our leave. I suggest you put some thought into this, Edwin."

Moments later, the front door closed. Giselle took this opportunity to yank Lottie back into the kitchen. "Did you notice Edwin didn't deny the charges? Didn't demand an investigation to prove his innocence? And I know his excessive anger was a show, but not certain for whose benefit." Giselle inhaled deeply. "I need to talk to Nora before Edwin confronts her." Or worse, Giselle thought grimly.

"What about you?" Lottie asked.

"First things first, Lottie." She squeezed Lottie's hand for assurance. "Would you please call a taxi?"

"What if Nurse Nora won't go?"

Giselle bit her bottom lip. "Let's hope she's smarter than that. However, the ride won't go unused. I will need the taxi to warn Elspeth in person rather than over the phone." Lottie flashed a knowing grin, which Giselle chose to ignore—even if her light complexion did not.

Either way, Giselle intended to warn Elspeth immediately so she could adequately prepare for any ramifications. She prayed Nora wouldn't give her any difficulties because of the warning.

"Maybe you should ride with her. It might be best if you weren't here after all that nastiness in the parlor. I'll have the driver come to the side of the house, not the front." Lottie's concern was evident in her paling skin and tearful eyes. Giselle nodded. Lottie moved to the phone to place the call, and Giselle ran upstairs.

It would be a long night, and indeed not as pleasant as last evening. Giselle hadn't expected this new turn of events. It might force her to break her promise, which Giselle was usually unwilling to do. But she knew the welcome she would receive at Elspeth's. Giselle didn't know what would happen with Edwin in this mood.

Chapter Twenty-two

Giselle retrieved the last of her belongings, put on her coat, gloves and hat, and went to Nora's room. Gratefully, when she explained the conversation she heard from the parlor, Giselle hadn't needed to press too hard to get Nora to agree to leave. After a quick hug with Lottie, Nora and Giselle took their belongings outside to the waiting car. Nora gave the driver her address, and the driver put the vehicle in motion.

The car reached the end of the drive when a dark figure walking away from the Gardiner house caught Giselle's attention. It was a bitterly cold night, so excessive outerwear was warranted, yet she could tell the heavily bundled figure was Edwin.

"Slow down and pull over, please," Giselle directed the driver. She pulled paper bills from her reticule and handed them to the man, with a verbal change in direction. Then, to Nora, she said, "Please, take my bags to Elspeth. Let her know where I am." To the driver, she added, "Could you take her to the original destination, after that? Thank you." Giselle opened the door and got out. When the taxi pulled away, Giselle followed the route Edwin had taken stamped by footprints into the snow.

Sporadic streetlamps dully lit the night, which worked in her favor as well as against her. It would assist in concealing her from Edwin yet could prevent her from following his every move. Giselle yanked her coat tighter around her, her breath wisps of smoky puffs with each exhale. For three and a half blocks, Giselle trailed him, only twice needing to press herself deeper into shadows. Near as she could tell, Edwin hadn't noted her presence.

Then, closing on the fourth block, Edwin stopped near enough to a streetlamp to make him out. Too bad she couldn't determine what he was doing to make him pause. Giselle pushed herself into the darkened doorway of a flower shop. He appeared to remove something from his overcoat pocket and then dropped it onto the sidewalk. Edwin stomped the item enthusiastically into the snow. His task completed; Edwin continued up the street.

Giselle waited until she could no longer see Edwin, presuming he wasn't aware of her and went to the area he'd abused with his booted feet. She reached down into the disturbed snow with one gloved hand and came away with a miniature object that appeared to be a broken, and now empty, capsule. Giselle thought it harmless enough to ignore, but for the fact of Edwin's strange manner in its elimination.

She dug around for some moments to find four others in similar states, pulled a scarf from her coat pocket, and wrapped them inside, and tucked them in her pocket. Giselle rose and brushed her hands, just as a car pulled to the curb.

****

Elspeth hopped from James's car as soon as it was safe to do so. She had been in a panic from the moment Nora Hunter knocked on her door with Giselle's bags. When she'd explained that Giselle had followed Edwin Merrick, the time it took to call James and enlist the aid of his vehicle, Elspeth was nearly panic-stricken. "Giselle, are you alright?" Without forethought, Elspeth yanked Giselle close to her chest. "Why would you put yourself in danger?"

"Hey, love, let a girl breath." Giselle chuckled, then raised a gloved hand. There was a strange—

She gently stilled Giselle's hand. "Giselle?"

"Can we take this reunion someplace warmer?" James said, exiting the car.

"Elspeth, what's wrong?" Giselle asked, tugging to release her wrist from Elspeth's grasp.

"James, what do you make of this?" Elspeth asked. Fear began to cloud Giselle's gaze. "It will be okay, just bear with me."

"Beg pardon," James said, as he brought his nose close to Giselle's gloved hand. Elspeth knew the moment he recognized the odor. His brow furrowed. "Sweet and bitter. Uh-oh."

"Uh-oh?"

Elspeth brushed her ungloved hand to Giselle's cheek and grinned. "What have you been up to on your evening walk, dearest?" She removed the soiled glove from Giselle's hand.

"Let's get you home," James said, striding to the driver's door. "It's freezing out here. Our conversation is too lengthy for the outdoors."

Giselle slid into the car beside James, Elspeth beside her. Within moments they'd arrived at Elspeth's home. Giselle tossed her outerwear on the coatrack by the suite's door and headed for the kitchen. "I'll make tea."

She returned with a loaded trolley and sat beside Elspeth, who took the opportunity to grasp Giselle's hand in hers. "Are you sure you're alright?"

"Of course. I would tell you if it were otherwise." Giselle leaned over, kissed her cheek, and poured out the tea. "The first thing you need to know is the elder Doctor Trent and a Doctor Jenkins paid a visit to Rosie, and the Merrick's a couple of hours ago to let Edwin know he started an investigation."

"Rupert Jenkins?" Elspeth asked James.

James shrugged. "He's the hospital administrator. Trent, the younger, Gerry, had to start somewhere to get things rolling."

"You two know him?"

"Yes, we do," James said. "Me personally, Elspeth by word of mouth." Elspeth wanted to slap the smirk off his face. If Giselle noticed it, she didn't comment.

"Well, Edwin is blaming the nurses, threatening to sue, so I thought it best to get Nora out of the house, and come tell you. As we were leaving, I saw Edwin rushing down the street, so I followed him. That is when I saw him drop and stomp something." Giselle rose from the couch and retrieved something from her coat pocket and handed them to James. "These are what I found, and what must have made the smell on my glove."

He opened the scarf and shot Elspeth a confirming gaze. "Cyanide."

"So, what happens now?" Giselle asked.

Elspeth put her teacup down and then draped an arm around Giselle's shoulder. "One more piece of the puzzle, dearest. Combine enough, and we've completed the picture. If we can get an inquisition started, they can autopsy—" Elspeth felt the color drain from her face, not wanting to bring some of the more distasteful parts of that procedure to Giselle's attention. She was used to all aspects of what an inquisition entailed, but now they were talking about digging up the Colonel's, who were family to Giselle.

"Don't worry. I remember it mentioned before. It's disturbing, but not making me squeamish." Giselle gave a wry smile. "Preston and Uncle Reginald deserve justice, even if the means are unsettling."

"Yes, and that's my cue," James said. "I'll take these with me." He stood. "Elspeth, my dear, keep our little detective safe." He dropped a kiss on top of her head. Shifting, he moved in front of Giselle and lightly kissed her cheek, before standing straight. "Thank you for the tea. But, from this point forward, stay as far away from the Merrick's and the Gardiner's as possible. At least until this matter is resolved."

"Thank you, James, for coming to my aid so quickly." Elspeth stood, prepared to walk him to the door. "If anything had happened—"

"Ah, but it didn't. No need to follow. I'll lock up after myself." He drew her into a hug and whispered in her ear, "Tuck her in nice and tight. Try not to let her out of your sight."

"I'll put my best effort into it," Elspeth said. When James left, she heard the click of the key and returned to Giselle. Elspeth felt simultaneously uneasy and relaxed. It comforted her when Giselle automatically entered the kitchen and prepared tea. After tonight's events, she wanted to suggest Giselle share her room, as much to lessen her distressing emotions as Giselle's. Would the offer be welcomed? "I placed your bag in your room."

"Thank you." Giselle rose and put the used teacups on the trolley. She appeared to avoid making eye contact with Elspeth purposefully. "Have you eaten? I'm stress-famished, but I could go without food. I don't want to take advantage—"

Elspeth realized Giselle was nervous too. Was Giselle uncertain how to openly broach her feelings, her expectations, as much as Elspeth? Softly blowing out a breath, Elspeth moved behind Giselle. She wrapped her arms around Giselle's waist, drawing them flush. "Continue as you did when we came in. This is your home, too, now. As for available food," she said, whispering in Giselle's ear. "I've only fixings for sandwiches. We need to shop."

Giselle twisted in her arms and grinned. "Is this where I should offer to do the cooking?"

"No, that's not—"

Chuckling, Giselle said, "I was teasing. But I don't have a problem with that, actually." She lowered her gaze to Elspeth's neck. "I can stay in your room tonight, right?"

"Any time you feel comfortable doing so, dearest." Elspeth leaned down and kissed her slowly, only stopping when Giselle gave a gentle push to her waist.

"Food first. Then we continue this."

"Good idea. You make the sandwiches, and I'll clean these." Together, they went to the kitchen. Elspeth beamed. Giselle was here in her home, their home. If all fared well, there would be many more nights to end as pleasantly as this was heading.

****

"Please, Tori, dear, hurry," Edwin said. He stuffed the last of his belongings into his luggage, then began tossing her items into her luggage until she sharply slapped his hand away. Edwin stepped back, pushed his glasses up his nose. "I refuse to stay a minute more than I must."

"You brought it on yourself, Carson," Astoria said.

The sneer curling her lip caught him by surprise. "How can you say that?"

"How can you not? Bad enough you nearly bled Preston before he died, you couldn't wait to kill off Reginald. You had no concept of time management. To top it all, people are suggesting you coerced me into marriage." She snorted indelicately—an endearing characteristic shared with him. To anyone outside their private space, Astoria was ever the lady. "Like you ever could."

Edwin recognized the insult but knew the stress of the situation was speaking. "What do we do now?"

"We go home and regroup, think of a way out of this mess."

"Do you think we can salvage this?" he asked.

The ice in her gaze caused him to shiver. What could she have possibly thought at that moment to produce that expression? Astoria was his rock. He had ideas, and she formulated plans. In the five years of their marriage, she had never let him down. Edwin needed to follow her direction, needed to compose himself. He picked up the luggage. "Do you need to say goodbye to Mother Gardiner?"

"Hmph. Get the car, Carson."

"Yes, my dear." Laden with luggage, Edwin left the library and took the bags to the car he'd parked in front of the house just moments ago. He reentered to escort Astoria out. Passing the parlor, Edwin peeked in. Rosie was always in this room, whether day or night. Yet, on this occasion, his mother-in-law was nowhere to be seen. Oddly enough, Edwin was disappointed.

"Let's go," Astoria said, tugging at the fingers of her gloves. "Take me to dinner, then home. We have a lot to discuss."

Edwin nodded. "As you wish."

Chapter Twenty-three

The last place James wanted to be was visiting Edwin Merrick at home. He understood the request was given to a few other colleagues and tried to anticipate what Edwin planned. Something melodramatic, James assumed. Did the man know how to act any other way? Prepared for nearly anything, he took his medical bag with him. Two could play games.

He hoped this wouldn't take too long. Elspeth and Giselle invited him and Helen for dinner tonight, understanding he would take Helen to his mother's home Christmas Day. James knew little time passed in their courtship but, aside from being adorable, Helen stirred feelings in him about the long term. Feelings his sister must also have for Giselle if the gentled edges to Elspeth's stoic persona were any indication. And the tender gazes, he thought with a touch of mirth, when Elspeth didn't realize anyone noticed the loving expression as she watched Giselle. If asked what he believed the perfect gift for him was, James would request what he thought Elspeth found in Giselle.

At the door to the Merrick home, James gave two solid raps. The door swung open to a doorman, or maybe the butler. He couldn't be sure as the time of domestic servants was reduced with the addition of modernized household devices. "Hello," James said. "Doctor Campbell to see Doctor Merrick."

"Of course, sir." The man stepped back and to the left. He closed the door when James entered the foyer and walked to a room off to the right.

James heard the mumbled voices before being led to

the home's parlor. Inside, positioned by the window, was a hospital bed, curtains drawn, and six straight-back chairs, four occupied, were arranged in a semi-circle facing the window and a bed. He shook hands with the elder and younger Doctor's Trent, Doctor Jenkins, and to his surprise, Doctor Barrett Keaton, who was responsible for the autopsies—which Edwin shouldn't know about. The attendees were an intriguing selection considering recent events James and Gerry instigated. Mrs. Merrick sat in a wingback chair at the head of the bed, her attention entrenched in a magazine article.

"So, what are you up to, my man?" he asked, turning his attention on Edwin.

"The damnedest thing," Edwin said. He pulled himself into a sitting position as if every movement costly to his wellbeing. "Ran some blood tests before this got the best of me. It appears I've contracted typhoid."

"Really?" James said, feigning puzzlement. "That's not good." He pulled out a syringe and moved closer to Edwin.

"What do you plan to do with that?" Edwin asked, scooting backward a lot faster than he had a moment ago.

"Oh, really, Edwin, do be a man," Gerry Trent said, slouching in his chair. His friend clearly didn't want to be here. Gerry came as a duty to his father, obviously.

"We have an obligation," James said. He tried to keep his tone solicitous. "If there's an epidemic in this town, I should think you'd want to isolate it as much as we do." Edwin couldn't very well argue with an audience of his creation. He nodded, and James took a blood sample, safely securing it in his bag. He and Gerry would make the sample their priority when this visit ended.

"There's no accounting for this," Gerry said. "It has all the appearances of intentional maliciousness."

James took this as his chance to stir the pot. "There

hasn't been an issue with your specimens, right, Edwin? The vials are secure?"

Rupert shot a look at James, then turned his attention to Edwin. "Have you been dallying with typhoid?"

"Are you suggesting I had anything—" Edwin scowled. "What would I gain by infecting myself?"

"I believe you're avoiding the question," Gerry said.

The elder Trent shook his head. "Gentlemen, please. Let's not upset Mrs. Merrick with an interrogation."

The missus didn't seem the slightest bit disturbed; in fact, her expression never changing from the bland perusal of her reading material. James decided to tone the tension down. "No one is accusing anyone of anything. Maple Woods has a medical issue we need to address. Deduction and elimination are the beginning."

Edwin snorted. "I bet this is because of that horrible child. She's upset because Muir died."

Gerry shook his head. "Are you suggesting Giselle Saunders created the illness at the Gardiner home?"

"Who is she?" Trent asked.

"Colonel Muir's ward," Gerry said.

"Ah," Trent said, nodding. "The pretty young woman who raises the children."

James didn't hide the grin at that, and was pleased outsiders were aware of the care Giselle provided. "Edwin suggests Ms. Saunders set the hounds on his trail, I believe," James explained.

"It's inconceivable to believe I could harm my own family," Edwin said. "The girl never liked me." Because she has excellent taste and smarts, James thought. "Thought I saw her following me to my lab the other night. She probably asked that hag of a nurse to implicate me."

That information was unsettling. Giselle believed she'd gone unnoticed.

It wasn't easy, but James held his tongue. He wanted

to defend his sister, hating that few people saw beyond her looks, but James would get more information if no one realized their connection. Trouble was he didn't want to spend another minute in this house, in this pathetic man's presence. "No matter who is responsible, placing blame isn't the answer. I'm certain the guilty party, if there is one, will be brought to justice."

Edwin removed his glasses, wiped the lenses with a linen handkerchief, and put them back on. "Well, once I've been cleared of this ridiculousness, I aim to prosecute those responsible for maligning my good name. My money's on Muir's ward."

James bent to pick up his medical bag, hiding his eye roll. It bothered him Edwin seemed so focused on Giselle. "Much as I enjoyed this visit, gentlemen, I have a Christmas Eve dinner to attend. Enjoy your holiday." Before anyone could stall his hasty exit, James strode from the room, glad the doorman-slash-butler was already opening the door.

****

The afternoon felt surreal to Elspeth. Earlier, they both made a trip to the grocers for much-needed supplies. She couldn't believe tomorrow was Christmas, and she was found so unprepared. The high note of the expedition was Giselle's assistance. She had grown used to most of her time being without someone present and thought she might find a constant presence of a companion to be stifling. The opposite held true.

For the last couple of hours, she and Giselle worked side-by-side to prepare a holiday meal for James and Helen, and Lilly, who she hoped didn't feel like the odd person at the table. And again, Elspeth wondered at the oddity. The instant immersion in their version of married life hadn't frightened her as much as she expected.

They agreed on the traditional meal of roast beef, chicken, goose, oysters, chestnuts, pheasant, and stuffing. Giselle prepared the stuffing, which consisted of sausage, chestnuts, and apples while humming or singing. Elspeth inwardly cursed her invitations, wanting nothing more than to draw Giselle into her arms, rain kisses across her body, and make love to her repeatedly throughout the house, starting right here in the kitchen. Instead, Elspeth settled for stolen kisses and touches as they worked.

"Hello, anyone home?" Lilly's voice called out. Elspeth hadn't locked the doors in anticipation of guests. "It smells wonderful, so don't stop what you're doing. I'll come to you." A moment later, Lilly strode into the kitchen.

"I'm glad you could make it," Giselle said. "Manners, Lilly," she said, slapping at Lilly's fingers as she stole a taste of the stuffing.

"These are my manners," Lilly said. "I take what I can from the ladies before they cut me off." Lilly raised an eyebrow, gave Elspeth an exaggerated wink, then pursed her lips. "Besides, I'm doing you a favor."

"What favor would that be?" Giselle asked with a smirk.

"Making certain you're ready for domesticity."

"How could you doubt it?" James said from the doorway.

Startled, she hadn't heard them enter. Elspeth turned toward him. "Doubt what?"

"That you're both ready for home life. A person only needs to look at the two of you, the way you simply ooze gooey—like corn syrup—love when together or talk about the other."

Elspeth could feel the heat from the blush infusing her face. "James, please."

James drew Helen into the kitchen, then planted a kiss to Elspeth's forehead. "Be at peace, Mairi." His whisper was for her ears only. "All present are happy for you and Giselle. She's quite the girl." Elspeth nodded her agreement. "And so are you. I'm glad Giselle sees it since you can't."

"Everything is ready," Giselle announced, saving Elspeth the need to respond to James. "Take your seats, and we'll get this meal started."

They each grabbed the plates, bowls, and platters of food to take with them to the dining room. They devoured the meal with vigor, amid pleasant conversation and lots of laughter. Elspeth felt blessed to have these people, even if one was her brother who was bound to familial obligations.

As everyone slowed their consumption of food, the dialogue slackened. James cleared his throat. "I don't wish to change the wonderful mood created by Elspeth and Giselle, but I have something to share."

Helen inhaled sharply. Apparently, Helen was aware of what James wanted to say. "James, don't ruin their evening."

"Helen, my dear," James said, giving her a wry grin. "We can better enjoy the remainder of the evening once the news is out in the open."

"What's going on, James?" Elspeth asked. Helen's concern doubled hers.

James explained his call to Edwin's house, noting who was present, and the reason for the visit, namely Edwin's strangely contracting typhoid. "Gerry's repeating the test, of course, to be certain. Our results concluded that Edwin had such a low exposure to the germ as not to have it at all. At most, he'd probably have a headache or upset stomach.

Nothing to send the man to his bed."

"James believes Edwin is attempting to throw suspicion elsewhere and off of himself," Helen said.

"Sounds like a typical Merrick move," Giselle said.

"Yes, which is why I felt the need to bring this up." He glanced between Giselle and Elspeth. "Edwin's newest complaint is that Giselle is setting him up, even following him." Elspeth blanched at that, worry for Giselle increasing. "He's also claiming that you, Elspeth, are her accomplice."

Lilly chuckled. "Who would have thought you were so diabolical, Giselle. And to subvert the good Nurse Keillor in your plans, too."

"Please, be careful, the both of you. Anyone who would willfully tamper with cyanide and typhoid germs won't have qualms with dispatching two women that he views are in his way to whatever goal he wants."

"Money. Gardiner money," Lilly said. "There's lots of it."

"Agreed," Helen said.

"Be wary, that's all I ask. And, now," James said, rising and picking up his plate and utensils. "Don't tell Mother or I'll have to do this tomorrow. I offer my services to clean up this outstanding meal—many thanks to the chefs—so we can move on to a lighter side of the evening." The clean up went quickly, with five people assisting in various duties. The laughter and teasing returned, and the chore proved more fun than work.

"Thank you all," Elspeth said. She couldn't remember a night she'd enjoyed more.

"Is it game time?" James asked. "I vote for the kissing game."

Lilly snickered. "How about the game where we snatch brandy-soaked raisins from the flames." She shrugged. "Or we could just get soaked drinking brandy."

"Charades?" Helen asked.

Games were a large part of the holiday for most families. History hadn't let Elspeth feel comfortable enough to participate. She wasn't sure she could let her guard down enough to do so now. But she would follow whatever Giselle wanted to do, hoping to give her a Christmas Eve to remember. Her heart filled with relief when Giselle said, "Oh, let's build up the fire and tell ghost stories." The gentle squeeze to her hand told Elspeth that Giselle understood more than she ever could have believed someone would. Elspeth loved Giselle at that moment, more than each previous moment. Each passing second grew her love for Giselle exponentially.

Chapter Twenty-four

All night, Giselle felt a bit like a ninny, and Lilly happily teased her about it every opportunity that arose. Not about being a ninny, but about her preoccupation through the meal in the hotel's restaurant, and then over drinks in Lilly's suite. Giselle refused to feel remorse. She missed Elspeth, and Lilly caught her staring at nothing when lost in reflections of her adorable lover.

At the time, she wondered if it was normal for new relationships. Would it always be like this? Then, she dismissed it just as quickly, not caring. Elspeth was essential to her, filled her heart, made her body respond in ways Giselle never believed possible.

"So, how 'bout a sleepover?" Lilly asked. She sat on an embroidered wingback chair, one leg dangling over an armrest. "Still plenty to catch up on."

"Well, I hadn't planned on it. Don't have anything—"

Lilly groaned, then burst out laughing. "I'm kidding. You're too new to this relationship for extended separations. Granted, I'm not familiar with the concept. But I've had a couple of women that I couldn't easily part from after just one night." She paused, a glint in her eyes. Then her tone grew serious. "I never considered my life otherwise, Cousin. Not until I saw the way you and Elspeth look at each other. Despite my teasing, I admit I envy you." She shrugged.

"You could always stay, maybe move to Denver proper, and find someone who can see and love you as I do." It was selfish of her, but Giselle wanted Lilly to stay close, wanted Lilly in her life. "I've missed you more than you can know."

"Never thought I'd admit it," she said, then scowled, "and I'll deny if asked, but I've missed you too." Giselle heard the tremor of contained emotion in her voice.

Giselle needed to change topics. Plus, she wanted Lilly's opinion. "Do you believe Edwin is responsible for murdering Charles and the Colonels? I mean, he and I have never been fond of each other, so maybe I see a demon where none exists."

"No, he's a demon. In fact, during our trip home, I believe Edwin tried to poison me, too," Lilly said.

The news startled Giselle. "Oh, dear Lord. Lilly, why didn't you say anything?"

"It's not like I had any proof. I'm glad my mother suggested I stay away from the house, even if for an entirely different reason. She assumed I could become ill because of the girls," Lilly said, then shrugged.

Curious, Giselle asked, "What do you suspect him of doing to you?"

"I had a headache and nausea on the train, which in itself isn't suspicious. Plus, I've done a lot of traveling and never become ill. However, the sickness only came on after Edwin gave me water. My health improved when I checked into this suite."

Giselle didn't believe it a coincidence. Using water as a means of delivery was how Edwin polluted the Gardiner house. "That's how he did it at the house. No matter her reason, Rosie probably kept you from a horrific illness." She sighed, and considered the extent of Edwin's perfidy. "Possibly saved your life."

"Will you hate me if I don't thank her?" Lilly asked with a wry grin.

"Certainly not, because what she doesn't know won't hurt her." Giselle had to share Lilly's experiences with James and Elspeth. The information would add to the ever-growing transgressions stacked against Edwin. She hoped

Elspeth would be happy with the news, pleased with her contributions. Now, it would be a good time to do just that—or after a snuggle and a kiss or two. It wasn't as if either of them could do anything with the news tonight.

Something must have bled into her face. "Ugh, go home to your woman. I know you're thinking of her since your expression got all goofy."

Giselle jumped from the settee. "Thank you, Lilly, for a wonderful evening and for your understanding." She slid into her coat and leaned over Lilly's near-reclining form on the chair, then kissed her cousin's cheek. "I'll keep you updated."

"Be sure you do," Lilly said as Giselle left the suite, happy with their visit, thankful to be on her way back to her home, and Elspeth.

****

Elspeth didn't think her life could get any better. Refurbishing work on the private suite, time consuming and exhausting, was worth the effort. The nursing facility portion almost complete. The Christmas Eve dinner proved to be a success. Giselle kept her room as a prop for the few days she'd been a permanent resident. The thought of Giselle spending their nights in Elspeth's room filled her heart with happiness. And now, Giselle didn't spend time at the Gardiners. Best of all, out of the reach of Edwin and his immediate retribution, away from Rosie and her demands. Elspeth was able to watch over Giselle, keep her from harm.

She made a concession today, and the tension in her body from her anxiety was painful to bear. Elspeth agreed Giselle could visit Lilly, share information in case Rosie hadn't shared all the pertinent details with her daughter. But the niggling of warning wouldn't leave Elspeth. Was she overreacting? Was she paranoid?

Giselle was a grown woman, and Elspeth didn't have a right to refuse her chances to spend time with Lilly, even if letting Giselle out of her sight was difficult. Lilly would leave for New York soon, their remaining time together precious. So, Giselle had gone to the hotel after assuring Elspeth she'd use a cab for all activities. Granted, Giselle would be on her own with the taxi driver. But limiting the chances of Edwin finding her alone was of the utmost importance.

All morning, Giselle had examined the receipts and expenditures, got Elspeth's accounts in a manageable order. They even collaborated efforts on the work needed to get the facility staffed and operational before spring. One thing became

When Giselle announced it was time for her to meet Lilly for dinner, Elspeth reluctantly let her leave with assurances to be careful, and a passionate kiss to, hopefully, remind what awaited her at home. Since that time, Elspeth sat at the desk, staring into space, accomplishing nothing of importance, unless you counted making herself sick with worry.

"This is pathetic." She stood and peered out the window, only to see herself in the glass, instead of into the night. It was a startling reflection.

Elspeth glanced at the clock. Ten at night. Should she wait up? Would Giselle think her foolish? Go to bed, as if Elspeth weren't worried? Not that she would be able to sleep. What kind of sane person obsesses like this? None. If she couldn't find balance, if Giselle learned of this moment, these neurotic emotions could separate them before they planted the proper roots for their relationship to grow. Of course, there was a real threat out there.

Edwin. Until he was held accountable for his actions, neither of them would ever be safe.

The phone on her desk rang, and Elspeth picked up the receiver before it could complete the second ring. "Hello?"

"Elspeth Keillor?" A female voice, high pitched and muffled from what sounded like hysterical crying, but not Giselle's, even if she didn't recognize the caller otherwise.

"Yes. Who is this?"

"Please, hurry, James Campbell—"

A part of her frowned as something felt wrong, but not the obvious with the full use of his name.

"James? What's wrong with him? Helen? Is this you?"

More crying and undecipherable words. Then, more coherently, "Hurry. I don't know what to do." Then the phone disconnected. Panic divided her heart, created a fissure in her responses. Giselle would return soon. Elspeth didn't want her to come home to an empty house. What if Giselle worried about her?

On the other hand, something happened to her brother. She had a familial obligation beyond his being her sibling. She needed to help him if she could. If she hurried, she could be here for both.

Elspeth grabbed her outerwear, uncaring that she wore her at-home clothes and rushed outside, running in the direction of her bother's home. She hoped to flag down a conveyance before long, or before she froze in her attempts to reach James in time. A buggy-for-hire was trotting down the street from the opposite direction, and she flagged the driver down. When he stopped, she climbed inside after shouting the address to him, offering twice the fare if he hurried. Luck was on her side. The driver arrived in excellent time.

"Thank you," she said, producing enough money to more than cover her doubled fare. Elspeth wasn't surprised to find the front door unlocked, men didn't concern themselves with personal vulnerability, as she pushed the door open and rushed inside, pausing in the hall with indecision. Where would James be?

Elspeth first heard soft laughter, lover's laughter. She followed the sound, and a surreal feeling consumed and then tore a cry from her. James and Helen were in a tight embrace on the couch. There wasn't a traumatic situation, her brother near death.

Her sob caught their attention. James sprung from the couch and rushed to her. "Elspeth, what's wrong?" Helen moved closer to them. Both now wore a concerned expression.

"I got a call from a woman. She said you were hurt," Elspeth said, glancing toward Helen. "I couldn't understand why Helen—" Then the magnitude of the situation, the real intent, occurred to her. "Giselle." As quickly as she entered, Elspeth ran out.

"Elspeth, wait," James yelled. Her forward momentum came to an abrupt halt when a vise-like grip bit into her left arm. "I'll drive." Helen caught up to them, passing James an overcoat. They hurried to James's car; Helen silently slid into the back seat. "What's going on, Mairi?"

She ignored the sting on her face as the cold night air froze the dropping tears. "A woman called. I couldn't make much out, not even who was on the other end. I did know it wasn't Giselle."

James nodded. "You came to my rescue, thanks. But what about Helen?"

"I believed she was too upset, afraid of the worst, and wanted me there for you." Elspeth glanced out the window as the scenery spread passed. The night seemed so peaceful, the snow blanketing the sidewalks and streets glistening beneath the streetlights. Fear for Giselle consumed her. A fresh sob escaped. "I didn't think beyond you were in trouble. Now I know someone wanted me out of the house." She savagely swiped the tears from her face. "I'll never forgive myself if anything happens to Giselle. I can't fail her, James." Elspeth began an internal mantra. Let her be safe, let her be safe, over and over.

"You shouldn't take on this burden, assume guilt for something you have no control over."

"James, you don't understand." The part of the call that had niggled in the back of her consciousness burst through like a thunderbolt. "I should have known. It bothered me at the beginning, but not enough to halt my flight." A headache built behind her eyes, piercing her skull. Elspeth tiredly rubbed her forehead, hoping to alleviate the pressure. "Helen wouldn't need to use your last name."

A hand squeezed her shoulder, and Elspeth realized Helen offered her support. "We'll get through this as a family."

"She shouldn't have to sacrifice her freedom. Her decision to visit with Lilly was normal, and I can't fault her for making it. But I knew it was risky for her to be alone, especially in the evening. I should have hired someone to protect her, watch over her."

James clamped her thigh. "Stop that. This isn't a circumstance the average Joe expects in life."

"Stay positive, Elspeth," Helen said.

"Here we are," James said, pulling as close to the house as the drive allowed.

Elspeth jumped from the car, stumbling a step as she stared at the house.

The front door gaped open like the maw of a giant, dark monster.

Chapter Twenty-five

Giselle expected Elspeth to be home, but was surprised to find the building dark and the front door locked. Well, she expected the locked door, but not to have the outside light extinguished. That wasn't like Elspeth. Not that Elspeth had to share her schedule with Giselle since she spent the evening doing her own thing. But she was startled to realize, with a stab of disappointment, that Elspeth hadn't counted the minutes Giselle had been away.

She slid the key into the lock, turned it to unlatch, and then realized the danger when she heard the crunch of glass sounded beneath her booted foot. Giselle twisted to the left, intent on reaching the street and safety when she slammed into an immovable object. She heard the opening of the door before being physically picked up by a man who smelled of sweat and cheap cigars, and carried into the house, then deposited in the hall. No lights were on, but enough moonlight filtered through to illuminate two large male forms, each at least six-foot, even if she couldn't make out their faces. Which meant they probably couldn't see Giselle was terrified.

"Never told us you was such a looker," said the smelly one.

"Knock it off, Jake. That's not what we're paid for." The second man hadn't moved closer yet. Since she anticipated the worse, Giselle wondered if he was second-guessing his mission.

"Heh, guess we get a bonus, Pete." Jake ran a thick finger down the side of her face.

Giselle hoped her terror wasn't noticeable in her voice. "Whatever you're getting paid to do, I can offer more not to, and won't tell anyone."

Pete said, "Our employer would know."

"Who's your employer?" she asked. She needed to stall with conversation until she could work out an escape.

"Didn't ask questions," Pete said. He stepped closer. "Snooty lady did tell us to give you a message."

Snooty? Who the hell would— Giselle knew and was saddened by the implications. Astoria.

"You're to leave Edwin alone," Pete said. "Or it will be worse for you next time."

Jake guffawed. "Ooh, I like repeated jobs." He moved quicker than she thought possible for his size, slamming a fist into her cheek. She dropped to the floor; excruciating pain radiated through her face. Jake clasped the front of her coat, jerked her to her feet, and slammed her into Pete. "Hold her."

"Not like she's going anywhere," Pete mumbled.

"Yeah, but can't keep pulling her off the floor." As Pete held her, Jake ripped her coat open and slammed his fists—left, right, left, right, and left again—into her torso. He followed with another crash of fist to her face, just under her eye.

Giselle's pummeled body hung loose in Pete's grasp. She was close to passing out, her legs unable to hold her up of their own accord. Astoria had to suspect her goons would do more than verbally warn her off. Was that part of her orders? How much more of a lesson did they intend to give her?

"Enough, Jake. Think she gets it."

"Let her go," Jake said. "I'm not finished with her."

A cold wash of dread filled her and exponentially increased when Pete did as told, and she fell limply to the hall floor. Evidently, the voice of reason feared the brute too. Pete would not stop Jake from his intended task.

Jake straddled her prone form, releasing the buttons on

his pants. Giselle tried to prepare herself for what was about to happen, but how does a woman do that? Instead, she worried about how Elspeth would react when she found Giselle later. Had she told Elspeth she loved her before leaving today?

"This isn't right," Peter said, tugging on the back of Jake's collar. Had Pete's conscious overpowered his cowardice of a moment ago?

Then a dark blur crashed into both men.

****

Conscious thought or planning didn't enter Elspeth's mind as she raced into the house. Instantly, the scene before her came to vivid life as three shadowed forms filled her vision, the smallest lying on the floor. Dear God, Giselle. Using surprise and the momentum of rage, Elspeth slammed into the standing figures dropping all of them to the floor. Before the men could gain the upper hand in this attack, she raked fingernails down their faces and then pummeled aimless fists at anything below her.

A massive fist smashed her jaw, but fury numbed her response. Giselle's moaning filled her ears, the only sound registering about the coursing of blood pounding in her ears from the exaggerated beat of her heart.

Light exploded around her, then the roar of a discharged pistol. One man howled in pain before both tried to rise to their feet. "Don't move, I have no qualms relieving my Colt of all the bullets," James said, voice deep with anger. He handed a key to Helen. "Call the police." Neither man moved, except for some squirming by the man shot in the leg, as Helen hustled away.

Elspeth crawled across the floor toward an

unconscious Giselle, aghast at the blood, swelling, and bruising on her face, her breath a wheezing rasp. Fury warred with remorse, knowing her actions put her lover in the position to be alone, to be attacked. Despite the overcoat making Giselle bulkier, Elspeth slipped a hand beneath Giselle's shoulders and knees, drawing her into her chest. Her balance faltered as she stood with Giselle's weight clutched to her. Helen returned from her phone call, gripped Elspeth's upper arm to steady her, and keep her from stumbling.

"Take her inside, Mairi," James said. "I'll be in shortly. Helen, go with her."

"Do you think that wise?" Helen asked, glancing at the two men on the floor.

"It'll be fine." The sound of the police car's bell rang nearer. "See?"

Taking quick but careful steps, Elspeth carried Giselle toward their room as the beat of hard soles sounded in the hall. Relieved she wasn't leaving James alone, Elspeth continued to her bedroom, where Helen turned down the covers. She tenderly laid Giselle on the bed.

"I'll get Jimmy's bag from the car," Helen said, heading toward the door.

"No need, Helen. I have one in the armoire." While Helen retrieved the bag, Elspeth removed Giselle's coat, boots, and loosened the laces on her dress.

"I'll get some hot water and towels, and some ice is probably a good idea." Helen rushed from the room.

Elspeth finished undressing Giselle; tears blurred her vision when she saw the angry bruising to the tender flesh of her stomach as she pulled the sheet over Giselle. "I'm so sorry, beloved," she whispered. Elspeth lightly prodded the facial damage with trembling fingers, noted the bleeding from a cut to her lip, and her nose, but teeth were aligned, the nose unbroken. With her left eye swollen and unconscious, she couldn't say whether Giselle would lose sight in her eye.

Helen returned, James with her, and headed straight for the bed.

"How is she?" he asked, opening the medical bag, while Helen placed her supply-burden on the nightstand.

"Blunt abdominal trauma and—" Elspeth's voice broke. She realized her hands weren't the only body parts trembling. Helen wrapped an arm around her waist, and James turned to her with a mix of sympathy and question. Elspeth shook her head and listed her findings. James raised an eyebrow, then turned and checked the movement in Giselle's jaw. "I was about to check that."

"Not broken," he said. "Helen, take Elspeth to the kitchen for a cup of tea."

"No, James," Elspeth said, moving toward Giselle. She trusted James to do his best for her, but another factor bothered her.

He turned to her again, ran a finger down her cheek. "Please, Mairi. I'll get her fixed up. You need to calm down. I need you in the best shape possible for her recovery."

"James, it's just—" Elspeth cleared her throat. "Could you wait outside, let Helen and me take care of this?"

"Don't you trust me?" He seemed genuinely confused.

Helen apparently understood. "James, the two of us can tend to your sister-in-law."

"My… Oh." His face flushed scarlet. He cleared his throat. "Sure, I'll make the tea. Let me know if I can fetch more bandages for binding. She has broken ribs." James quickly left the room.

"Thank you," Elspeth said to Helen.

Smirking, Helen said, "I did it for me, too, in case your brother is serious about us. It would be hard to look at her knowing James was privy to her, um, well, au naturel."

Elspeth nodded. Together, they cleaned up the blood, applied ice compresses, and wrapped Giselle's broken ribs, constricting the ribs below for good measure. One bone surely was broken, but with the discoloration and tenderness, marked by the whimpers from a still unconscious Giselle, Elspeth worried about a second.

"Why hasn't she come around?" Elspeth asked when they'd finished. She sat on the side of the bed and clasped Giselle's hand.

"It was quite traumatic, I'm sure," Helen said, a hand on her shoulder, then a quick, gentle squeeze into her flesh. "Let's get her in a nightdress, then see if James needs to check on her." Elspeth nodded. They gently raised and lowered Giselle as they dressed her. "If you don't mind, I can stay in Giselle's room tonight, in case you need me later." Helen's concerned gaze met Elspeth's, who nodded to her. "Good night, then."

James poked his head in the room as Helen left. "Mairi, honey," James said. "I'm sure you and Helen did fine, so I'm going to sleep on the couch tonight. I don't think anything else will happen tonight, but I don't feel right leaving you ladies alone."

She didn't take her gaze from Giselle, hoped he could hear the sincerity in her voice. "Thank you, James, for all you've done tonight. I know I lost my mind for a moment, and don't know what would have happened if you and Helen hadn't been here."

"Not necessary. Rest, you'll need it as much as Giselle does."

When the door closed, Elspeth quickly put on her nightclothes and gently and gradually crawled into bed beside Giselle. Though concerned Giselle still hadn't woken, Elspeth conceded that rest was the best medicine right now.

Elspeth arranged the covers over them both, kissed the

side of Giselle's battered face, and snuggled as close as she could without touching any of Giselle's injuries. "I'm sorry I wasn't here when you needed me. Please know that I love you." Despite every nuance of her mind and body rebelling against the idea, Elspeth's stress exhausted body fell asleep moments later.

****

Two things drifted into Giselle's conscious. First, the excruciating pain, second, the warm body pressed into the side of hers. She attempted to open her eyes but found only one complied. The room was dark; only a small ray of moonlight lit the room. Slowly, she extended the hand closest to the heat beside her, and felt Elspeth, her touch waking her.

"What do you need?" a sleep husky Elspeth asked.

"Nothing." Giselle winced as her lip protested. "Ow. I suppose if I feel the pain that means I'm alive."

Elspeth gave a strangled sob. "I'm so sorry." Giselle regretted her attempt at humor. "I should have been here, would have been here, but I had a call James was hurt."

"Astoria," Giselle said. She tried to shift, needing to see Elspeth, offer reassurances, but pain radiated from her torso. "How bad is it?"

"Broken rib, maybe two since one is iffy, cut lip and, well you can probably tell, a swollen eye. Lots of bruises, slugger." Elspeth said the last word hesitantly. Was she trying for humor, too?

"Any long term damages?"

Giselle didn't care for her hesitation. Her heart began to pound in her ears. Finally, Elspeth said, "Overall, no. We can't be sure about your eyesight until the swelling goes, and you can open your eye."

The thought of losing her sight frightened Giselle, but she took some solace in the fact that she was alive and otherwise unmolested. The last being the most significant relief. She gave a warbly chuckle. "Good thing I have a girlfriend to help me through all this, to take care of me."

"Forever, Ellie, dearest." She drew in a sharp breath. "Sorry, I didn't mean to use the Colonel's nickname."

"I enjoy hearing the way you say it," she admitted. Preston and Reginald always used it with teasing tenderness. Elspeth said it with such love. "May I call you Mairi, like James does? It's such a beautiful name."

"It would please me greatly. Plus, it's much nicer than Elspeth."

"I happen to adore both." There was something she wanted—needed—to share with Elspeth, about the events tonight, but she grew so weary, with sleep tugging ruthlessly at her.

A tender brush of fingers stroked the side of her face. The action sent a frisson of warmth from head to toe. "You mentioned Astoria when I spoke of the call. Why do you think so?"

Ah, that was it, Giselle thought. "One of the thugs mentioned a message from a snooty lady to leave Edwin alone." Her breathing became more labored and painful. Her fatigue started to overwhelm her. "She had it planned, you gone, me here alone."

"Sleep now, Ellie. James is on the couch and Helen in your room. We aren't alone tonight. We'll deal with this tomorrow." Elspeth raised herself onto an elbow, and lovingly planted a kiss on Giselle's lips, across her face, and Giselle felt the love in every cell of her body. "I'm sorry—"

"Oh, dearest, please don't do this to yourself." Giselle couldn't bear Elspeth blaming herself for her beating.

"This isn't your fault." Then, the memory of a shadowed blur flashed in her mind. "Besides, how lucky am I you appeared when you did and pummeled those hooligans? Will you kiss me?"

"But your lip?"

"Please?" Then soft lips covered hers. The pain was minimal in contrast to the flood of heat Elspeth's closeness created. All too soon, Elspeth pulled away. Lethargy filled her, but so did pleasure, knowing Elspeth would be beside her now, tomorrow when she woke, and for as long as Giselle wanted. That knowledge was the healing balm she needed; knowledge she'd hold in both hands—in her heart.

Chapter Twenty-six

The swelling lessened considerably, and the reds and pinks of the damaged skin were purpling on Giselle's face and body. Elspeth apologized again this morning as she assisted Giselle into a dress since she refused to stay in bed any longer. James and Helen woke, made them breakfast, which they took in bed, and left to change their clothes. She'd offered Giselle the use of her trousers and shirt, but she declined. "Besides," Giselle said. "I could never look as sexy as you do."

They'd moved to the couch in the living room. "Sexy? How hard where you hit?" She placed a kiss to Giselle's forehead. "I'll have James check on that."

"Stop, Mairi, and quit hovering. Gosh, I love calling you that name." And I love hearing it, Elspeth thought. Giselle tugged on her hand, and she sat down. "No matter what others say or have said, dearest, I find you beautiful. Especially in your at-home outfit." As Elspeth currently wore the stated outfit, she shouldn't have been surprised when Giselle arched her eyebrows then winked, but she did feel a startle, nonetheless. Would she ever get used to Giselle's playful adoration? Elspeth hoped not.

"I want to ask James about buying a car," she blurted.

"Okay. That could be useful for you."

She shook her head. "For us. I want you to use it, too. You shouldn't be out late and relying on taxis or carriages. The safer I can make your life, the better."

"Safer for us." Giselle clasped their hands. "Don't go through too much trouble because of me. I'll heal, we'll get over this Merrick debacle, and your dream will become a working reality. Are the workers—"

The reverberating sound of the knocker at the main door echoed into their suite. They were only expecting James to return, and he had a key. Elspeth wondered, and worried, it might be the police. If another attack were imminent, the culprits wouldn't knock. She gave a swift pat to Giselle's thigh. "I'll be right back."

Elspeth, not expecting anyone other than her brother and Helen, hadn't dressed appropriately to entertain guests. She hoped whoever was here would quickly depart. The last person Elspeth expected to see when she opened the door was Madeline Brewster, now Jenkins. "Maddie?" She hadn't changed much, still petite at with her, medium-blonde hair. Unlike their college days, Maddie reeked of money.

"Hello, Elspeth, nice to see you in one piece," Maddie said, tugging the gloves from her fingers. Her thin lips and a pointed nose added to an air of superiority. "May I come in?"

She reluctantly stepped back, the comment not registering. "Why are you here?"

Maddie raked her gaze up and down Elspeth's frame; her expression flashed distaste before transforming into her social-bland facade. "Thought you'd grow out of this horrendous stage of dressing."

"I find it comfortable. Again, why are you here?"

"Rupert may have mentioned a meeting with James Campbell and Nurse Keillor. Not a common name, so had do be you. I told him we were college friends and insinuated myself into this little get-together. He and Gerry Trent should be here soon." Maddie raised a perfectly manicured eyebrow. "Gives us time to catch up."

Lucky me, Elspeth thought, wanting to usher her out. She wouldn't mind, under other circumstances, but a battered Giselle sat in their suite. She and Maddie departed on civil terms, and Elspeth knew the danger in their situation should their affections be recognized, even if Maddie remained silent. Maddie got what she wanted and had no reason to bring up the past. A past that would not bode well for her should anyone become aware now. Elspeth would not respond well if Maddie said anything discourteous.

Despite her better judgment, she led Maddie to the living room. Elspeth nearly ran into her back when she stopped at the threshold.

Giselle raised an eyebrow and, unlike Maddie's, hers exhibited curiosity. Elspeth didn't resort to social conformity by offering to take her coat; instead, she pointed to the coat bench and returned to her place by Giselle. "Can I get you anything?" The glimmer of amusement in Giselle's open eye made Elspeth smile.

"This is Mrs. Rupert Jenkins. Previously known as Madeline Brewster."

Maddie sat primly in the chair opposite the couch. "Oh, dear. Rupert said there was an attack last night, but he hadn't mentioned the extent." Ah, that explained the "in one piece" comment. Maddie thought Elspeth was the victim. Did she come there out of worry? Why ever for? She'd made her position quite clear at their separation.

"I'm sure it looks worse than it is," Giselle said kindly.

"Hmm, at least Elspeth is the best nurse you could hire."

Giselle grinned, reached for Elspeth's hand, and drew it into her lap. Then she glanced at her with adulation, causing Elspeth to beam her affection right back. Giselle recognized who Maddie was to her. "Didn't have to hire her. She happens to hold my heart, and I can't be too far from her without it."

Elspeth drew Giselle's hand to her lips and placed a kiss on her knuckles. "Such a precious possession, too."

From her peripheral, Elspeth noted Maddie's sneer. "Really, Elspeth, is that necessary?"

"Not like you haven't received the same from me."

Her pale complexion became vivid red. "You mentioned me by name?"

"She didn't," Giselle said. True, James was the one to bring up her name. "There's something in your body language that gives you away when you glance at her. Unlike me, you obviously decided not to follow your heart." Giselle glanced into her eyes again, and Elspeth saw love reflected there.

James's voice sounded at the front door; Helen's giggle followed before they strode into the room and to Giselle. "How are you feeling?"

"Fine, but tired."

"To be expected. Hello, Madeline," he said simply. James glanced at her. "Doctors Jenkins and Trent, the younger, are right behind us."

"I'll get some tea and coffee brought in," Elspeth said. She stood and planted a kiss to the top of Giselle's head.

Helen said, "I'll help, Elspeth."

"No, please," Maddie said, leaping from the chair. "Let me."

Elspeth couldn't decline the offer without drawing questions from Helen. She nodded curtly and headed to the kitchen, knowing Maddie followed. Busy with boiling water for the tea and getting the coffee ready, Elspeth managed to avoid eye contact with her former lover. She pulled the trolley from the corner of the kitchen and brought it closer to the counter.

"Are you serious about her? You know the behavior is unacceptable." Maddie rearranged the cups on the trolley. "You aren't providing any favors to the child."

"Giselle is not a child." Elspeth poured the hot water into the teapot.

"She needs a husband, not dabbling in youthful escapades." Maddie shrugged. "A husband could protect her from events like last night."

"I protected her." It wasn't easy for Elspeth to reign in her irritation. "I haven't forced her into anything she doesn't want. Giselle cares for me deeply." She whirled on Maddie. "Just because it didn't suit your long term goals, doesn't mean it can't be viable for others. You cared for me once."

Something shifted in Maddie's expression. Was it regret? Did their history mean more to Maddie than she let on? "Not that I'd admit it openly, but, yes, I did. On occasions of introspection, I even miss you. Miss that you made me feel what no one else has, even Rupert. Not that he's been unkind." She stepped close, too close. "Do you ever think about me?"

Elspeth finished preparing the trolley, keeping it between her and Maddie. Maddie wasn't being unkind, hadn't been insulting, just inquiring. Her knee jerk response was honesty. "I loved you, Maddie, but it wasn't enough for you. I understand what we had made you uncomfortable—and disposable. Do I think about you? Yes. Do I yearn for what we could have created together? No. You made your decision. No matter it broke my heart, I understood. I never expected to have that feeling again." Giselle's image flashed in her mind's eye, and she smiled. "Will it last forever? I don't know. But I'll give her my heart and soul, do everything I can to make her happy. Giselle completes me, fills all the empty places within me." Her heart filled; her body tingled with the recognition every word was the truth.

Maddie nodded. "I never meant to hurt you, Elspeth. In my way, I did love you back." She shrugged. "Just not enough to turn my back on social conventions. Or the shame that what we did was wrong, even with the guilt for hurting you. I've never been strong like you."

"I'm not strong, not really. With time, I healed and never placed blame at your door. Well, not entirely," Elspeth said, then gave her a wry grin. "And I've never dismissed our friendship." Not really, but her hurt overshadowed it, Elspeth admitted to herself. "Let's finish this up, shall we?"

The kitchen door banged open, and Lilly burst inside and pulled Elspeth into a tight hug. "Giselle told me about last night. Thank you for saving her life." She stepped back, and her brow furrowed when she noticed Maddie.

"This is Doctor Rupert's wife, Madeline," she said.

"Ah, one of the men in the living room."

"Guess that's my cue to bring the trolley out," Elspeth said.

Maddie cleared her throat. "Shouldn't you change out of those unattractive clothes for your guests? It's offensive."

Elspeth paused, then shook her head. "Of course. Would you take the drinks out?" She didn't wait for a response but rushed from the kitchen to her bedroom. Elspeth wouldn't be able to sneak passed the people gathered in her living room but didn't care. She wanted to get everyone out of here as quickly as possible. She needed to hold Giselle in her arms to comfort and be comforted.

****

Giselle grew tired, but this gathering was important. She sat on the couch between Lilly and Elspeth, glad for the support they provided. Luckily, she hoped it would be winding down soon. She didn't want to appear weak, even if they'd understand her situation. James, Gerry Trent, Rupert Jenkins, and Elspeth all discussed the specifics and timelines of events around the deaths, illnesses. Lilly mentioned the train ride and a few things she'd noticed since returning to Maple Woods.

More important than the dread of showing fragility, Giselle didn't want to leave Maddie an opportunity to get Elspeth alone for a second time. She doubted—knew in her heart—that Elspeth no longer pined for Maddie, and that their romance happened years ago, but Elspeth became tense after the encounter. Much to Giselle's dismay, Elspeth changed into a skirt and blouse hurriedly. Knowing her lover as she did, Giselle suspected Mrs. Jenkins overstepped a line she shouldn't have crossed in criticizing Elspeth's clothing preference. The results could work in Giselle's favor. If there were a niggling of returned caring between them, insulting Elspeth's clothes would be like cutting at her personality. Giselle would hold that against the older women. She hadn't a right to disparage Elspeth.

"I believe we have everything we need," Rupert said. He stood and extended a hand to Madeline, who also rose. "I'll get with you, James, should we have further questions, or need to set another meeting."

"Yes, I believe all this should do," Gerry Trent said. He turned and faced Giselle. "Our apologies that you had to become another victim in this horrible mess, Miss Saunders. We may not have stopped what happened to you, but we'll do everything in our power to stop him from harming anyone else."

She nodded, then smiled at him. "Thank you, Doctor Trent. Everything is irrelevant to the fact Edwin needs to be stopped." Giselle inhaled, then exhaled. "What of Astoria?" Even with no love lost between them, Giselle still recognized Lilly was Astoria's sister. It bothered her no end that Lilly had to see the perfidy of her oldest sibling. Hated that she was the one to bring Astoria into the conversation with Lilly here. But Giselle believed Astoria as guilty as Edwin.

"Not enough evidence to point to her involvement or culpability," Rupert said. "We spoke with the police, and the two men who attacked you aren't pointing fingers at anyone but themselves. I believe Doctor Merrick the real objective here. I'm sure Mrs. Merrick is simply another pawn." Of course, Giselle thought, because women couldn't possibly commit crimes without the encouragement or direction from a man.

Gerry and the Jenkins's made their goodbyes, followed by James and Helen, with a promise to return the next day to check her progress.

After the room cleared, Lilly twisted to focus her attention on Giselle. "Everyone's gone, honey. Tell me, are you really okay?"

"I'm fine. I told you, Elspeth saved and cared for me," she explained to her cousin. "I'm glad you stopped by today. I appreciated your support."

Lilly patted her hand. "You look tired. Go rest now. I'll come back to see you after you have a chance to recover more." She took one of Giselle's hands in hers but gazed at Elspeth. "Is Mrs. Jenkins a friend of yours?"

"In a manner of speaking."

Giselle squeezed Lilly's hand. "They went to college together," Giselle said, not wanting to share Elspeth's past, as that was Elspeth's place if she so desired.

"Well, she was sorely wrong, you know," Lilly told Elspeth.

Curious, Giselle asked, "Wrong about what?"

"Your earlier outfit is neither offensive nor unattractive." Lilly flashed Elspeth a come-hither glance. "I happen to find the outfit sexy as hell."

"Ooh, so do I." Giselle smiled at Elspeth's sudden blush.

"Little Mrs. Doctor's wife doesn't know what she's missing." Lilly snorted.

"Yes, she does," Elspeth said, then jumped from the couch. "That's not what...I mean..."

"Oh-ho, as I suspected. Her loss," Lilly said.

"Yes, and thankfully, my gain."

Elspeth sighed. "I need to clean up." Giselle silently thanked Madeline for her dismissal of Elspeth, leaving her heart available for when she and Giselle met. Giselle couldn't imagine not having this wonderful woman in her life. Elspeth's attention focused on Giselle. "You should lie down, beloved. You look exhausted."

"She does, and that's my cue to leave. Come lock up after me." Lilly placed a light kiss on her cheek, then she and Elspeth left the room.

Giselle patiently waited for Elspeth to return, locking the suite door too. She extended an arm toward Elspeth. "Save the cleaning for later, dearest. Will you come to rest with me, hold me?"

"Gladly," Elspeth said. She took Giselle's hand and assisted her to her feet. Giselle leaned into Elspeth, soaking all the warmth and strength Elspeth's body offered. Once she walked Giselle to the bed, Elspeth turned and locked the bedroom door. At Giselle's raised eyebrow, Elspeth said, "Better to be overly cautious than not vigilant enough."

When she drew the curtains and returned to the bed, Giselle didn't waste time tugging Elspeth into her side, hissed through her teeth when she moved too fast. She hadn't realized the extent of her exhaustion until her head hit the pillow. Before she fell asleep, Giselle had to ask about earlier. "Elspeth?"

A heated brush of air against her ear as Elspeth asked,

"Yes?"

"Did Madeline make a pass at you?"

Giselle shivered at another puff of hot breath. "No, she told me I was ruining your life."

"Ruining, how?"

Elspeth shifted but didn't pull away. "Not allowing you to realize you needed a husband to protect you from all the monsters in the dark."

"What did you tell her?" Giselle worried Madeline made Elspeth question their relationship. Would Elspeth leave her, believe the nonsense from her ex-lover? Make her sleep in her own room?

"Told her you weren't a child and capable of making life choices."

Giselle ignored the discomfort and tugged Elspeth closer, smiling. "Good answer." Sleep pulled at her, but Giselle fought long enough to say, "I love you, Mairi." And hear Elspeth's reply. "I love you, too, Ellie."

Chapter Twenty-seven

Three months later

The morning rushed in cold and bitter; a perfect pairing for the events to come. Even Giselle's wool dress and cloak couldn't keep the chill at bay. The stone structure housing the courthouse loomed behind Giselle as she waited for the building to open for business officially. Uniformed policemen stood at alternating positions from the top to the bottom of the stairs leading inside, ready to prevent reporters entering the building before they readied the courtroom. Already the vultures of the newspapers were circling. Giselle tugged on her gloves, not because they needed it but for something to occupy herself. And to stabilize her thoughts. So much had happened in the last few months. She felt relieved the bruising and broken ribs healed, more so that no damage occurred to her vision. Finally, the horrible actions conducted by Edwin Carson Merrick would now be addressed. She could only hope justice would prevail.

An unexpected touch to her elbow made Giselle startle. "I'm sorry," Elspeth's voice whispered in her ear. She twisted to better look at her love, and Elspeth rewarded her with a tender smile. "How are you holding up?"

"Fine," she said. "But, this hasn't started yet." Giselle leaned closer to Elspeth. Casual observers might believe it for the body warmth. Others might be less kind. Let them. Giselle needed comfort that only Elspeth's presence gave her. "Heard from Lilly that Rosie hired a night watchman to keep the press and the gawkers from trespassing."

Elspeth snorted. "Because the family hasn't been harmed enough, the press needs their pound of emotional flesh from the rich."

"Precisely."

Gently, Elspeth slid her arm through Giselle's. "You aren't doing fine, honey. I know how hard this is—"

A uniformed man, probably the bailiff, announced family and witnesses could enter at this time. Because of the anticipated draw of the proceedings, select "tickets" were provided to them, prepared by the court clerk, to authenticate their presence. Elspeth guided Giselle upstairs to the entrance.

Inside, they walked directly into the courtroom and took seats in the back, where they'd have a minimal degree of privacy, able to watch without being too close to the proceedings, and access to leave hurriedly should the need arise. So far, they had the back seats to themselves as others filed in, partly due to the stern glare Elspeth flashed when anyone came too close to their position.

Giselle leaned her head to the side when Elspeth shifted to whisper in her ear. "Are you certain you want to be here? No one will fault you for leaving. Especially me."

"I owe this to Preston and Uncle Reginald. Someone needs to represent them. We know the Gardiner's won't." Giselle shook her head, trying to dispel the irritation rising in her. If it weren't for the summons to testify, most of the family wouldn't be here. "Besides, I want to be here for you, too."

Elspeth leaned in closer to her ear. "I love you."

Giselle bit her lower lip to hold back the tears from nerves on edge. She put her face near Elspeth's ear. "I love you."

A shadow blanketed them. "Make some space, you two," a voice whispered playfully. Lilly stood next to

Elspeth, smiling down at them. Giselle couldn't believe they'd been so careless. Lilly must have noted the stunned expression. "Relax. I'm teasing." She tilted her head to indicate the people behind her. "Everyone's murmuring closely." She brushed against their knees to sit on the bench beside Giselle. "Only I would recognize that glint in your eyes."

"How are you, Lilly?" Elspeth grinned.

"Looking forward to seeing that monster condemned." Lilly removed her gloves. "I got off easy, compared to my sisters. Charles and the Colonels certainly didn't. They were tor—" Elspeth cleared her throat noisily, causing Lilly to wince. "Sorry, Ellie."

Giselle gave her a wry grin. "I understand." She did. The happenings in Maple Woods, in the Gardiner home, were sensational. Sensationalism would keep people tittering in gossip for months. At least until more dramatic events came along.

The papers reported much of the events in the inquest held by the coroner's jury. Whereas Giselle thought this would curb the need for people to leave their homes, it seemed the opposite resulted. The citizens of Maple Woods, Denver, and the other nearby cities came to witness the spectacle personally.

Not a Gardiner by blood, so not experiencing the level of invasion, Giselle still felt the public's assault. Yes, the Gardiners lost Charles. Yes, all the girls, Lilly too but not to the same extent, were poisoned with the intent to kill them.

Giselle lost two important men in her life, whom she loved dearly. She suffered anguish when the press released news of the exhumation of Preston and Reginald, even if they only learned Reginald's death was accelerated by indeterminate means. Accelerated? Indeterminate? What was that supposed to mean? She and Elspeth always believed both men murdered. But the knowledge their bodies were removed from their hallowed resting place, sliced open for inspection held a high level of dispassionate intrusion for her; two great and prominent men of Maple Woods nothing more than vessels for titillation for the magnitude.

Regarding the typhoid infection, no one was saying anything, which proved telling in what was left unsaid. Giselle held her suspicions. Edwin provided the bottled water, easily doctored beforehand. Edwin provided the box of chocolates right before Susan and Blanche showed symptoms of typhoid. Edwin provided the medicine and majority of the medical ministrations to the family. All evidence pointed to Edwin.

One thing would make Edwin happy. None of the Gardiners implicated him as the main suspect in the tragedy. A small glimmer of enjoyment for Giselle was knowing Rosie never wholly adjusted to Edwin's marriage to Astoria, her prized daughter. A wedge of contention that Astoria still verbally blamed her mother for on repeated occasions.

This room was the largest in the courthouse, the spectator area already at capacity. A uniformed man, Giselle presumed the bailiff, moved to stand before the audience, directing any witnesses to leave the courtroom. He also announced proceedings would begin in ten minutes.

Elspeth reached over and squeezed Giselle's hand. "Here I go. Save my seat for after my testimony." Giselle nodded as Elspeth left. Lilly stood and leaned close. "Save mine, too, honey," Lilly whispered with glee. Giselle swatted her arm as she moved away. She appreciated Lilly's sense of humor. Glad for her return and the resurgence of their friendship.

Not long after, the proceedings began, lawyers took

their place, Edwin and the jury brought in and seated. Then, the judge entered from the door behind and to the right of the bench.

Now it begins.

Giselle barely focused on the opening statements. She knew the two sides. One lawyer believed Edwin guilty, one lawyer intended to prove otherwise. She thought the questioning would begin with the professional testimony, but Mrs. Lowell B. Gardiner was the first called to the stand.

Rosie was dressed entirely in black, a broad-brimmed hat with black lace draped over her face, as she sat primly in the witness chair. Walsh hurled a barrage of questions at her, which she responded to smoothly, as if at a tea party. Most of her answers were typical responses concerning household activities.

But Rosie did give a couple of fascinating facts. One: Merrick knew Uncle Reginald planned to change his will. His intent to provide one million to the businesses for the management of the poor children. Two: Rosie knew Edwin used medicinal mixtures containing strychnine.

Frank Walsh would frown at each response. Walsh never denied his conviction that Edwin was a victim of injustice, which made him the ideal person to represent him. Giselle didn't believe she misread his expression, but at each mention of poison, a broad smile spread on Edwin's lips. It made Giselle shudder to see.

Neither Astoria nor Edwin were called to the stand, legally exempt from doing so. Wouldn't this cause later negative speculation why Edwin hadn't made an effort to produce his defense? Giselle believed it would.

Her beloved Nurse Keillor impressed the jury, and Giselle, with her damaging testimony, bolstered by the statements provided by Nurse Hunter. Then, Lilly explained the train trip and events after her return home.

Giselle was glad to have Elspeth and Lilly return to her side. So far, events looked to favor a verdict against Edwin. She only had to wait.

****

The trial continued for days, each one dispersed to the public with coverage on the front page of every newspaper, national and independent. With her part done, Elspeth sat beside Giselle each day, offering support as she could. It was comforting to have Lilly's presence, complete with her personal brand of humor that helped relax them all.

But the events weren't issue-free.

For her own eight hours on the stand, Elspeth had endured a constant onslaught of objections and hectoring challenges from Walsh. Giselle, with all her heart and support, assured her the evening of her testimony that she'd conducted herself with deportment on the stand. She thought it the actions of a young woman in love. Her surprise came when the press confirmed Giselle's observations, adding the words "awe of her demeanor" when relating her time on the stand. They labeled Nora's testimony as a skilled member of the nursing profession; Lilly touted as the Gardiner daughter whose words were as stylish as herself.

An issue to present was the passing of Doctor Trent two nights before he was to give testimony. Questions concerning the numerous charges, only two for murder. The question arose whether the other charges were truly admissible as murder charges. The most startling disaster came with discovering the grand jury notes were missing. Speculations circulated, of course, settling on an act of espionage.

There was some surprise when the State's attention swung from the family to the ominous science predicated by the alleged murderer.

After the first day, Walsh, probably suspecting he required more sympathy for his client, called upon Astoria's assistance. Walsh worked the juror's emotions by directing attention to the anxious wife, who sat behind his defendant. In his closing arguments, Walsh labeled Astoria the second victim in the injustice perpetrated.

Closing arguments concluded, instructions were provided to the jury, and sent on their way.

Elspeth and Giselle now snuggled on the couch, Giselle tucked against Elspeth's chest. She had an arm at Giselle's waist. They listened to Lilly, decorum aside as she lounged in the chair facing them, her legs and shoeless feet dangling over the chair's arm, as she replayed her latest exploits to a secret club location for women who loved women. Lilly offered to take them, show them a place where they wouldn't be judged and could socialize and relax in their romantic attentions.

"Not as fun as the places in New York, mind you," Lilly said. "But any opportunity to mingle with like-minded women like myself—ourselves—is worth the exploration."

"Explore to your heart's content," Elspeth said. "I have all I need here to discover."

Giselle turned her head and kissed Elspeth's cheek. "Thank you, honey. But I don't want to prevent you from any expedition into women's studies. Heaven forbid I be the example of clingy."

"But I like it when you cling."

"Ugh," Lilly moaned. "Next time, I bring a nuzzle-partner of my own." She chuckled. "Sad thing is, I can't complain because you two are just so cute. I'd have been in full-blown make-out by now, were it me."

"You and any friend," Giselle said, "are always welcomed."

"I don't know, honey," Elspeth said. She gave a wink to Giselle and feigned a frown at Lilly. "If the situation were to happen, and we want to have any conversation with Lilly and her date, we'll have to go to a public restaurant. Otherwise, she'll be too busy with the petting and smooching to conduct a reasonable conversation."

"Ah, too true, too true," Lilly said, followed by a heavy sigh.

"When are you going to settle down, anyway?" Giselle asked, then sat straighter without entirely leaving Elspeth's embrace. "You aren't going back to New York after the trial, are you?"

"First answer. And deprive women of the chance of me? I think not. I have an appetite to satiate." Lilly gently swung a leg. "Second answer." She flashed a sisterly smile at Giselle. "Not soon, no, Ellie. Coming back, I've realized how much I've missed you." She cocked her head to the side. "Besides, I like Elspeth and want to see this nursing facility of hers get off the ground. But I also need to make sure she'll take good care of you."

Elspeth squeezed Giselle a little tighter, caressed Giselle's neck with a brush of her lips. "I will always care for her, look after her. Even when she realizes I'm too old for her and moves on."

Giselle sat up and spun so quickly, the top of her head collided with Elspeth's chin. "I'm so sorry," Giselle said, her hand stroking the injured area on Elspeth's face. "You're not old." As she looked into Giselle's eyes, Giselle cupped her cheeks. "I'll always be with you for as long as I have breath."

Elspeth leaned in for a kiss.

"Okay, maybe I should leave you two alone," Lilly

said, laughing. Both Elspeth and Giselle shifted away from one another, blushing and apologizing.

"No, please," Elspeth said. She gently pulled Giselle back against her. "Guess we are so comfortable around you we forget ourselves."

"We should probably be more careful," Giselle said.

"That's what friends and family should be for. To put you at ease with your feelings." Lilly sat primly in her chair, adjusting the material of her dress but not putting her shoes on. "How could a decision take so long? His guilt is obvious."

Giselle tittered. "Honestly. And, was it only me, or did you see the smug expression every time Edwin heard the poison word?"

"He barely batted an eye when they read the charges," Lilly added.

Elspeth nodded. Edwin had always been strange, but his reactions were bizarre, even for him. "Maybe he believes his charismatic charms will decide the case in his favor."

"Then he's in for a surprise," Lilly said. "He's not as charming as he thinks he is. A young man died, and the children were poisoned. Someone has to pay to make the public feel safe. Edwin is all the people have to offer up. Even if he didn't do this—"

"Which we all know he did," Giselle interrupted.

"Edwin is the only one available for examination." Lilly bent to pick up her shoes. "I should be going, let you two get some rest. Thank you for dinner, and the pleasant visit."

She and Giselle stood. "Nonsense, Lilly," Elspeth said. "You shouldn't be out so late on your own. Stay in Giselle's room. She and I will try to bear the hardship of sharing a bed. This way, we can all return to the courthouse together tomorrow." When Lilly seemed poised to argue, she added, "Please. Between Giselle and I, we should be able to outfit you with fresh clothing in the morning."

"Yes, please stay." Giselle moved away from her and tugged Lilly from the chair. "We will feel better if you accept our invitation."

Lilly whisked a kiss to Giselle's cheek. "I welcome the offer, actually. Thank you." Elspeth turned out the light. When Lilly reached Giselle's room, Giselle stood at the threshold of theirs. Lilly spun around and giggled. "Try to keep the moans to a minimum." She smirked. "On second thought, do the opposite. For the evening, I can live vicariously through you two. Night."

Elspeth rolled her eyes. "Good night, Lilly."

As soon as their door closed, Giselle gave her a heated kiss. "Thank you."

"For what?"

"Looking out for Lilly. For a wonderful evening." Giselle kissed her again. Her body responded by warming instantly, in a manner only Giselle could conjure. "Because you make me giddy with happiness just by being you."

She turned off the overhead light, the cast iron stove in the corner provided enough of a glow to make out the objects in the room. Not that she didn't know every square inch. Elspeth lifted Giselle into her arms, walked to the bed, and gently placed Giselle atop the duvet. "The feelings are mutual, I assure you."

Giselle raised her hands and worked the buttons of Elspeth's dress. "Always good to hear."

"Mhm." Elspeth covered Giselle with her body. "Speaking of hearing. If you don't mind, I'd rather we didn't provide Lilly with fodder for teasing in the morning."

"Of course not," Giselle whispered. "However, I

considered it more as not making her envious."

Elspeth moved away from Giselle and quickly shed her clothes. Giselle also got up and undressed. Once they both had changed into their nightgowns and returned to bed, Elspeth kissed Giselle lovingly, tore herself away when both were breathless, and then tugged Giselle flush against her front. "We're talking about Lilly," she murmured into Giselle's ear. "She'd invite herself to join." Giselle giggled. Before long, both fell asleep.

****

The jury took three days to come to a decision, once released after closing arguments. Giselle would be glad to have this procedure finally over. Life would go on without her uncles, she'd still have an empty spot for them, but at least Edwin would pay for his vile acts if the jury did their job.

Giselle, Elspeth, and Lilly sat on the bench at the rear of the room as with the previous trial days. This was it. The decision Edwin Merrick was guilty of murder or innocent. He looked like he always did. Reddish-gold hair parted in the middle and slicked down, his suit expensive and pressed, and deep-set eyes behind his spectacles. Not what one might picture as a murderer, which could work in his favor, especially since he continued to sit as if waiting for teatime with the wife.

Giselle hadn't realized her hands were shaking until Elspeth clasped them. "It'll be okay. The jury will do right by your uncles and the children."

"I hope so," she said. "One can never tell, even if the verdict seems obvious."

"I concur," Lilly said, leaning forward. "We have a

group of people we want to have seen the evidence as to the same. When has any group of people agreed on everything?"

"Still," Elspeth said. "Ellie needs to relax. She's not doing herself any favors being anxious. She'll make herself sick."

Lilly smirked. "There is that, of course." She gave a mischievous glare at her. "If you're going to barf, do so in Elspeth's direction. I'm in borrowed clothing."

"All rise," the bailiff ordered. The entire courtroom did. With the trial over, the verdict to be given, they had a cramped courtroom. It was with the original crowd and the addition of any reporters earlier withheld from the proceedings. The lawyers, judge, and the jury went through the formal procedures before the verdict. As the jury foreman stood, Giselle clasped a hand each of Elspeth and Lilly. Today would conclude months of mourning, emotional turmoil, and days wracked with fear.

Finally, the part Giselle had awaited:

Two counts first-degree murder: For the deaths of Colonel Reginald Gardiner and Charles Gardiner.

Manslaughter: For negligently killing Colonel Preston Muir by bleeding him to death.

Poisoning—three counts: On the life of Rosalind Gardiner; 1) by use of typhoid germs; 2) by hypodermic injections; 3) by use of strychnine.

Four counts poisoning with typhoid germs—Lilly Ann Gardiner;
Jayne Price, a visitor in the Gardiner home; Blanche Gardiner; and Susan Gardiner.

Giselle trembled harder, this time in relief. She heard a groan, suspected it came from her lips, confirmed when Elspeth squeezed her hand tighter. Edwin was led from the room. She couldn't be certain of the meaning but thought Edwin had given a wink to Astoria. It wasn't the supportive it-will-all-be-okay wink. The look conveyed a silent code of conspiracy. "Did you see that?" she asked.

"Let it go," Elspeth said. She must have questioned the wink, too, as she frowned.

The murmurs of conversation were deafening simply by their quantity as people filed out. Giselle and her companions remained seated until the courtroom had cleared. She had to ask the question in her mind. "Do you think it possible for Edwin to buy his way out of jail?"

Elspeth draped an arm across her shoulder, tugging her a little closer. Giselle didn't fight it, needing the comfort, publicly or not. "No, honey, I don't."

"Let's get some lunch," Lilly said. "We can talk more openly away from here."

At Lilly's suggestion, they found a nice restaurant specializing in Italian cuisine. A bit of flirting with the maître d' had them seated in a private and quiet area. "Ugh," Lilly said with a shudder. She leaned in and lowered her voice. "The things one does to get special treatment."

"I, for one, appreciate the sacrifice," Elspeth said, smiling.

"The cause thanks you," Giselle added. They placed their orders and received their meals before returning to the topic that brought them here. "Please, Lilly, tell me the Gardiner money won't get Edwin Merrick out his ruling, out of jail time. Is that why he winked at Astoria?"

"No, I don't believe that's possible. Edwin's actions

involved a prospective attack on all the citizens of Maple Woods." She sipped her tea. "Besides, even if Edwin believes my sister is on his side, Astoria has other ideas."

Elspeth frowned. "What do you mean?"

"Well," Lilly said, drawing out the word. "True, I've limited my time at the house, obviously because I have a social life. However, I'm neither blind nor deaf. Astoria's planning her future, but I don't see how she's included Edwin in it. She's told our mother how her nerves can only be unfrazzled by world travel."

Giselle sat straighter. "All the more proof she may have made plans with her husband included. Take him out of the limelight but removing him from the country."

"Anything is possible, of course. But I don't get the impression Astoria has those thoughts. Astoria plans to take advantage of a wife flummoxed by a charismatic husband. One who had no idea her convicted husband planned to murder her entire family."

The waiter neared the table, and Elspeth gained his attention with a raised finger. "Please bring a bottle of champagne." After the bottle was brought to them and three glasses filled, Elspeth smiled warmly at her, then Lilly. "A celebration, ladies." She raised her glass, and they followed suit. "No matter what happens with the Merrick duo, I have a new friend to be thankful for, and the one person who makes my life whole."

"To friendships," Lilly said.

Giselle returned the warm smile, hoped her eyes conveyed the love in her own heart. "To friendship. To love." She may have suffered a tragedy. But Giselle also had the return of Lilly, her sister of heart, though not blood. More fulfilling, she received the love of her life. She could move on with her life and work with Elspeth. Spend time with Lilly and not need to worry. There was no reason she would have to engage the others, ever again.

Pluses far outweighed the minuses.

She warmed at the thought Preston and Reginald would approve.

Chapter Twenty-eight

Edwin couldn't be as happy to see someone as at this moment. Finally, the last part of this scheme was complete. He smiled broadly when Astoria somberly made her way into the area, within the jail, and his cell. Edwin became more confident in the plan's completion— although wished he'd been informed of this part—when two men carrying large wicker baskets followed his spouse. Last to enter was a police officer, who rushed ahead of Astoria at the last moment, the folding table he carried banged on his leg.

"Step back against the wall," the officer ordered, leaning the table against the bars. Edwin did, his gaze locked on his beautiful wife, as the cop released the lock. The two men entered the cell, deposited the baskets on his bunk, and put up the table. When they left the cell, Astoria entered. The cop grabbed the lone chair in front of the next cell, put it in the cell, and closed the bar door behind her. "You've been allowed an hour, ma'am." He glared at Edwin, then turned his attention to Astoria. "I'll be just outside. Holler if you need me before then."

"Noted. Thank you, Daryl." Astoria smiled too brightly, making him cringe inwardly.

He waited until the three men were out of sight before he rushed to Astoria and pulled her into his arms. His mouth slammed into hers in a harsh kiss. Long moments passed before he realized his ardor was unreturned, and he took a step back from her. "Tori?"

"Daryl is just outside the door, Carson."

"The cop? Who is he to you?" he demanded.

Astoria rolled her eyes. "Oh, do stop. I used a little

honey." He scowled. "Sweet talk, Carson, nothing else. How else do you think I was able to bring you a meal, and an hour with a convicted murderer?"

"Please, Tori, must you talk like that?"

"Put the table up, and we'll eat."

Edwin knew when to let a topic drop with his wife. It was probably best to ignore this battle, too. There would be others once he was released. He did what she asked and opened the baskets. There were a plethora of assorted foods. He pulled out sandwiches, fried chicken, ears of buttered cob corn, a bottle of wine, tableware, cloth napkins, and so much more. Lastly was the small plate with a large slice of Tiramisù, his favorite dessert. He would get the entire piece as Astoria never acquired a taste. "Quite the feast. Thank you. But why? You make it seem like this is my last meal."

"Do you really want to eat what the police would feed you?"

"Well, no, but—"

"Three points." An exasperated sigh, and another exaggerated eye roll. Astoria was angry with him. "One, you need proper food, and it's the best reason for a long visit. Two, this is what a wife would do, visit her convicted husband. Three, we don't want you drawing attention to yourself."

And there it was. Confirmation that Astoria had a plan in place. There were moments of utter silence while locked in the cell, with nothing to do but wonder at what point everything fell apart. Edwin finished laying out the table. He sat in the chair provided by Daryl, while Astoria sat at the edge of the bunk bolted to the wall and poured them each a glass of wine. "So, how have you been, Tori?"

"Really, Carson?" She nearly snarled the words. "I've had reporters camped outside, dogging my heels, barraging me with questions. Mother had me move in with her. She's hired watchmen to keep everyone as far from the house as possible so that I can avoid the frustration for the most part."

Edwin flinched at her tone. "At least—"

"Eat. We can talk afterward."

"Yes, dear." He agreed to keep her harsh attitude at bay. They consumed the meal, her mostly picking at the food. Edwin devoured as much as possible, neither conversing beyond a comment on the food or the cold weather. Astoria had been correct. Jail food was far from consumable. Their time was nearly up, and they had yet to talk about what would happen next. Surely Astoria had a plan for his release. The table was almost empty of food, except for his wife's plate, and his dessert, which he devoured greedily. The stress evidently wreaked havoc on her appetite. Edwin cleared everything away, containers and tableware back into the baskets. Astoria covered her plate with her linen napkin and shoved it under his pillow. He smiled. She couldn't help herself, always seeing to his well-being.

He restored the table to its travel position, put both baskets beside the cell door, and returned to the chair. Edwin took Astoria's hands in his, rubbing her knuckles with the pad of his thumbs. "I've missed you, darling." He winked suggestively, then lowered his voice. "Every inch of you. Can't wait 'til we are together outside these concrete walls. I'll take you so often that you'll be confined to bed for days."

Astoria stared at him stone-faced. "That is what you're focused on?" He turned their clasped hands and placed a wet kiss to her inner wrist. "This is not the time, Edwin."

Edwin shot back against the chair as if pushed, which figuratively he had. She hadn't used his first name since they'd dated, which meant Astoria was miffed with him. "All right, Tori," he said. No need that both of them should lose their tempers. "I apologize for not considering your experiences at the hands of the public and those awful reporters. Having to deal with low life police officers. It's just that I miss you so. Miss how powerful you make me feel."

Her features twisted until she glared at him. A chill skittered down his spine. Astoria's voice became a menacing whisper. "And whose fault is that? Who promised fault wouldn't fall on us? 'We can't be held accountable for indiscriminate germs?' That's what you said." She paused and gritted her teeth. "You were supposed to have thought of every contingency. Where was your control?"

"You know what happened. Reginald was changing his will. The plan needed to start sooner to prevent the adjustment he proposed." She knew this. Why was she questioning him? The fault wasn't his. The failure belonged to that above-herself nurse. "The blame belongs to the damned nurse who didn't know her place. She never liked me, always interrogative of my diagnosis."

"Which was your doing." Astoria's pale features resembled marble, her tone level again, her back stiffer than usual. "You should have dealt with the questioning by ignoring it. Keillor would have overlooked her dislike of you had you not bled Preston to death. Then, a day later, her employer dies." He tried to resist the tug but allowed her to pull her hands free from his. "That is what triggered her attention. You. Your actions."

Edwin shook his head. He still blamed Keillor's nosiness. "She never should have been allowed back in the house."

"But she was, which means you should have been more careful. Then, you had to botch the handling of Rosalind. Why did it take so many attempts, Carson?"

Why was his beloved questioning him? Her support

shouldn't be waning. He shrugged noncommittally. "I couldn't know her body would be so resilient." A cramp spasmed through Edwin's stomach. He clutched a hand to his abdomen; sure it was from the tension created by his wife's actions.

They heard the door at the end of the hall open. Daryl made his way to them. "Are you ready, Mrs. Merrick?"

Astoria stood. "Goodbye, Carson."

"No, wait," he said, grabbing her arm before she could move away.

In his peripheral, Edwin noted the hand on the gun before Daryl demanded loudly, "Step back against the wall."

Edwin did, not wanting to cause a ruckus. "Tori, honey?" Daryl unlocked the cell. Astoria stepped into the hall, waiting as the guard removed the chair, table, and two baskets. Once the guard relocked the cell, Edwin raced forward, staring pleadingly at his wife.

"Could I have a moment more, Daryl?" Astoria asked, her tone dripping sweetness. Surely one of them would get a toothache.

"Of course, ma'am. I'll be back in a minute." Daryl picked up both baskets and walked out.

Edwin knew he hadn't much time left, so he got directly to the point. "When can I expect you to have me released?"

The smirk his beloved flashed Edwin clenched his stomach with a different pain. The look didn't bode well for a response he wanted to hear. "Never darling. You botched everything. Now you can deal with the consequences."

His face burned hot in his rage. "I'll tell them you were an accomplice."

Astoria chuckled menacingly. "No one would believe you."

"It's the truth," he said.

"A little late for that now, isn't it?" Daryl returned, picking up the table and shoving the chair, so it was out of Edwin's reach. Astoria's expression changed to reflect sadness. She pulled a tissue and dabbed at her eyes. "I'll visit when I can." She turned toward the door, and Daryl took the cue she was ready to leave.

"Tori?" he called after her departing figure. "What do you mean? When will you come back?" Astoria disregarded him. Was that a smile gracing her lips? "Tori? Tori, please." The outer door closed. Clutching the bars, Edwin gave one last try as loudly as possible. "Tori!"

He'd been ineffective in her eyes. She could no longer believe in him. He breached her trust, promising, and then not delivering. They could fix this, couldn't they? She was just angry; she'd be back. As effectively as the closed-door behind Astoria, so was the outcome in his heart. Edwin threw himself onto his bunk. All their plans—

Tears formed in the corner of Edwin's eyes. No, not their plans. Astoria's plans, he only the instrument of those plans. He laughed aloud and at himself. This was Tori's plan all along. Astoria would come out as the poor wife whose husband tried to murder everyone in her family—for money. The money they were both to share. Most might suspect her death would be part of his nefarious plan.

"Ah, Tori, darling. You're smarter and more wicked than even I realized." Edwin inhaled deeply, resigning himself to his blinded-by-love-inevitable-fate. Another, more painful stomach spasm caused him to convulse. Edwin considered calling for Daryl to produce a physician, but what was the use? Instead, Edwin mentally congratulated Astoria for her final move, grit his teeth and buried his face in the pillow, regardless of the food resting there. He knew the dessert had been the catalyst to his own poisoning. It was his favorite, and only his.

As his breathing become more labored, the spasms more painful, Edwin gave a rictus grin. No one would suspect Astoria, though she was the last to visit, had brought the food. Plenty of people wanted to see him dead. Anyone could have poisoned his food, because the proud Mrs. Merrick wouldn't have made the meal herself.

"Touche, Tori," he whispered through gritted teeth. "I accept your last move, and await you in hell."

Chapter Twenty-nine

The morning dawned cold, but the sun gleamed bright this early Sunday morning. Not surprising for early January in Maple Woods, neither was the two-inch layer of snow covering the ground. Hopefully, the weather would keep visitors away from their home today. Giselle spent the time after bathing and dressing, to cook in the suite's kitchen. She wanted to surprise the woman she loved with breakfast in bed.

The woman she loved.

A broad smile split her face. One she never considered holding back. Giselle didn't care what other people thought. Elspeth made her deliriously happy. More than she'd felt with her uncles, but they were family. Elspeth filled her heart with warmth, safety in her wellbeing, and peace Giselle never expected to have in her life. And she would spend the rest of her life demonstrating she returned those feelings.

She'd made over-easy eggs, bacon, fried potatoes, toast cut in triangles, and a pot of coffee, all covered with a linen cloth. Not the caliber of Lottie, but practice would improve in time.

Giselle tucked the newspaper under her arm, picked up the tray she'd prepared, and made her way to Elspeth's bedroom—their bedroom in private. She used her room for dressing, or if they had visitors, so her items were seen. But nights were for and with Elspeth.

As was this morning.

She hipped the slightly ajar door, placed the lap tray on the night table with newspaper on top, and sat on the bed beside Elspeth, caressing her cheek while leaning to kiss her lips. Her long, dark hair framed her face, adding another layer of softness not witnessed by anyone but Giselle. "Morning, my love."

Elspeth's eyelids fluttered open. "An angel visits me," Elspeth whispered huskily.

"Not hardly. I brought breakfast."

"I thought I'd dreamed of the heavenly smell. Seeing you only confirms your celestial position and the dream to be true." Elspeth shifted, fluffed the pillows behind her, and pulled Giselle into another, longer kiss. "You have far too many clothes on. Come back to bed. Let us enjoy your culinary creation together."

Giselle hesitated. "What if someone comes by?"

"Only you and I have keys to the suite, love." Elspeth raised Giselle's hand to her lips, and tenderly kissed the knuckles. "Should anyone stop by, someone with a key," she said, raising an eyebrow. "They'll have to wait until I've thoroughly ravished you while waiting outside the suite."

"And what of breakfast?" Giselle asked teasingly.

"Yes, you did put a lot of effort into the offering. Guess I can hold off on the physical activity."

She stood, looking down on her lover as she removed her dress, leaving the undergarments on, and draped it over the end of the bed. "Food first," Giselle said, handing the lap tray to her. She walked to her side of the bed. "In all honesty, the nourishment is required. I'll need my strength for my ravishment."

"Indeed, you will," Elspeth said as Giselle snuggled closer to her. She'd removed the newspaper and linen from the tray and presented Giselle with a rigid slice of bacon. "Just the way I like it. Probably also the time to ask if you dip your toast in the yolk." Elspeth raised her eyebrows. "Need to know every detail and nuance the makes you precious."

Giselle leaned forward and took a bite of the bacon. "Definitely a dipper," she said. "However, be aware, should you spill any on me, you're responsible for its removal."

Elspeth's eyes darkened. "Gladly. In any manner I see fit, I presume." She felt the warmth of a full-body flush at the images the words conjured. Was a response required? Or did Elspeth see how the words affected her? Elspeth kissed her cheek. "Relax. My intent isn't to make you uncomfortable. It's only that you mean so much to me, have my heart. I can't get enough of you."

"Nor I of you. Your words didn't bring a flush of embarrassment, but an anticipation of fulfillment."

"Good to know," Elspeth said. Her lips split into a wide grin.

They jointly consumed breakfast, sharing the cup of coffee and utensils. The meal was both intimate and comforting. Giselle couldn't imagine being happier than at this moment. When they'd finished, she hopped out of bed long enough to rush the tray to the kitchen, foregoing the night robe Elspeth offered. She returned to her cuddled position against Elspeth, who currently perused the newspaper.

Giselle had already scanned the headlines, deciding she didn't need a reminder of all the deaths at Edwin's hand. A gasp escaped when she noted the death of Doctor Edwin Carson Merrick announced. She believed Astoria was the catalyst for his crimes, and entirely complicit in all Edwin's evil deeds. The fact no one raised the opinion didn't change hers. Astoria must believe she needed to remove any future implications by removing Edwin. Giselle said as much to Elspeth.

"I happen to agree with you, even if there's no evidence. Justice isn't always fairly portioned," Elspeth said. "Now it's between her, Edwin, and God. I'm just glad the matter resolved without any more death of innocents. Thankful that you needn't contact any of them." Her brow furrowed. "Unless you wish to, of course."

Giselle nuzzled into her shoulder. "I won't ignore or avoid them if our paths cross. But I won't make a point to initiate the encounter, either. I feel bad the children were used, but encountering them means seeing either Astoria or Rosie. It's too soon for me to handle that properly."

"Understandable."

"Besides," Giselle said, splaying her fingers across Elspeth's abdomen, delighted when her muscles tensed. "My current responsibility is to you. Well, to us, I guess. We have a nursing facility to staff and open. That's a lot of work still ahead of us."

Elspeth placed a kiss to the top of her head, and Giselle felt goosebumps. "Your priority is to finish your education. If you decide to do—"

She lightly slapped the warm flesh beneath her palm. "There's nothing else I want to do, honey. I want to be here with you and for you. Together."

"I can't imagine anything I want more. I want you with me always." She cleared her throat. Giselle suspected what would follow. "But know I would understand if you ever needed to move on. There's a lot you haven't experienced in life."

"True," Giselle said. "But in this, I've been blessed." She focused on Elspeth's eyes. Her hand skimmed upward, brushing across, then caressing a breast. Elspeth inhaled sharply. "I've experienced you. There isn't a need to look for more adventure than is already within my grasp."

Elspeth shifted, drawing Giselle lower and positioned under her. The initial contact of Elspeth's warmth blanketing her sent a thrill through Giselle. "I love you, Ellie," Elspeth said, her voice husky.

Giselle's heart filled with so much joy it would surely

burst. "I love you, too. Now and forever."

THE END

About the Author

Creating characters and situations is an often risky business, especially when, in lieu of the homework he expected, an American History teacher gets a short story the student has written. Somehow, Sharon managed to graduate and move on, doing an eight year tour of duty with the Marine Corps. She has also worked as a computer specialist, a substitute teacher, and currently, as a telecommunications analyst. Having toured in numerous countries must be an omen, since her life has been one giant research project. Sharon currently resides in Colorado.

Email: lilsarge60@aol.com
Web site: www.sharongclark.com

Bringing rainbow stories to life.

Flashpoint Publications welcomes submissions from writers of every
color and books featuring characters of every color. In addition,
Flashpoint Publications encourages job applicants of every color
whenever a staff position becomes available. We believe that
EVERYONE is entitled to a seat at our table.

www.flashpointpublications.com